Under the COVERS

D0038473

SCORING

Kristin Hardy

HARLEQUIN®
Live the emotion™

Visit us at www.eHarlequin.com

BLAZE™

ISBN 0-373-79082-1

EAN

AVAILABLE NOW:

To the pool shark," Mace toasted

He clinked his beer bottle with Becka's. "You're definitely a better player than I am, but I usually don't stink as badly as this. I think I need a goal." He glanced at the table. "I think we ought to bet on the next game."

"I don't play for money, Duvall."

"No money. Something better." He set his bottle down and traced a finger along her jawbone. "You win, the evening's over and I never bother you again.... I win, we go to bed."

She opened her mouth with the intention of telling him to go to hell, but stopped before the words got out. It was the perfect setup, she realized. He was offering her a chance to reel him in, to get him turned on and, thinking he had her, then take the game from him and show him who was *really* in control. "I think that's a bet I can live with."

Mace walked behind her, sliding a slow hand down her hip, and she jolted. He leaned over the table with his pool cue, looking sexy and a little bit dangerous, yet more than capable of taking this game, of taking her.

Uh-oh. "Wait," she blurted, just as the cue ball cracked into the colored balls, scattering them around the table.

Damn. Too late.

Blaze™

Dear Reader,

The minute Becka Landon swaggered onto the scene in
My Sexiest Mistake, I knew she deserved a book of her own.
Fortunately, my editor agreed, and the result is *Scoring*, the first
book in my UNDER THE COVERS miniseries. I've always been
fascinated by spin-off characters, enjoying the way they unfold as
they move from their initial introduction through to a story that
focuses just on them. The UNDER THE COVERS miniseries
isn't anything as obvious as a family saga. As you read *Scoring*,
As Bad As Can Be (May) and *Slippery When Wet* (July),
your challenge is going to be figuring out which secondary
character in each book will become the hero or heroine of the
next.

For now, though, just sit back and enjoy as Becka strikes sparks
with hunky Mace Duvall, ex-baseball heartthrob. Be sure to drop
me a line at kristinhardy@earthlink.net and tell me what you think.
Or drop by my Web site at www.kristinhardy.com for contests,
e-mail threads between characters in my books, recipes and
updates on my latest book.

Have fun,

Kristin Hardy

Books by Kristin Hardy

HARLEQUIN BLAZE
44—MY SEXIEST MISTAKE

SCORING

Kristin Hardy

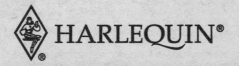

HARLEQUIN®

TORONTO • NEW YORK • LONDON
AMSTERDAM • PARIS • SYDNEY • HAMBURG
STOCKHOLM • ATHENS • TOKYO • MILAN • MADRID
PRAGUE • WARSAW • BUDAPEST • AUCKLAND

To Shannon Short for a great critique,
to Teresa Brown for being generally wonderful,
and
to Stephen,
luz de mi vida,
for everything.

ISBN 0-373-79082-1

SCORING

Copyright © 2003 by Kristin Lewotsky.

This edition published by arrangement with Harlequin Books S.A.

® and TM are trademarks of the publisher. Trademarks indicated with ® are registered in the United States Patent and Trademark Office, the Canadian Trade Marks Office and in other countries.

Visit us at www.eHarlequin.com

Printed in U.S.A.

1

———

"GOD, I LOVE IT when you have your hands on me." The husky words broke the stillness of the room.

Becka Landon slid her fingers over the muscled back of the half-naked man lying in front of her, the warm oil slick under her palms. Skin slipped against skin as her breath came faster, a faint dew of moisture forming on her flushed face. The scent of the oil wove its way into her senses, the warmth of his body heated hers. She caught her lower lip between her teeth in concentration.

"I don't want to share you," he groaned. "Let's just run away, you and me."

Becka's mouth curved. "Sammy, you try running away with anyone and your wife will track you down and brain you with a frying pan." She slapped him smartly on the shoulder. "Off the table, coach. Time to go teach these kids to play baseball."

Sammy Albonado, manager for the Lowell Weavers minor league baseball team, sat up and ran his fingers through his grizzled hair. Years of crouching behind the plate as a major league catcher had given him dickey knees and chronic bursitis in his shoulder. Only Becka's skilled hands could banish the aches on those days when the arthritis gnawed at him. "You got yourself a great touch, kid. I'm gonna have you teach my wife."

"I don't know." Becka put her hands on her hips and gave him a sassy look from under the bangs of her red hair.

"If I were you, I'd be a little nervous about bringing Essie in. I might have to tell her you're threatening to run off on her unless you make it worth my while."

"Aw, you know I was just joking." When she only looked at him, he slumped his shoulders in defeat. "What do you want?"

"New hoses for the whirlpool."

"That's a hundred bucks. I'll have to fill out a req."

"You're the one asking me to keep a secret, Sammy," she reminded him, fighting a smile. "I'm only here as long as Ron's out with his carpal tunnel problem, and who knows how long that will be. I've got to do what I can to get this place in shape before I leave."

"You're not goin' anywhere," he insisted. "Whether Ron comes back this season or not, I'm gonna find a way to keep you on. Even if you do push me around."

Hope ballooned up inside her before she could hold it down. "I don't push you around, Sammy, I just... encourage you. But it's all for the sake of the team." She gave him an impudent grin and shoved her hands into the pockets of her khaki walking shorts, trying to ignore the leap of excitement. She knew that keeping her spot as team trainer was a long shot. It didn't do to count on things that might not happen.

Sammy walked out of the clubhouse and into the shadowed space underneath the grandstand, following the sloping walkway that led to the field. A couple of players skidded up from the parking lot in street clothes.

"Hey, Sammy, is it true?"

"What? You should be dressed and on the field stretching, not bugging me," he barked in the gruff tone he imagined gave him authority. "It's almost time for practice. In my day we cared enough to be early."

"But is it true?" asked Paul Morelli, the tough, good-looking catcher with the makings of major league talent.

"Is what true?" Sammy's voice rose. "Is it true that all of ya are gonna be out on the field in fifteen minutes or I'm handing out fines? You'd better believe it."

"No, for real, we heard that Mace Duvall is coming as a batting instructor."

Sammy took his time hitching up his trousers and adjusting his cap, then nodded. "Yep, he'll be the batting instructor all week, and he'll go on the road with us." His look turned to a glower. "But unless you guys get changed and out on that field in ten minutes, you ain't never gonna meet him."

"You just shaved five minutes off the time, Skipper," protested Sal Lopes, the team's center fielder.

"That's nothin' compared to what I'm gonna shave off you if you don't get your butts out on that field," Sammy thundered, and the players scattered toward the clubhouse.

BECKA STRETCHED a new cover over the massage table, idly listening to the chatter of the players as they dressed for practice. When she'd first joined, a few of them had tried to put the moves on her, but she'd laughed them off. Becka had been around locker rooms most of her life, whether competing or assisting the coaches, and locker rooms frequently contained half-naked, testosterone-laden men who found it hard to believe that a lush-mouthed redhead like Becka could resist their charms.

Over the years, she'd gotten very good at doing just that.

The buzz of a locker room energized her, and okay, so she'd gotten an eyeful once or twice. Admittedly, it was sometimes…entertaining, especially when her social life was almost nonexistent. Still, it didn't throw her off her stride. She'd perfected a slightly bored matter-of-factness that made her one of the boys, even though she was all female. And maybe to their own surprise, the Lowell players found themselves treating her like a bossy older sister rather than date bait.

"Look it up in the book. I'm telling you, he had a .360 career batting average." That was DeWalt Jefferson, aka Stats, resident baseball trivia fiend. "Why do you think they called him Mace? He was like tear gas, left all the pitchers weeping."

"You're full of it," Morelli's voice came back. "That's almost as high as Ted Williams. Next you're going to be telling me his season high was .400."

".383," Stats said triumphantly.

"That's a line of bull."

Becka glanced idly out the door of the training room and into the locker area.

"Hey, if Stats says that's the number, that's the number," Chico Watson, the team's burly first baseman, broke in. Twenty-three and married, Watson was the elder statesman of the team.

"Man oh man, what I'd give to bat like that in the big leagues," said Sal Lopes, dreamily pulling on his jersey.

"Me, I'd settle for having his batting average with the ladies," Morelli grinned as he leaned down to tie his shoes.

"Who's this?"

Four heads whipped around to stare at Becka before they went back to dressing. "Mace Duvall."

Even Becka had heard about Mace Duvall, seen his caramel-blond good looks as he'd escorted actresses and models to swanky benefits and premieres. He'd also escorted them to his bed, if the media was to be believed. There was something else about him that nibbled at the edge of her memory, something she couldn't quite dredge up.

"He retired or something, didn't he?"

"He got retired, more like it." Morelli stood and gathered up his catcher's gear, tucking his leg guards under his arm. "Car accident. A big rig took him out. He's lucky to be alive."

LUCKY WAS HARDLY the way the man in the Bronco would have put it. Mason Duvall pulled into the parking lot at Lowell's LeChere stadium and turned off his truck, listening to the ticks of the cooling engine. Lucky would have been knowing he was going to be back on the diamond. Lucky wasn't losing the only thing that he'd ever wanted to do with his life.

He climbed out of the truck, frowning at the stiffness in his back and leg and then ignoring it as he habitually did. To favor it was to give in to it, to say that the accident had won.

The accident had already won too much.

He absently tucked his gray T-shirt more securely into the back of his worn jeans, the faded material stretching over his lean, hard-muscled frame. During the long months of rehab, the Florida sun had streaked his light hair with tones of bronze and gold. It curled thickly down over his collar. Back in his playing days he'd kept it trimmed short for convenience. Now, he only bothered to have it cut when it hung down in his whiskey-gold eyes or tickled his neck enough to distract him.

A slight limp marred his loose, athletic walk, a limp that faded as he crossed the street to the back fence of the minor league park. He leaned on the wall and stared at the diamond. It exerted an almost irresistible pull, beckoning him to vault the fence and join the game. Instead, he watched the players complete their fielding drills. They looked like a litter of young puppies, still loose and joyfully gawky, their playing infused more with raw talent than finesse. And now he, of all people, was supposed to come here and show them how it was done.

Once, his job had been to slam balls out of the park like artillery shells, to field anything hit within fifty feet of him, to help propel his team to the playoffs half a dozen times in a single decade. That had been before a trucker long past his legally mandated sleep period had lost control of his tractor-trailer and taken Mace off the road. Before the weeks in ICU and the surgeries, the months of rest.

Before the news that he was never going to play baseball in the major leagues again.

Baseball had been all he'd ever wanted, all he'd dreamed about ever since he'd been a kid. He'd been one of the chosen handful that had had the skill, talent, and drive to live that dream. And indeed, baseball had been his life. When he hadn't been playing, he'd been working out. When he hadn't been working out, he'd been watching game tapes. When he hadn't been doing either, he'd kept the media entertained.

Now, there was a giant hole where baseball had been, so Stan Angelo, his onetime teammate and self-appointed savior, had bullied him, or conned him, rather, into trying out as a roving instructor.

"Just one season, Duvall," Angelo had said as they'd shot pool in Mace's half-finished Florida home a month before. "I'm telling you, you'll like it a hell of a lot better than laying around here bored out of your mind."

"I'm not bored out of my mind. I'm building a house, I'm working out. I'm fishing." Mace watched as Stan put a shot wide and cursed. Studiously careful not to smirk at his friend's mishap, he leaned over the table and stroked a ball in smoothly. "I'm enjoying my life instead of hopping on a plane every other week for nine months out of the year. Just because running around the country working for the organization works for you doesn't mean it'll work for me."

"I doubt it will." Stan put one in, but missed the next.

"And you're right," Mace said too quickly.

"That's why I'm telling you about the roving instructor spot," Stan continued, unperturbed. "I talked with the organization about you and they want to give you a try." His ball bounced too hard off the rails and missed the pocket.

"Yeah, well, thanks but no thanks." Mace shot smoothly and put the seven ball in the corner pocket and set up for the next shot. "I'd rather just stay here and work on my pool game. Yours could use some work, too, by the way."

"Hey, I've been on the road," Stan said mildly, watching Mace sink the eight ball. He began pulling balls out of a corner pocket and stacking them into the triangular rack. "Okay, let's make it a bet. You win the next game, I never mention it again."

Mace snorted and took a swig of his beer. "The way you've been playing, we can just save ourselves the time and agree to stop talking about it."

"Humor me." Stan pulled the rack off the balls and gestured to the triangle of color. "I win, you take the roving instructor job for a season." He chalked the end of his cue and walked to the other end of the table. "So maybe you can't play. You can still teach. Better than sitting around here all season driving yourself crazy."

"I'm doing fine."

"I suppose being here gives you a lot of time to practice your pool," Stan said placidly.

"Shut up and break."

"Oh no, I'm the one who set up the bet. You first."

"Break," Mace snarled.

"Okay, okay." Stan leaned over the table, stroked the cue a few times to get the feel, and slammed the cue ball into the balls, sinking two immediately and scattering the rest across the table. "I guess that makes me stripes," he said, stepping around the table to sink two more colored balls in quick succession with machine-like strokes.

Mace's eyes narrowed. "Tell me I didn't just get hustled."

"A bet's a bet, Duvall," Stan said with relish as he sighted along his cue and sank another ball in the corner pocket. "You're not a carpenter, for Christ's sake. Or a fisherman. You belong in a ballpark, and you know it." He put another ball in the pocket. "Try the roving instructor gig. Maybe you'll like it." His bank shot put in the last ball.

"Maybe I'll stop inviting pool hustlers to my house."

Stan squinted down his cue at the eight ball. "Maybe you'll invite me to the clubhouse the first year you're managing in the World Series." He slammed the ball into the pocket and straightened up with a guileless grin. "Looks like I win."

Too bad he wasn't better at sniffing out pool sharks, Mace thought, as he stood leaning on the Lowell ballpark fence and shaking his head.

He'd promised Stan he'd try the job, which as far as he was concerned meant showing up for a couple of days. They'd only taken him on as a favor to Stan anyway.

Mace pushed off from the fence and walked away. If he'd learned one thing in the past year, it was that reality could purely knock the hell out of any plans he might cook up for the future. He was through with doing what he was supposed to do in pursuit of some long-term goal. Nope, from now on, he was going to take life day by day. He'd do what he felt like now instead of constantly focusing on tomorrow. Starting today he was going to live the good life.

BECKA SAT in the dugout watching the players. "You know he won the Gold Glove three times in a row?" Stats asked Morelli before walking past him to take his position at first base, ready to run the minute the hitting coach at the plate slammed a ball into the outfield.

Becka rolled her eyes. She knew without asking that the "he" in question was Mace Duvall. In the past two hours she'd learned enough about the training regimen, lifestyle, achievements, batting stance, favorite shoes, and hobbies of baseball's number one playboy to last her a lifetime. God help her, she even knew the recipe for his favorite protein shake.

"Sammy says he's going to stay in the dorms with us," Morelli said, watching Stats get thrown out at second. "I got an empty room next to me." Most of the Lowell players didn't bother to get their own apartments. They just took rooms at the University of Massachusetts dormitories that stood across the street from the stadium, which were empty during the summer break. Management encouraged it; it was easier to keep an eye on young players when they were nearby.

"You better not take all his time, Morelli, ya motormouth," Chico threw back as he stepped out of the dugout. "Give the rest of us a chance."

Next, they were going to start arm wrestling over who got to have the locker next to "him," Becka thought exasperatedly as Sal Lopes moved into position at first and got prepared to run. They might have been old enough to vote, most of them, but they were all as starstruck by the great Mace Duvall as any Little Leaguers would be.

Becka watched the hitting coach knock a ball into the outfield, with Sal Lopes rounding second and heading for third in a feet-first slide. She couldn't have said whether it was luck or premonition that had her watching Sal intently as he slid into the base, but she saw the exact moment his ankle folded against the bag at an angle that made her cringe. In seconds she was sprinting out to the field.

"I can't believe I'm such an idiot," Lopes groaned as Becka helped the pitching coach carry the player into the training room and lay him on the massage table. "Of all the stupid things to do, the day before Duvall gets here."

"It'll be okay," Becka soothed, fitting a cold pack around the ankle, which was already swelling alarmingly. "Now you just sit and keep it elevated. Once the swelling eases a little, I'll tape it for you." She rummaged around the meds cabinet for ibuprofen. "Swallow a couple of these and lie back for a bit." The phone rang and she turned to her desk.

"Landon," she said briefly.

"Hey, sis."

Becka blinked. "Nellie? What are you doing there? I thought you and Joe were still on your honeymoon."

"We got back on Sunday. Joe wanted to have plenty of time to get me moved. Speaking of which, Mom said you wanted some help moving?"

"Not exactly. I was just trying to find that buddy of Joe's who carries loads for hire. I can't stay on the phone, though, I've got a hurt player here to deal with."

"Oh, you don't need to hire Charlie to move you," Nellie said airily, ignoring her. "Joe will do it."

"Nellie, give the poor guy a break. You just got back two days ago. You can't just sign him up for duty."

"Sure I can," Nellie laughed. "I got my permission slip three weeks ago when he said 'I do.' You were there."

"You've been watching Mom too much," Becka muttered. "Joe might have something to say about that."

"I know how to take care of Joe, don't you worry."

Actually, it was probably true, Becka thought. Her baby

sister had always had her fiancé—now husband—wrapped around her little finger, and used the fact mercilessly. Becka glanced over at Sal and tapped her fingers restlessly.

Nellie chuckled again. ''Joe's asking if it can wait until the weekend.''

''I have to be out by Friday morning,'' Becka said. ''Let me just hire his friend. It's not that big a deal. Look, Nellie, can I call—''

''What about tomorrow?''

''Nellie, you guys took that time so you'd be able to get your stuff moved into Joe's place. You don't need to spend it moving me. I just want Charlie's number.''

''No way. Joe and I will help. How much do you have?''

''Five or six pieces,'' Becka said, giving up. Somehow, in a way she never figured out how to resist, this always happened when Nellie and her mother were concerned. It was like playing Pin The Tail On The Donkey. One minute she knew exactly what direction she was going, and the next she was spun around until she didn't know which way was up and let herself get pushed wherever they would push her. And the worst part was, they always meant well, which was what made it all but impossible to fight without being utterly ungracious. Becka sighed. ''A couch, the table and chairs. My dresser. Oh, and we have to stop by Ryan's. She's giving me her bed. Now, please, I've really got to go.''

''Ryan's not getting married for weeks, is she? Where's she planning on sleeping?''

''With Cade, I assume. If you're dead set on the moving thing, it'll have to be early. I work tomorrow.''

''How early?''

Becka considered. ''It'll probably take a couple of trips, even with Joe's truck. Could you guys do nine o'clock?''

''How about eight?''

Becka shrugged. "The earlier the better as far as I'm concerned."

"We'll see you then."

"Great. Thanks for calling."

"You want to talk to Mom?"

"I've got to get back to work," Becka said rapidly. "Bye."

"Hey, you didn't have to rush on my account," Lopes put in as she put the receiver in the cradle.

Becka rolled her eyes. "Believe me, it wasn't on your account."

2

MACE WALKED through the door to the administrative offices of the Lowell Weavers. The stadium was new, but its weathered brick and iron blended with the turn-of-the-century factory buildings that surrounded the ballpark, reminders of Lowell's heyday as a textile center. Though the mill buildings now housed upscale housewares stores and trendy boutiques instead of steam-powered looms, the town still held the faded dignity of a bygone era.

Turning back into the locker room area, Mace heard Sammy Albonado before he saw him.

"Just give me another coupla weeks to straighten him out, Rick. Don't jump the gun on this."

Mace knocked on the open door. Albonado waved him in, nodding vigorously to the unseen caller on the phone.

"I really think he's got what it takes, we've just got to get him focused." Mace took a seat, looking around the cramped office with its battered metal desk and file cabinet. An insurance company calendar dangled from the putty-colored wall, next to faded schedules from seasons long gone. Tacked to a beat-up corkboard on the door was that night's lineup.

Sammy paused to listen, nodding again. "Okay. Have a good one." He hung up the phone and grinned, sticking out his hand. "Well, glory be, it's Mace Duvall."

"In the flesh." Mace gripped Sammy's hand.

"You know, I was at that game a couple of years ago

where you hit for the cycle. Single, double, triple, and homer in the same game. What a night.'' Sammy shook his head in admiration, standing up to shut the door that led into the locker room. ''Want a drink? Got Gatorade, Coke, water, you name it.'' He dropped back in his chair and rolled back to flip open the door of the mini-refrigerator that sat behind his desk.

''Water?''

''Sure.'' Sammy passed Mace a bottle and cracked open a Coke, leaning back until his chair creaked in protest. ''I gotta say, I'm happy to see you here. If you can get a tenth of what you know about hitting into these kids' heads, we'll be way ahead of the game.'' He took a drink, sighing in satisfaction at the first taste. ''I can teach 'em fielding, but we really need someone like you to help them understand how to look at the ball.''

Mace twisted the cap off the bottle of water and took a swallow. ''Well, I'll do what I can, but I'm not making any guarantees.'' He stared into the clear plastic bottle. What the hell was he doing here? And what was he hoping to accomplish?

Sammy examined him shrewdly, then gave a smile that Mace didn't trust. ''Of course you can't,'' he said jovially, ''but you know hitting and that's what counts. Watch the game tonight and you and I can talk over breakfast tomorrow morning. Practice starts at 1:00 p.m.'' The phone rang and Sammy gave it a baleful glare. ''Okay, take a look around while I get this. I'll be out in a minute.''

Mace opened the door to step into the empty locker room. Then he heard a throaty female laugh.

''TIME TO TAPE UP that ankle, Sal.'' Becka turned to where Lopes lay on the training table. Trying to be gentle, she pulled off the cold pack. The sight underneath made her wince. Though the swelling wasn't as bad as it could have been, angry red and purple streaks overlaid a hard-looking knot just over the joint.

Lopes raised himself up on his elbows. "How's it look?"

Becka lifted his ankle gently, moving it slightly to test range of motion. His breath hissed in. "Hurts, huh?" she asked softly.

"Not too bad," he managed in a strained voice. "I'll be okay tomorrow."

Becka took another look. "I'm thinking you'll be lucky if you're actually walking tomorrow. We need to get this X-rayed," she said decisively and checked her watch.

"I got to get playing tomorrow," Sal protested. "Duvall's only here a week."

"He's an ex-ballplayer, not a god," she said impatiently, pulling a tensor bandage from the supply cabinet. "You rest this and let it recover now, or it'll just keep giving out on you. Even if it's just fractured, you're going to need to take it easy for at least several weeks."

"They'll put me on the disabled list," Sal groaned.

"Two weeks or so on the DL isn't going to ruin your career," Becka chided him. "It's not broken, that's something at least. Let me tape it up and I'll drive you to the E.R." With gentle, competent hands she wound the tape around his ankle until the ankle was supported and restrained. "Okay, big guy, sit up and let's get you on your feet." She turned to rummage in the supplies closet, digging back toward the rear. "I have some crutches here somewhere that you can use...." She emerged with them just as Lopes tried to slide off the table.

As soon as the injured foot touched the floor, he yelped and lost his balance.

"Dammit, Sal!" Becka dropped the crutches and leaped to catch him. He slumped against her, face screwed up in pain, one arm hooked over her shoulder. The locker room rang with post-practice silence.

"Okay, let's get you on the table first." Becka puffed with exertion as she struggled to hold him. Even for someone in her shape, moving him was a job. "Let's move back toward the table a bit at a time. Just let me carry your weight when you need to put your bad foot down, and take little steps. Okay?" She took his grunt for assent and moved him slightly, first one step, then two.

It was like the clumsy, shuffling slow dances she'd done in junior high, Becka thought, or maybe like a pair of dancing bears. They made progress, though, until Lopes began laughing. Caught in the ridiculous clinch, Becka couldn't keep from joining him.

His shoulders shook. "Hey baby, I got some moves for you."

Becka smothered another giggle. "Stop it or I won't be able to hold you up," she ordered as she propped him against the table. She took a breath of relief before leaning in to wrap her arms around him for the final push. Then laughed again.

"You know, in ten years in the majors I can't say I've ever seen physical therapy like that." The voice was like warm molasses, with just a hint of a drawl. Becka jerked her head up to see Mace Duvall in the doorway, watching them.

Her mind stuttered to a stop.

He was lean and tawny like a jungle cat, with the same sense of coiled energy waiting to spring. The face that had merely been good-looking on television was taut and honed down, almost predatory in person, made more so by the thin scar that ran along his left cheekbone. He looked at her like he wanted to snap her up. In some indefinable sense, he was more present in his body than any man she'd ever seen. The blood thundered in her ears.

Sal, meanwhile, was hyperventilating with excitement. "Oh wow, man, you're Mace Duvall. It is truly a pleasure to meet you." Sal's words snapped Becka out of her daze, and she finished helping him up onto the table. Sal grinned. "Hope you don't mind if I don't get up."

Mace stepped over to shake hands with the young ballplayer, but he never took his eyes off Becka. "What happened?"

"Bad slide. Just a sprain, though. How long you here for?"

"A week."

"Florence Nightingale here said I'd be back up tomorrow," Sal said, hooking a thumb at Becka as she leaned over to pick up the crutches.

"I think I said we should go get it X-rayed, Sal." Becka slapped the crutches into Lopes' hands.

He ducked his head in embarrassment. "Oh. Well. Yeah," he mumbled, "but I gotta make a pit stop."

"Okay," she said with a glance at Mace. "Then I'll drive you to the E.R."

"Right. Gimme five minutes." He swung out of the room, still grinning. Oddly, the space seemed smaller with just her and Mace, Becka thought, struggling to banish the uneasiness. Maybe it had to do with those mocking eyes. Maybe it had to do with the unexpected edge of desire that suddenly sliced through her.

She struggled to breathe deeply and slow her system down. So she was attracted to him. Big deal. She'd been attracted to plenty of guys in her life. No way was she going to pat his ego and fall at his feet like every other woman he met. This was her territory and her job. She wasn't about to let some pretty boy make her uncomfortable.

His mouth curved up in a slow smile as though he knew what she was thinking. It brought out the temper in her.

You're a professional, Becka reminded herself. Act like it. "I take it you're the infamous Mace Duvall." She stuck her hand out. "I'm Becka Landon, the infamous trainer."

"SO WAS THAT your version of bedside manner?" Mace asked, shaking her hand, intrigued to feel her pulse jump unsteadily under his fingers. He'd always been partial to redheads, and this one had the glowing, luminous skin that was a combination of good fortune and complete, utter fitness. Deep, dark red without a hint of orange, her hair feathered down to end just above her shoulders, framing exotic cheekbones and slanted green cat eyes that stared out at him from under a fringe of bangs. Her lush mouth looked soft and sulky.

He didn't blame the player for trying to grope her or whatever had been going on. She obviously took her own medicine when it came to working out. Even camouflaged in a polo shirt and long walking shorts, her taut, curvy body made him wonder just what kind of things she could get up to in bed.

Becka raised her chin belligerently. "He was hurt, I was doing my job. You have a problem with that?"

He might just have a problem with her, he thought, wondering how those full lips tasted. "Only when it means distracting players in the clubhouse."

"Oh, get over it," she said impatiently, turning to jerk the cover off the table. "His foot wouldn't hold his weight and it was either catch him or scrape him up off the floor."

Something about the way her eyes snapped at him

tempted him to push her a bit, just to see how she'd react. "Happens a lot that way?"

She flushed. "Now you're being insulting. These kids like to play tough guy when they're hurt. I was just trying to keep him from making things worse."

"Looks like you distracted him from his pain just fine."

Her cat eyes narrowed. "What's that supposed to mean?"

"I don't usually see trainers in a clinch with players."

She laughed then. "Are you kidding? To these kids I'm like their old Aunt Edna. Sal's thinking about the games he's going to miss, not me. His mind doesn't work that way."

Just for a heartbeat, his gaze flicked down to the buttons on her polo shirt. "Sugar, every eighteen-year-old's mind works that way."

She wanted to be annoyed. She wanted to be offended. She didn't want to feel this flush of heat. Then she saw amusement flicker in his eyes and irritation rescued her.

"Gee, Duvall, are you always such a charmer or did you cook up the sexist routine just for me?"

Oh, belligerence suited her, he thought. She had herself a temper, Miss Becka Landon did, and she wore it well. And if she looked this good in shorts and a polo shirt and mad, he couldn't help wondering what she looked like in nothing at all. "No offense intended, just a friendly warning. You don't want to underestimate these boys. Half of them just got out of high school two months ago. Their hormones are still kicking in. Something you think is harmless might have them daydreaming about you when they're on the field."

"Oh stop, Duvall, you're flattering me."

He stepped closer to her, and her heart jumped in response.

"You don't want to underestimate me, either," he said softly, staring at her throat where the pulse beat madly under translucent skin. Flattery didn't even come close to what he wanted to do with her.

She should haul off and put him in his place, Becka thought, but her mind kept focusing on the flecks of copper in his golden eyes, and the heat she could feel radiating from him. Seconds stretched out, until she heard Sal's voice as he crutched back toward the training room.

"I'm ready, Florence."

Becka turned and got her keys and purse. She glanced at Mace.

"Well, this has been fun, Duvall, but I've got to run. Guess I'll see you tonight when the game starts."

The corners of his mouth curved in a slow grin and his eyes flickered with a heat she felt down to the pit of her stomach. "Funny, I thought it had started already."

3

EARLY-MORNING SUN SLANTED across Becka as she helped Joe tie the last of her kitchen chairs onto his pickup. The final amalgamation looked a lot like something out of the *Beverly Hillbillies,* but it all fit, even the bed picked up that morning from her girlfriend Ryan's house.

"We're ready to roll," Joe called, dusting off his hands as he walked over to stand with his wife. "Everybody in." Blunt-featured and stocky, he seemed to adore Nellie beyond reason. And like Becka's father, he was endlessly patient. Maybe patient enough to be in a relationship in which his sweetheart always knew best—or at least thought she did.

As for Becka, she'd go down kicking and screaming before she'd let someone control her, particularly a lover, she thought, squeezing next to Nellie in the cab. She wasn't, however, always as quick to notice if they were so self-absorbed like her ex-boyfriend Scott had been. Having a boyfriend was a relatively small part of her life, all things considered. Except for the sex, of course. Still, no one she knew had died from doing without, she thought, trying not to count how long it had been. The image of Mace Duvall popped into her head and she pushed it away with baffled irritation. One thing was for sure, next time she had a lover, he wasn't going to be a playboy.

"So how's the new job going?" Nellie asked, her hand on Joe's knee. "It's sort of like what you used to do for

Dad's team, right? I always envied you, running off with Dad to the big games all the time.''

Becka smiled as she thought about all the Saturday evenings she'd spent volunteering for the college basketball team her father coached. And getting up at the crack of dawn even on the weekends. ''It wasn't all fun and games,'' she said. ''Those weight rooms and locker rooms smell like something died in them.''

''Couldn't bother you too much if you're back in one.'' Nellie winked at Becka. ''So, have you walked in on any of the players in the buff yet?''

''Hey,'' Joe protested good-naturedly. ''You're a married woman, you shouldn't be thinking about guys in the buff.''

''No guys in the buff at all?'' Nellie asked coyly, running her fingertips up the inside of his leg.

Joe shifted in his seat. ''You're gonna feel real funny if you make me run off the road,'' he said gruffly.

With a delighted giggle, Nellie bussed him on the cheek until a flush bloomed up his neck and across his face.

They were good together, Becka thought suddenly, looking at them. In some indefinable way they'd melded since she'd last seen them. The thought warmed her. Okay, so maybe their type of marriage would send her to the nuthouse within five minutes, but the important thing was that it worked for them.

''So, your team any good?'' Joe asked, cheeks still stained a faint pink.

''Oh, so-so,'' Becka admitted. ''These guys aren't going to be in the majors any time soon. They're just a step up from high school.''

''Still goofballs?''

''I wouldn't say that,'' Becka said protectively. ''They've got talent, some of them. They're just still figuring out how it all works. We have lots of instructors coming through to give them hitting clinics and stuff.''

"Anybody famous?" Joe asked, linking his hand with Nellie's.

"We've got a big name in now. Mace Duvall, used to play shortstop for the Braves."

Joc whistled. "Hey, I saw him play in the World Series on TV a couple of times. Guy swings a hell of a bat."

"You think that's big, you should see his ego."

"It ain't ego if you can back it up," Joe said thoughtfully. "I read an article on his training routine one time. That's one guy who works his butt off. And that was in the off-season. I'd hate to see what he does when he's playing."

Becka hesitated a beat. "He doesn't anymore. He got hurt. That's why he's here instructing."

"Oh, yeah, that's right." Joe drove for a moment. "Boy, what a drag."

"What happened?" Nellie asked.

"Car accident."

"That's so sad."

The tug of sympathy Becka felt caught her by surprise. It *was* sad, she realized, both for the sport, which had lost one of its superstars, and Duvall himself, who had so nearly lost everything. However much he might annoy her, a huge part of his life had been snatched from him, she thought slowly. What did a person do after that? What else could possibly come close?

HE LIKED MORNINGS best. Perhaps it came from growing up on the farm, getting up before dawn to feed the stock. Perhaps it came from his early playing years, when the morning was the only time he had to himself. Maybe it was purely constitutional. In any case, he had always woken up chirping with the birds.

Mace leaned an arm on the cracked red vinyl seat of the diner booth, looking across the Formica tabletop to where Sammy Albonado sat hunched over his coffee cup. It was hard to be sure, but he thought that Sammy's eyes had actually opened a fraction now that the caffeine was hitting.

Some people were morning people and some people weren't.

The waitress sauntered up to refill their mugs. "You're a goddess, Bernice," Sammy said without looking up.

"Don't mention it." She set down the pot and pulled out her order pad. "What'll it be, boys?" she asked, pen poised.

"Three eggs over easy, fried ham, and a bagel," Sammy ordered.

Bernice didn't write, she just stared at him.

Sammy shifted in his seat. Seconds passed by. "What?" he burst out pugnaciously.

"Your wife called. Reminded me your last cholesterol test was 290."

"She what?" he yelped. "Oh, come on, it was a little high, but give me a break. The woman gives me porridge for breakfast. Porridge." Sammy gave a pained look, whether over the idea of the cereal or over actually opening his eyes, Mace couldn't tell. "Now she's cutting me off at my favorite diner? I should never have brought her here."

"So you're telling me that after the doctor's warnings and all the worrying your poor wife is doing, you'd rather order the heart attack special than eat what's good for you?" Bernice folded her arms over her chest and gave him a disapproving stare.

Tinny honky-tonk music played on the mini-jukebox a few tables down. Gradually, Sammy's belligerent look faded into sheepishness. "No." He cleared his throat. "I'll just have orange juice, toast, and uh," he flinched at Bernice's stare. "Oatmeal."

Bernice kept a straight face. "There's hope for you yet, Sammy Albonado." She patted him sympathetically and turned to Mace. "How about for you?"

"Three eggs, scrambled with cheese, bacon, toast and orange juice," Mace rattled off, enjoying Sammy's anguished look. "Don't worry, Sammy, I'll let you smell it."

"You're lucky I don't run you out of town, Duvall," Sammy muttered, glowering as Bernice walked away with his order. "Woman's worse than the drill sergeant I had in the army. I oughtta start going to Denny's. That'd show her." He added creamer and three packets of sugar to his coffee cup and stirred until the spoon clanked against the porcelain.

"So whatdja think about the game last night?" he asked. "We hammered that Brooklyn team."

Mace watched him drink and tried not to wince. "I think you've got some talent here. They're rough, though." He took a swallow of his black coffee, strong and unsweetened, just as he liked it. "They need a lot of work." And he was the last guy in a position to give it to them. It was a damn-fool idea, one that he'd decided the night before to give up. All he had to do now was figure out how to break the news to Sammy, who was nodding wisely at him.

"Settling 'em down is what A ball is for. Half the time, they're just here to grow up enough that they can focus on the game." Sammy stirred his coffee again. "I figure you can be a good influence on them. Steady 'em down, especially Morelli."

He wasn't a stable pony, Mace thought, glancing out the window. He felt a surge of annoyance toward Stan, and then at himself for agreeing to be in this spot. He was damned if he'd take a job just because someone in the organization pulled strings for him. The thing to do was quit and go back to Florida, leave the spot for someone who wanted it. He'd do some fishing, surf a little, maybe play a little golf.

And go back to going quietly mad in his sprawling beach house by the sea.

He tuned back in to Sammy, who was still talking.

"I don't know, Sammy, I've been thinking about this and I just don't know. These kids need to be taught by—"

"By a champ, and here's what I've got planned," Sammy said. "We work on batting practice and go to fielding."

"Sammy, that's great, but I'm not the guy—"

"I know you're not here for the fielding drills this time, but I figure it doesn't hurt to overlap assignments."

Mace looked Sammy in the eye; Sammy looked back. Mace gave up. When he'd been a player, Sammy had been famous for his single-minded focus on the game. Obviously, he'd gotten it in his head that Mace was the right man for the job and wasn't about to take a hint. Mace prided himself on dealing straight with people, but he also knew when it was time to throw in the towel. Maybe it would be easier to just write a resignation letter and do it that way.

"All the game reports and player files are in the top drawer of my cabinet." Sammy stopped to sip his coffee. "Ask Becka for a look at their training records if you want."

"Where'd you find that one, anyway?" Mace asked idly, as the memory of green eyes and luminous skin vaulted into his mind. He'd been out with plenty of beautiful women in his time, but something about Becka Landon lingered in his imagination.

Maybe he was being too hasty about this quitting thing.

"Where'd I find who, Becka?" Sammy asked as Bernice set their breakfasts on the table. "The Boston College trainer recommended her. Our guy came down with carpal tunnel so we had to find a sub at the start of the season. She's top-notch."

Mace gave him a skeptical look before digging into his eggs. "How is she with the players?"

Sammy stared at Mace's plate with starving orphan eyes. "I'll give you five bucks if you slip me a slice of bacon," he offered. When Mace just looked at him, Sammy sighed and began slathering jelly on a piece of dry toast. "They call her Attila behind her back, and Florence Nightingale to her face, if that gives you a clue. She's a demon in the weight room. These boys are in better condition this year than any team I've ever had before." He bit into the toast.

"They're probably pushing themselves to impress her."

Sammy chewed thoughtfully, then shook his head and swallowed. "Nah. At first, maybe, but every time one of them tries to hit on her, she gives them the brush-off. I saw her once, acted like a third-grade teacher would at one of her kids feeding her a line. Didn't even bother to get on her high horse. She just laughed. Cooled him right down."

It would take a lot more than a simple brush-off to cool him down if he made a pass at her, Mace decided, remembering the unsteady feel of her pulse under his fingers. "You're not concerned with having her in the clubhouse? Breaking the players' concentration?"

Sammy shrugged. "We're only two games out of second place. They're playing hard and they're improving. What more do you want?"

A certain curvy redhead wrapped around him naked, Mace thought before he could block it. It had been a long time since a woman had climbed into his head like Becka had. A slow grin stole over his face as he remembered her provocative pout. Maybe he'd drop by and see if he could worm loose her phone number before he left. For years he'd been tagged with a rep for scoring with women. Maybe it was time that he actually earned it.

Starting with the delectable Ms. Landon.

BECKA SAT at her desk in the training room, updating player records, absently wrapping a twist of red hair around her finger.

"Got a minute?"

She recognized the slow drawl even before she glanced up to see Mace leaning against the doorway to the locker room. The quick frisson of excitement that whisked through her had her scowling. It had only been a few months since she'd unloaded her cheating bum of a boyfriend. The last thing she needed was to get caught up in more trouble on two legs, and Mace Duvall definitely qualified as trouble. Okay, maybe she'd felt bad about his situation earlier that morning, but too much sympathy could be a dangerous thing. Be too sympathetic to a jungle cat and you might just wind up being a snack, she reflected.

"What do you want?" she asked briefly. "I'm working."

"Looks like my timing's perfect," he said easily. "Sammy said you could review the training records with me."

She ignored a flutter somewhere in the vicinity of her solar plexus. Sports trainers weren't supposed to have flutters on the job. "I'll need time to finish this report first."

"That's fine," he said equably, not moving.

Trust him not to take a hint, she thought. "Batting practice isn't for two hours. Why don't you go back into your office and I'll come get you when I'm done." He'd kept his distance during the game the night before, but time and time again she'd looked up to find his eyes on her. Time and time again she'd found him on her mind. Okay, if she were honest, she'd thought about him before she'd even seen him. His presence just made it worse. Hoping that sheer rudeness would drive him away, Becka bent her head back to her reports dismissively and tried to ignore the figure in the doorway.

Out in the locker room, the vacuum cleaner of the custodial staff whirred. On the other side of the wall, in his office, Sammy argued with what was probably the stadium manager over letting an Elvis impersonator do a pregame show from the pitcher's mound. Life in the minor leagues went on.

Mace smiled to himself and pushed away from the doorway to walk toward Becka. Her head jerked up like a deer scenting a predator, her eyes wide and startled. He caught a hint of her fragrance and leaned in close to her to get a better whiff. Like sunkissed wildflowers, he thought. "I'll just grab a seat," he murmured into her ear. "I don't mind waiting when I want something." Enjoying her reaction, he moved past her to retrieve a chair from the back of the room.

Sitting across from her, Mace watched her pore over the reports, trying to understand why she fascinated him, trying to understand why he'd woken in the night thinking of her. He'd escorted internationally acclaimed beauties, women who worked at their mystique as though it were a career. How was it that tomboyish Becka Landon crept into his dreams?

It wasn't as though she'd given him the come-on, he thought as he leaned back in the chair. Maybe she had a mouth that a man found hard to ignore, but she'd made it clear that she was no fan of his. So why was he getting hung up on her? He wasn't a glutton for punishment. A woman said no to him, that was that.

But Becka's body seemed to say yes. Despite herself, she responded to him. Perhaps therein lay the fascination. Mace studied the coppery spill of hair that trailed across her cheek as she worked. An energy hummed around her, a glow of vitality that radiated from her skin, taut warm hide stretched over perfectly toned muscles. He had the sudden urge to touch her, to see if he could feel that energy, like some kind of magic force field.

Becka was digging for a paper clip in the tray of odds and ends that sat at the base of her desk lamp when she glanced up at him and her hand froze. For a long instant, he stared into the cool green of her eyes, trying to divine just what it was about her that had its hooks in him. On impulse, he reached out to take her hand, just as she pulled a paper clip out of the tray and bent back to her paperwork. She fumbled as she clipped a sheet into the file. Minutes passed while she stared at the papers without writing or turning a page.

Finally, she put down her pen with a snap. "Fine. What do you want to know?"

"Are you sure you're done?"

"You know I'm not done. Let's just get this over with."

"Are you sure?"

"Take advantage of my generous mood, Duvall," she advised him. "It may not last."

"Who are you working on?"

"Morelli."

"Ah." He leaned forward with interest. "Kid's got some good moves."

Becka handed him the file. "You think he's got the goods?"

Mace shrugged diffidently. "Too early to tell, but I like

the way he handles himself." His eyes flicked to her mouth. He liked the way she handled herself, too, now that he thought about it. "So what do you do with yourself when you're not working?" he asked abruptly. "What about dinner?"

Becka's mouth opened in surprise, then shut. "Sorry, Duvall, I don't date colleagues."

"Don't worry about it. I'm not going to be a colleague any longer than it'll take me to turn in my resignation."

"What do you mean? You just got here. Your assignment's supposed to be for a week."

He was only here because they were humoring him, he reminded himself. It wasn't like he was running out on the job. "It was a dumb idea. I shouldn't have started it."

"But you did start it." An edge entered her voice. "You should at least finish the assignment."

"What does one week matter?"

"To these kids? It's everything. You're a minor deity around here, you know. The amazing Mace Duvall, baseball superhero. They've memorized every detail they could dig up about you." She shoved her chair back and paced across the office. "They talk about you every waking minute. I've got a kid with a severe high ankle sprain who won't stay off it because he's got the chance to work with you while you're here. And now you're telling me you're going to leave without even getting into your assignment?"

"Hey, disappointment is a part of life. They might as well get used to it." The words tasted bitter in his mouth. "Besides, they're grown-ups. They can handle it."

"No, they're kids. *You're* the grown-up and you're supposed to be responsible," she shot back, jerking her chin up.

Like a girl protecting her kid brothers against the neighborhood bully, he thought, surprised at just how sexy it was. An enticing flush ran along the tops of her cheekbones. "Look, it's not that big a deal. I mean, really, what does it matter if I resign? I could walk out of the front door right now and get hit in the head by a falling brick and be just as gone."

"Unlikely," she said, sitting down reluctantly.

"So are a lot of things that happen, believe me."

"All the more reason you should control what you can, and keep to your word."

"What word? I made a stupid bet over a game of pool. I lost, and the stake was being a batting instructor for a season. I've got no real business being here, so I'm pulling out. It's nothing personal." He picked a steel ball the size of a walnut out of the tray of paper clips and began rolling it idly back and forth across the desktop.

"I'm not taking it personally," she returned hotly. "I could care less if you stay or go but it's important to these kids. They're trying to do something here they care about. All you seem to be in it for is the moment."

"There are worse ways to live than just enjoying the moment."

"Some of us believe in getting the job done, not laying back and singing all summer long."

"The ant and the grasshopper?" he asked, his voice amused. Then it turned serious. "So what happens if you're the ant and you get crushed? You never get to enjoy the results of all your hard work and you never get to appreciate life one day at a time like the grasshopper. You lose out on everything because you think you're going to be lucky and have things work out like you expect." Whiskey-gold, his eyes abruptly flamed with heat. He let the gleaming sphere roll, his attention focused on Becka.

"So you live your life planning to be unlucky?" Her

fingers reached out to catch the ball before it rolled off the desk.

"No." With a lightning-quick move, his hand trapped hers. "I plan to get very lucky indeed."

Her system jolted. She tried to jerk back from the heat that licked up her arm, in sharp contrast to the cool steel.

"Not so fast," Mace said, holding on. "You have very shaky hands for a therapist. I noticed that yesterday. Why do you think that is?" He turned her palm up, tracing a finger down the soft, sensitive flesh there.

Becka snatched her hand back. "Get lost, Duvall. Go flatter one of the girls in the front office. I've got better things to do."

He stared at her a moment, a smile playing on his lips. "You know, I might just stick around here after all."

"Do tell. Is your conscience getting the better of you?"

"No, but wondering what you'd be like in bed is."

For a moment she just stared at him, eyes darkening. Then she seemed to recover. "Find another reason, Duvall," she said witheringly. "I don't do ladies' men."

He gave a look of pure amusement. "Then it's a good thing I'm not one, isn't it?"

She snorted. "Yeah, tell me another good one."

"It's a mistake to believe everything you read, you know."

"We're finished with this conversation, Duvall. I've got enough to do without wasting time on quitters."

A brief shadow flickered in his eyes and was gone just as quickly. He tossed the steel ball back into the tray. "See you around, Florence."

"Not if I see you first."

4

MACE LEANED on the dugout fence in the afternoon sun and watched batting practice. He'd always loved being out on the diamond, feeling the spring of power in his muscles, the excitement of knowing the game was just hours away. The nights he had good batting practice were the nights he felt like he could do anything.

"That was a ball you just swung at, Jefferson," Sammy bawled as Stats stepped out of the batting box. "What, these pitchers such good friends of yours that you wanna give 'em gifts? Make 'em work."

Mace grinned and stepped up to the batting box to talk quietly into Stats' ear. A few pitches later and the young shortstop was waiting out balls and slamming the strikes into deep left field.

"You do that in a game, you've got yourself a .340 average, buddy." The buzz of triumph Mace felt surprised him. Grinning, he turned to size up the next batter just as Becka stepped into the dugout, video camera at her side.

She spared him a glance. "Where do you want me?"

"I get a choice?" He couldn't resist running his gaze down her legs, long and smooth in her walking shorts.

"Don't get cute, Duvall. Sammy asked me to help out. How do you want the batters filmed?"

"From the side. Film the entire at bat, even if Sammy and I are up there. I want to see everything they do."

She nodded and moved back into the background as Morelli came to the plate.

"Okay, Morelli, show me what you got," Mace said.

Becka put the video camera to her eye and began filming. A miniature version of Morelli appeared in the viewfinder, then Mace moved into the frame. Somehow, in the electronic image he looked even more lean, even more male. The sunlight on his hair brought out the gold and bronze; sunglasses hid his eyes. Something about the frame of the viewfinder made it impossible to look away.

Mace finished talking to Morelli and moved back. Becka ignored a ridiculous twinge of disappointment, focusing instead on the task of filming the young player. At the next pitch he swung late and the ball thumped into the catcher's mitt.

Mace stepped back into the frame, slipping on a batting helmet and gloves and taking the bat from Morelli. The polished wood whistled through the air as Mace took a few practice swings to loosen up. When he was satisfied, he stepped into the batting box and raised the bat over his right shoulder, lowering into position with taut precision. His stance spoke of coiled violence. Becka's pulse began to thrum.

The pitching coach on the mound threw one low and outside. Mace merely adjusted his position and focused more intently. The next pitch came nearer the plate, but Mace just looked at it.

"Come on, Duvall," the pitching coach called. "You don't really want to relive all those times you whiffed when you were up against me in Cincinnati, do you?"

"I'll be whiffing in your dreams, Butler. Those were balls. Get it over the plate and we'll talk."

Butler wound up, kicked, and threw a curve ball that barely made it into the strike zone, low and outside.

And Mace exploded into motion.

The curving snap of movement seemed to deliver every bit of power in his entire body to a single point on the bat. Becka swore she could see the ball flatten where it made contact with the wood, before it slammed out of the park on a trajectory headed for New Hampshire.

"Oh man, he crushed it," someone cried out behind her.

It took her breath away. It was one thing to see Mace standing before her, loose and rangy. It was quite another to see him do what he'd been born to do. The tiny figures that performed athletic feats on television bore no relation to the burst of power that she'd just seen. A little curl of desire twisted through her.

The players surrounded Mace like groupies around a rock star. Becka turned off the camera and lowered it shakily, raking a hand through her hair. She took another glance toward the crowd, and found Mace's whiskey eyes locked on hers.

"Man, do you realize that tomorrow is going to be our first day off in twelve freaking days?" Morelli asked hours later, after the team had played and won. He shifted as Becka worked on his shoulder to loosen up the knots. "I'm gonna go out and party tonight and sleep 'til noon."

Chico Watson sat in the whirlpool bath, trying to soak away a sore hamstring. "Laying around sounds good to me. What are you gonna do, Florence?"

Becka pressed the heels of her hands against a knotted muscle in Morelli's shoulder. "I don't want to think about it. It'll only depress me."

"What, you going in for a root canal?"

Becka flashed a grin. "Almost as bad. I'm moving tomorrow."

"Moving? What the hell for?"

"Call me crazy, but something about spending two hours a day driving to work is starting to get to me."

"Where's the new place?"

"Just across the river." She shrugged. "It shouldn't be too bad. The furniture's all in. All that's left is boxes, and I'm getting a cargo van." She laid a heat pack on Morelli's shoulder.

Chico stirred. "Why you renting a van? I've got a truck. Tell me where to go, I'll help you out."

"It's your day off, Chico. You don't want to help me move. Trust me, I don't even want to help me move."

"Hey, I got nothing better to do. My wife was supposed to come up from New Jersey with my kid but she couldn't get off work. Helping you move is better than sitting around and feeling sorry for myself. Buy me pizza and beer and you've got a deal."

She looked at him for a minute. "Vegetarian pizza."

"You ever eat anything that's not all sprouts and tofu, Florence?"

"I'm supposed to be setting a good example for you. Pepperoni's full of fat and nitrites."

"Puts hair on your chest. Tomorrow's your day off. You can go back to setting a good example when we're back on the clock." He folded his arms over his chest. "Pepperoni and beer, or I don't help you move."

She eyed him as he stared blandly back, then her face relaxed into a smile. "Pepperoni and beer it is."

BECKA WIPED down the training tables with alcohol, glancing at the whirlpool to check that the water was draining properly. The noise of the locker room gradually died away as the players finished changing and headed back to the dorms.

Sammy stepped into the training room. "I'm heading out for the night. You all set here?"

"Sure thing, chief."

"How's Sal's ankle looking?"

"We were lucky that it didn't turn out to be a break. He can start doing some basic stretching and strength exercises in a week, but right now he's got to stay off it and let it rest."

"He's really hot to work with Duvall while he's here."

The thought of Mace was like a splinter under her skin. Despite what he'd said earlier, Mace had apparently made no plans to move on yet, which could mean almost anything. She frowned. "I'm sure Sal will get a chance to work with another instructor. If he tries to push this now, he'll only keep himself sidelined longer."

"You're the expert. He's on the bench until you give the word."

"Thanks. Have a good night, Sammy."

He waved and ducked out of the room.

The outside door shut with a rattling clunk and Becka listened to the silence rush in. There was something soothing about being in the clubhouse after everyone had gone home. During the day, it was crowded with bodies and noise, the rising scents of leather and exertion. Now, a quiet peace settled over the rooms. Finally, she could relax. She wasn't shy about being the lone woman in an organization of men—actually, she kind of liked it—but sometimes it was nice to have a break from all the testosterone. She rolled her head in a circle and rubbed her shoulders, easing the tight muscles of her trapezius.

"I'll rub yours if you rub mine."

She caught a breath at the sudden voice, whirling to see Mace standing at the doorway. "Don't ever sneak up on me like that,'' she burst out at him. ''You took ten years off my life.''

''Sorry. I thought you knew I was still here.''

''I assumed you'd left like everyone else. I usually have the clubhouse to myself by this time.''

He stepped closer to her. ''I guess you're going to have to get used to sharing, then, aren't you?''

''What are you doing here? I thought you were quitting.'' She refused to back up, even as her pulse began thudding.

''I haven't decided.'' He stared at her a moment. ''That batting practice today kind of did a number on my back. I was hoping I could get you to work on it for a little.'' He reached out and traced a finger down the side of her neck to her shoulders. ''We could trade. I give as good as I get.''

Becka jerked back from his touch. ''Don't tell me that line has actually worked for you in the past, Duvall,'' she said, trying for scathing, trying to ignore the shiver of butterflies in her stomach. ''I'd expect better from such a big-league player.''

His smile turned wolfish. ''Just for the record, I don't bother using lines. I've always favored the direct approach.'' His hands dropped down to the buttons on his shirt. ''You're missing out if you don't want me to rub your neck, though. Guess I'll just let you work on me.''

Becka gave him a dismissive glance. ''Sorry, we're closed for the day.''

''Not 'til the team's gone home, you aren't, and until something changes, I'm a member of the team.''

''I give you a rubdown tonight and you quit tomorrow.''

''Who knows? Maybe I will, maybe I won't. I haven't decided.''

She stared at him for a moment. ''Fine. Get your shirt

off and get on the table. But next time, you tell me you want treatment before I get everything all cleaned up.''

''Sure thing. You'll be happy to know you've got me thinking, by the way.''

Becka snapped a cover over the table, then opened the metal door of the supplies cupboard to get to the massage oils inside. He wanted a rubdown, fine, she'd give him a rubdown and send him on his way, just like she did all the players. She snatched a clean towel off the linen shelves, then swung around.

And the shock went through her entire system. Mace stood with his shirt off, looking at her inquiringly. For an instant, everything stopped while she stared at the corrugated muscles of his belly, trying to remember how to breathe.

As a physical therapist, she had studied the human body exhaustively. She had been around athletes of various levels for years, both clothed and unclothed, but nothing had prepared her for the way Mace Duvall looked with his shirt off. Flat ridges of muscle defined his abs and pecs. The taut, cannonball lines of his shoulders and arms spoke of power and control, of energy coiled into muscle built by effort and determination. The sun had darkened his skin, bleaching the light dusting of hair that ran in a suggestive trail down his belly to disappear in the waistband of his jeans.

He gave her an amused look. ''Face up or face down?''

''Huh?'' she said blankly.

''You want me face up or face down?''

Her brain simply refused to work. ''Uh, where do you want me to work on you?''

His grin widened. ''You really want me to answer that?''

Becka flushed, unable to keep her own eyes from straying to follow his gaze. "On the table, Duvall, or I'm out of here."

"Yes, ma'am," he said smartly and laid down, folding his hands under his chin.

She took her time moving to the head of the table, trying to compose herself. Trying to convince herself that touching him would be just like touching any other patient she'd ever had. Becka squeezed the massage oil on her hands and rubbed them together for a moment. As friction heated the oil, the scent of citrus wove into the air around her. She took a deep breath to clear her head, then lowered her hands to his shoulders, hesitating for just a moment before she touched his bare skin.

The warmth surprised her. It was as though he was stoked by some inner fire. She caught her breath for an instant and pressed downward, sliding her hands from his shoulders to the small of his back in one smooth motion. Her palms registered the texture of his skin, the cords of muscle that lay beneath. He was hard and rugged, smooth and streamlined, powerful, all hardened sinew and coiled strength.

Her practiced hands searched for knots, working to release the pockets of tension from muscles that had been asked to do too much that day. His broad back tapered to a narrow waist, a small patch of soft hair nestled at the very base. Now using pressure, now using deep strokes, she worked at him.

Time seemed to stop as she sank into the mesmerizing sensation of flesh against flesh. Smooth skin over bone and sinew, his body beckoned her to keep touching as she worked the tension from his back and shoulders, pushing on the hard muscles in the lumbar spine where his back dipped low just before rising to the tight, hard curve of his ass.

Becka moved to the side of the table, down by his waist, and ran the heels of her hands up the lines of muscle on either side of his backbone. Again and again she repeated the movement, now using her thumbs, now using her palms, coaxing every bit of tension from the muscles.

She stretched out over his body, her fingers curling over the edge of his shoulders, the skin of her forearms resting lightly on his back.

And suddenly, her mind filled with the vivid image of them naked together, her bare skin pressed against his, his hands tormenting her until she was hot and mindless.

She jerked upright, pulling her hands away as though they'd been burned. She opened her mouth to speak, but no words came.

Mace turned his head to look at her inquiringly.

Becka licked her lips. "Okay, that's it, you're done," she said, backing away. Then she glanced at the clock and gave a heartfelt curse. "How did it get to be midnight?" She wiped her hands and tossed the towel into the hamper.

Mace pushed himself up to sit on the edge of the table. "I thought it seemed like it went on for a while." He stood and stretched. "Guess you lost track of time."

"Get dressed so we can get out of here. I have to get up at the crack of dawn tomorrow to move." Becka crossed to her desk, fishing her purse from the bottom drawer. She didn't want to look at him standing there with his shirt off. She definitely didn't want to remember what it had felt like to touch that body. Quickly, she snatched her keys, then rose and turned.

And found herself face to face with him.

He topped her by about eight inches, which left her looking at his clavicle. She dragged her eyes up from the hard planes of his chest, only to find herself drowning in his eyes.

"I dreamed about you last night," he said softly, his drawl whispering over her skin and along her bones. "I'm trying to figure out why that is." He touched his hand to the side of her face, running his fingertips down her cheek and tracing them into the open collar of her polo shirt. She shivered. Her purse dropped from nerveless fingers with a soft thud.

"I'm thinking it's because of your mouth," he said, staring at her. "I'm thinking it was because I was wondering what it might be like if I did this—" he dipped his head to take a light nip at her lower lip, sliding a hand around her waist to draw her nearer. "Or if I did this—" he brushed her lips with the tip of his tongue, featherlight, tempting them to part as her breath shuddered out. "Or maybe I should just do this," he whispered, and he closed his mouth over hers in a hard, urgent kiss that sent her spinning into passion, unable to think, only to feel.

Hot and demanding, his mouth made no pretense of gentleness. The rough scrape of his beard was a sharp counterpoint to the silk of his tongue, to the teeth that scraped at her lips. His body was hard against her, the insistent pressure of his desire sending little shudders through her.

The heat overwhelmed her. His hands ran down her back, molding her to him. Though she might have satisfied her need to touch others through massage, she'd been starved for the feel of a man's hands on her body. Need flooded through her, had her almost whimpering for more.

Long minutes passed as they dove into one another, mouths locked, hands roving. The soft release of breath punctuated the silence. Becka ran her fingers across his cheek and into his hair, even as Mace made a sound low in his throat and pulled her closer.

Mace had kissed her out of curiosity and desire. He'd no idea that kissing her would be like a fist in his gut, robbing him of air, making his head whirl, leaving him weak. Her mouth was a ripe, red fruit, tempting him to devour. It was too much, he thought dimly as he feasted on her lips, but he was powerless to stop himself.

The lithe, taut feel of her against him sent his system into overdrive and he made a small growl of satisfaction. For nearly an hour he'd lain on the table, feeling the stroke of her hands driving him mad, using all his control to keep from rolling over and pulling her to him, knowing it was too soon to touch her. Now, he needed to stop, but he couldn't resist tasting her just a little more deeply.

Mace's fingers slid down to the waistband of Becka's shorts, tugging her shirt loose so he could touch the smooth, silky skin of her back.

Becka sighed against him. The sudden surge of wanting overwhelmed her. Sensation vibrated through her, making her excruciatingly conscious of every atom of her body. She needed his hands on her everywhere, needed him to release her from the tension that was stringing her tight. It wrenched a moan from her and she moved to wrap her arms around his back. Her car keys slipped from her fingers to hit the floor with a jangle.

She jumped at the noise. Sanity came rushing back. What was she doing? Tumbling for him, just like every other woman he'd ever met? He wanted to know what she was like in bed, he'd said so, and he'd been halfway there. She pulled out of his arms and sucked in a long breath.

"Oh no, we're not done yet." Mace reached for her again, his eyes darkened to the shade of old amber.

"Yes we are." Becka put a hand on his chest. True, it trembled a bit, and she had to fight the urge to stroke him, but at least she was making a stand. Even though all she wanted to do was wrench his clothes off and... "I hope you've satisfied your curiosity, Duvall. From now on, hands off.''

''On work time, sure.''

''All the time,'' she retorted, tucking her shirttail back in. ''Let me be really clear about this. I'm not interested in being part of your parade.'' She looked him up and down. ''You've been around the block a few too many times for me. Now if you'll get your clothes on, I need to get home.''

Mace slipped his shirt on. Becka picked up her purse and keys and started to walk out the door. Swiftly, he reached out an arm and pulled her in close against him.

''Now let me be clear about something. There is no parade of women, I don't give a damn what people say. My life is my own, not what the media makes it. As for you and I—''

''There is no you and I.'' Becka pressed her hands against his chest and glared at him. ''And if you think I'm going to sleep with you—''

Wicked amusement filled his eyes and he brought his mouth down to ravage hers until he felt her arms weaken and heard her soft sigh. Then he raised his head. ''It's not a matter of if, darlin','' he said, staring into her dazed green eyes. ''It's a matter of when.''

And he walked out the door without another look.

5

THERE WAS NO DOUBT about it, moving sucked.

Becka took a deep breath and began lugging a box of pots and pans up the dark, narrow stairwell that led to her new apartment. Feeling blindly for each step, she concentrated on using her chin to stabilize the trio of stainless steel mixing bowls and plastic dish rack that she'd balanced on top of the box.

Bad enough she'd spent every spare minute in the past three days filling boxes, packing things in newspaper until her hands were black. Now she had to spend one of her rare and precious days off hauling them over to the new apartment. Only the prospect of eliminating her commute made the project even remotely tolerable.

A soft tearing sound warned her that the box she carried was failing rapidly. Obviously, it was going downhill more quickly than she'd expected when she'd packed it, she thought, trying to speed up.

The box gave another alarming rending sound as Becka emerged onto the landing. She lurched to get her fingers under it just as the mixing bowls slid from under her chin to cascade onto the battered hardwood floor of the hall. The dish rack followed as the box canted to one side, and Becka fought to get a grip on the weakening bottom. Just a few more steps, she thought, fumbling for her doorknob. Just a few more steps and she'd be able to—

The bottom of the box gave way. Pots and pans clattered

out, lids rolling to the walls or circling with metallic ringing sounds. Finally Becka gave up and just dropped the box in disgust, with grim enjoyment at the crash.

There was a loud thump from behind the door opposite hers, a barking voice that ascended in volume as Becka stared at the door in alarm. "Hey, can't a person get a little sleep around here?" The door banged open and a disheveled woman swathed in a white terry-cloth robe glared at her, face still pale with sleep.

Becka blinked. "Oh wow, I didn't think anyone would be here on a weekday. I'm really sorry. My box broke and I..." She waved a hand at the ripped cardboard, trying not to stare at the woman's smudged eyes and the wild waterfall of sable hair that tumbled to her waist.

The woman looked at her a moment longer. "Yeah, well, some of us work nights. Do me a favor and keep it down." She slammed the door shut without another word.

And nice to meet you, too, neighbor, Becka thought as she leaned down to pick up the pans. Fumbling through her door, she carried the pile inside to spill them on her couch. Yup, it was shaping up to be a daisy of a day. After the humiliation of the night before, irritation—she was sure it was irritation—had kept her amped up and awake into the wee morning hours. Bad enough that he'd kissed her, but he'd made her respond.

And then his smug parting shot. Becka huffed back into the hall and stomped down the stairs. A matter of when indeed. It would be a cold day in hell before she slept with Mace Duvall, no matter how magic his mouth might be. She'd only responded because it had been a while, that was all. Which was the absolute worst reason in the world to get involved with someone, she reminded herself crossly.

And just where was Chico, she wondered, smothering her annoyance as she checked her watch again and crossed the parking lot. He was over two hours late. Even stuffed to the gills, her valiant little Toyota could only carry about seven or eight boxes, which had been why she'd reserved the cargo van, since cancelled. There were very few immutable laws in life, but one of them was certainly that she who gave up a U-Haul reservation on the last Friday of the month was not about to get it back. Thanks to Chico's unreliability, she was going to spend her whole day ferrying boxes from Cambridge to Lowell.

"Need some help?"

Becka turned to see the woman from upstairs standing behind her, an ironic smile on her face. "I'm with the welcoming committee," she said, sticking out her hand. "I'm Mallory Carson, your neighbor." She'd swapped the robe for a T-shirt and shorts, and tamed her hair into a ponytail. The smudged makeup was gone, leaving her with the clean-scrubbed look of a high-schooler on a face that any high fashion model would envy.

Becka shook her hand bemusedly. "Becka Landon. Hey, I'm sorry I woke you up."

"I'm the one who's sorry. I don't usually jump on complete strangers, I swear." Mallory gave a brilliant smile. "It's just that I was at work really late last night. I'm a bartender," she explained, yawning into her hand.

"Well no wonder you were ready to strangle me."

She shrugged. "No big deal. I'm up now, so let me help. It'll keep me from having to do something really disgusting like vacuuming."

Becka popped the trunk and pulled out a box for Mallory and one for herself. As they crossed the parking lot to the broad side porch that led into the house, Mallory studied Becka with frank curiosity. "So are you from somewhere else or are you just moving across town?"

Becka balanced the box on her knee while she opened the front door. "Cambridge, but I work here."

"Why do you want to leave Cambridge for a backwater like Lowell?" Mallory asked, following her in.

Becka shrugged. "Cambridge isn't any fun if you're never there to enjoy it. Dealing with the drive and the traffic was making me crazy."

"Yeah, I guess I can sort of see that." Mallory started up the stairs. "So I guess I should fill you in on the rest of our little happy home here. Two apartments on the ground floor, Ed and Lorraine. Ed's in construction, so he's usually out of here at the crack of dawn. Helpful if you have something really heavy to lift, but kind of a dim bulb. He was having an affair with Lorraine, but he just broke up with her to see someone else, so we've got lots of slamming doors around here right now." Puffing, Mallory followed Becka onto the upstairs hallway and through her front door.

"Third floor only has one apartment. Anne, a grad student over at UMass Lowell. Psychology, I think. Terrifyingly earnest. Watch out about making any jokes when you talk with her. She'll get this really concerned look on her face and say things like 'That's a very interesting question, Mallory, but the more important thing to ask is why you're so concerned with how many male chauvinist pigs it takes to change a light bulb. We should talk about this latent hostility you have toward men.'"

Becka laughed. "I think you're exaggerating."

"Probably," Mallory said cheerfully, setting the box on the floor and walking to the kitchen window to look at the vacant lot next door. "Now Mr. Metzger is the one you want to watch out for. That lot next door is his property and you'd better remember it. He's got a lot of vegetables growing and he's totally paranoid about people coming along and stealing them. I'm not saying he'll take after you with a shotgun, but he's been known to be unpleasant.''

Becka looked over her shoulder and out the window at the white-haired old man moving among the lush green beds of vegetables. "Does he sell any of them?"

Mallory shrugged. "Couldn't tell you. I've never managed to have a conversation with the man beyond him barking at me. I guess I look like a zucchini-napper."

"Why are you being so nice to me?" Becka asked as they started back downstairs.

"Catholic guilt," Mallory said good-naturedly. "Helping you move is my penance for being rude. So what's the story with you? The neighbors will be wondering."

"I'm the trainer for the Lowell baseball team."

Mallory goggled at her. "You teach them how to play baseball?"

Becka laughed. "No, I do everything else. Supervise workouts, keep them healthy. It's a fancy version of a physical therapist."

"Small world. I run the sports bar just across from the park."

"Double Play?"

"Yeah. Some of your players come in after the games, especially the dark-haired one with the long eyelashes. He's real popular."

Becka's eyebrows rose. "You'd better take a good look at their IDs. Most of those kids are barely old enough to vote. Not to mention the fact that they're violating curfew."

They went down the front hall and out onto the porch.

"So it's kind of unusual for a woman to be a trainer on a guy's sports team, isn't it?" asked Mallory.

"A little," Becka admitted over her shoulder as she stepped out the door. "They were hard up and I was the best option they had. I'm trying to convince them I'm indispensable.'' She turned to walk forward and stopped. Across the parking lot, leaning on her car, was Mace Duvall.

''Do they give you a bad time?''

''Only some of them,'' Becka said darkly, forcing her feet to start moving again. His eyes never left her, making her conscious of every step she took, of the strands of hair trailing down her cheeks, of the thin, dust-smudged tank top she wore. She crunched across the gravelly pavement of the parking lot and stopped in front of him. ''What are you doing here?''

''Helping you move. Hi.'' He nodded to Mallory then took his gaze back to Becka. ''Chico's wife surprised him this morning, so he asked me to pinch hit for him.''

Ignoring the awareness that buzzed through her system, Becka walked past him to pull a crate of sheets and towels from the back seat of her car. He was not going to get to her. She knew what she wanted, and it did not include getting involved with another guy who played the field. ''I can handle it, thanks.'' She swung the door shut with unnecessary force.

''I'm sure you can.'' Mace caught the door neatly before it slammed and scooped another box out of the back. ''As long as you don't mind spending the entire day shifting your things in that little cracker box. I've got the Bronco. We can move your stuff in a couple trips.''

Becka kept walking as though she didn't hear. Mace shrugged and followed her across the parking lot.

''You're not ticked about last night, are you?''

The laughter in his voice made her keep control. ''Did something happen last night?'' she asked coolly. ''I must have missed it.''

''I don't know, you were sure breathing hard.''

She ignored him. Mallory watched avidly, dashing up to catch the door before it slammed behind Becka.

Mace glanced at her. "Thanks."

"Don't mention it. I'm enjoying this. I'll be up in a few minutes."

He grinned and ducked in the door. Ahead of him, Becka started up the stairs, and he watched her appreciatively. Whatever she did to keep in shape, it was working.

He took a better grip on the box he was carrying, glancing at its contents. Books, mostly, tossed in haphazardly. He wasn't surprised to see that they were mostly nonfiction. Becka didn't strike him as the type for novels. The book on nutrition fit his image of her, as did one on t'ai chi, and one on...

"Ancient Chinese sexual secrets for Western lovers?"

Above him, Becka stumbled and caught herself before stepping out onto the upper landing. She walked quickly into her apartment without a backward glance.

Mace followed. "Well, this looks like a useful reference book."

Becka dumped the sheets in her bedroom, next to the unmade bed that still stood in the center of the room. "Keep your paws out of my stuff," she snapped and burst back into the living room to find him fishing the book out of the box he'd set by her shelves.

"Oh, but I think I could really learn something here." He held the book out of her reach, stepping nimbly around her toward the bedroom. "Here we go, the *Tortoises of Spring*. 'The woman places her hands and feet on the bed. The man inserts his jade stalk into her cinnabar grotto and plucks her lute strings ten times,'" he read, somehow managing to stay just out of her reach as he dodged around the bed. "'He ceases when she rejoices. A hundred illnesses will vanish.'" Mace flopped down on the quilted surface of the mattress and sent Becka a wicked look. "We could cure those hundred illnesses right now, if you want."

"You're pushing your luck, Duvall. Hand it over, *now*." She stretched across him, groping for the book.

Mace rolled onto his back and held the volume away from her with one long arm. "Hey, look at this one. She's hanging from ropes coming down from the ceiling." He slanted her a look. "Your mother know you read this?"

Face flaming, Becka made another stab for the paperback just as her hand slipped on the slick cover of the mattress, sending her falling down on top of him.

For long seconds, the only thing that registered in her stunned brain was the hard length of his body against her. Hard and getting harder, she realized, turning her head only to brush her lips against the taut skin of his neck. She made a move, then, to get her hands under her and rise.

Swiftly, Mace rolled to pin her half beneath him. "No sense in rushing. You owe yourself a break after all that lifting."

She felt an alarming thrill of excitement, and a trembling that started deep inside. Oh no, she thought, this wasn't the way it was supposed to go. She was supposed to be impatient and worried about time. She wasn't supposed to wonder what it would feel like if he kissed her again with that mesmerizing mouth.

She wasn't supposed to want him.

"It seems to me we didn't get much of a chance last night to see where this could go," Mace murmured, nuzzling her throat.

Keeping a grip on her wits was vital, Becka thought, striving for the detached amusement she used on the players when they made passes at her. "Better brush up on your lines, Duvall. They could use some work." She fought to ignore the soft kisses he pressed into her skin. How could a man's mouth be so soft and gentle when his hands felt so hard sliding down the curve of her hip, running up to brush over her breast? She jerked as the heat scorched through the thin cotton of her tank top.

"Maybe I should just skip talking, then," he said, his eyes snaring hers, capturing her gaze until she couldn't look away.

Becka steeled herself not to respond to the whirlwind of sensation she knew was coming. And while she prepared to defend herself against it, he slipped in to seduce her with gentleness.

His lips were warm, soft, taking light, quick samples rather than drinking her in as he had the night before. Nibbling his way across her jaw, he left a trail of heat and awareness that teased, enthralled. Before she could adjust, he returned to her mouth for more of those teasing kisses, now on one side, now on the other, now on the lids of her eyes that had somehow fluttered closed. The better to focus on his kisses so she could ignore them, except they never came where she expected. Like the soft, random landings of a butterfly, his kisses touched from point to point, here then gone, over before she could register the little buzz of electricity they triggered.

More. It drummed through her in frustration. The light touches only ignited cravings she didn't want to have. She tried to think of all the reasons she had for keeping her distance from Mace Duvall, even as need began a slow twist in her gut. If she let her treacherous body take over, it was just like handing him the reins.

Becka cast about to remember just why it mattered but only wound up getting lost in the heat of his body against hers, the tantalizing pressure that made her wonder what it would feel like to have him naked on top of her, inside her.

She shifted against him, her arms coming around his neck. A puff of breeze came through the window.

Mace brushed along her jaw, sampled the softness of her earlobe, but always he journeyed back to her lips. Her mouth was addictive, he thought, like an irresistible dessert. One taste drew him back for another, and another. He could feel the heat simmering in her as she tried to bank it back, as she tried to ignore what he was doing to her. It made it all the more enticing to tempt her, to savor that full lower lip like it was taffy, warm and sweet.

He smiled inwardly when he felt her mouth begin to respond to his, moving to kiss him back. He liked knowing he could take her beyond where she wanted to be, lure her into forgetting and giving herself up to the moment.

Still, it strained his patience, and Mace thought of himself as a patient man. The brushing kisses amused him and aroused him, but they weren't what he wanted. What he craved, in a low, insistent throb, was the taste of her, dark and sinfully rich. He licked at her lips, savoring the flavor, enjoying the soft catch of her breath.

Then she flamed into desire, with a swift completeness that took him utterly by surprise. He was like the boy who throws gasoline on a fire only to see it explode beyond any imagining, beyond anything he can control. Her mouth was molten against his, her body hot and straining. His own desire billowed up to match as he dove into the textures of her, the firm, impatient lines of her body. Her fingers sliding under the belt of his jeans sent him to the edge of control.

There was a tapping sound in the hall, but he couldn't surface enough to process it. He couldn't get beyond the greedy temptation that was Becka. The rhythmic clunking sounded almost like steps, almost like…

"This is the last box." Mallory's voice drifted in from the living room. "Are you going to make another trip?"

They broke apart, breathing hard. Becka blinked dazedly, touching her lips with her fingertips. Then her eyes cleared and she bolted upright, shooting a baleful look at Mace.

"Guys? Where are—whoops!" Mallory jumped back from the bedroom door just as Becka got up from the mattress. "Sorry, didn't realize I was interrupting your, uh…" She paused delicately, her amusement only slightly suppressed.

"Actually, your timing is perfect." Becka walked out of the room, grabbing Mallory by the arm and pulling her out toward the hallway. "I've got a couple more things in the car. Help me out?"

"No offense, I mean, I hardly know you, but are you out of your mind, walking out on a guy like that?" Mallory asked.

"I'm out of my mind to get near him, more like."

"Yeah, right. Your eyes still haven't focused, you know."

It fried her to think that she'd been clawing at Mace like an actress in a bad porn film. "He's a jerk." Becka slammed the screen door open and stomped onto the porch. "He can't commit to anything, not even a job. He's here twenty-four hours and he wants to quit. He's had so many women in his bed it's probably got one of those take-a-number thingies like they have at the deli installed on the headboard." She clattered down the steps. "I just broke up with a creep a couple months ago. The last thing I need to do is get involved with another one."

"Who says you need to get involved?" Mallory asked as they crossed the parking lot. "You said he's ready to leave. Go for recreation. If it's been months since the creep, you can probably use it. And it's not like Loverboy will mind, judging by the way he looks at you."

Becka unlocked her trunk and turned to her. "You always jump into people's lives like this when you've just met them?" she asked without heat, grabbing her VCR.

Mallory pulled the last box from the car. "I'm a bartender, Becka. Most of the time I'm trying to do anything I can to stay *out* of people's lives."

Becka grinned, then turned to see Mace coming out of the house. Oh, and didn't she just itch to wipe that smirk off his face? She was very clear about what she did and didn't want. She wanted to focus on her job and not do anything to jeopardize her chances of staying on, like sleeping with a member of the team. She didn't want to sleep with another womanizer who seemed to have made it his mission in life to get her into bed.

She didn't want to want him as much as she did.

"You all set to go pick up another load?" Mace asked, eyeing her assessingly.

"I appreciate the offer, but I've got it under control."

Mace gave the tiny Toyota a glance of disbelief. "You're kidding."

"Never turn down help on moving day," Mallory put in helpfully.

Becka looked from one to the other. "What is this, tag team wrestling?"

Mace stuck a tongue into his cheek. "Threesomes aren't my bag, thanks."

"And you're not my bag."

Mallory gave her a look. "You need the help, Becka. Why turn it down? It's not like you have to sleep with the guy just because he helps you." She turned to Mace with a brilliant smile. "Is it?"

"I'm willing to entertain other offers."

"See? Take the help."

They were right, Becka thought resignedly. If she hoped to finish the move today, she needed a bigger vehicle and she did need help. Much as it made her teeth hurt to think about taking a favor from Mace, it was senseless to pretend otherwise. She gave him a wary look. "What is this going to cost me?"

"I'm sure we can figure something out."

"That's what I'm afraid of," she muttered as she locked her car.

6

BECKA SQUINTED at the early-morning sun, wishing she'd remembered her sunglasses. The metronomic thud of her footfalls on the surface of the UMass Lowell track soothed. The hint of coolness in the air made every breath cleansing, even as the relaxation of physical effort began to filter through her body. She knew some people swore by bio-feedback or meditation, but for her running was the thing. Whatever stress she felt melted away as she pushed her body to exhaustion. Becka lengthened her stride until she felt loose and fluid.

If only her mind felt the same way.

Mace Duvall... The man was making her crazy. It wasn't a problem that he was stubborn—she was more than stubborn enough to match. The problem was that no matter how much he ticked her off, her body kept betraying her. One of them, she could fight against. Fighting both of them was beginning to get exhausting. Okay, maybe it had been a while since she'd had sex, and maybe the man had a fabulous body and eyes a woman could drown in. She should still have some self-control.

For him, of course, it was about proving a point, winning a battle of wills. If she'd said yes, he wouldn't have given her a second thought. Only the fact that she was saying no made her memorable.

Of course, innate honesty forced her to admit it was her own fault that she was having to think about him at all.

He'd been halfway out the door a few days before. She should have just let him go, she thought, shaking her head at herself. She should encourage him now. It would be a relief.

Except for the disappointed players she'd have to face.

That was where the problem came in. Right now, the team was winning. It didn't matter whether Duvall was actually improving their hitting or not. The important thing is that they *thought* he was. He didn't realize the effect his disappearance could have. All it would take was a few more days for him to finish out his assignment. He could quit after and they'd never know.

Becka grimaced. The problem was that just a few more days might be enough to put her over the brink. Most of that time the team would be on the road, though, which would make it easier. Then Duvall would head out and it would be history.

All she had to do was hold out until then.

Far across the field, another runner hit the track and began to stretch. Becka frowned as she reached the far turn and began curving back. She'd known the privacy of having the track to herself, even at the crack of dawn, was too good to last. Seconds passed as she drew near enough to register that it was a man, the lines of his body vaguely familiar. Then she drew closer still and recognition flooded through her.

It was Mace Duvall.

She cursed fluently under her breath as he straightened to watch her approach. She thought she caught the gleam of a self-satisfied smile.

"Beautiful morning for a run, Florence," he said as she neared and he broke into a run alongside her.

"Well, isn't this a coincidence," she observed brightly. "You always hang around tracks at six in the morning?"

"I heard you talking to Stats yesterday about your runs so I figured I'd check it out. How's the battle of the boxes going?"

She made a face. "They were still there when I woke up this morning. Looks like the magic elves had the night off again."

"Life in the real world just sucks sometimes, don't it?"

"Moving sucks. 'Course, probably not for you. You're all primed to hit the road."

He slanted a look at her. "If you want me gone so bad, then why do you care?"

"I care because of the team. For reasons that escape me, it means a lot to Sammy and the guys to have you around. They think you're the reason they're winning and I don't want to mess with that."

He chuckled, the sound low in his throat. "Are you sure that's it? You sure you're not starting to get a little bit of a soft spot for me, Florence?"

"Oh sure, I'll cry on my pillow every night after you leave, Duvall. I'll send you pictures."

He raised his eyebrows. "Now that could be interesting. Do you sleep in the buff?"

She had a sudden vivid fantasy of being in bed with him, naked, the sheets twined around them, the two of them twined around each other. "In flannel up to my chin."

"Seems a little hot for summer," he said thoughtfully. "Always did like unwrapping presents, though."

A little bolt of desire flicked through her. "Who said I was yours to unwrap?"

"Dangerous stuff, Florence, tempting fate. Who knows what the next few days will bring?"

"So you're sticking around." Annoyance warred with triumph and won. It was in her voice and she knew Mace could hear it as well.

"You don't seem to know what you want, do you?" His lazy amusement made her grit her teeth. "One minute you're ticked off at me for running out, the next minute you're ticked off at me for staying. You seem a little confused."

"I'm not confused at all, Duvall. I know exactly what I want."

"Oh yeah? What's that?" He unzipped his warmup jacket and tossed it to the grass at the side of the track. The sweat-damp T-shirt underneath was just tight enough to make her aware of the body under it.

"I..." She opened her mouth to speak and then shut it. She wanted him to leave so she'd be rid of the aggravation of having him around. She wanted him to stay, though, only for the team. Going to bed with him would be absolutely the dumbest thing she could do. Entertaining as it might be, it was a complication she didn't need, and she was not about to give him the satisfaction of thinking he'd won.

Then she remembered the feel of his mouth, hard and hot on hers as the length of his body pressed her into the mattress. Entertaining probably wouldn't do it justice. Astounding, more like it.

"What's the matter, cat got your tongue?"

She threw him a dirty look. "Not at all. I just don't see this as a necessary conversation. You're going to do what you're going to do. It's not up to me to push you either way."

"But you already have."

She snorted. "Don't put your decisions on me."

"You're the reason I'm sticking around."

"And the moon is made of green cheese. Duvall, I get the feeling you don't do anything that's not exactly what you want."

"That's true," he said thoughtfully. "Currently, what I want is you."

Becka would have huffed if she weren't already out of breath. "Didn't we have this conversation already?" She looked over at him.

That predatory gleam flashed in his eyes for an instant. "I'm a patient man."

"And I'm running out of patience. New topic, Duvall."

"Okay," he said equably, "let's talk about you."

"That's an old topic. I'm sure you can come up with something more interesting. What about one of your ex-fiancées? Just what does Megan Barnes really wear at home in the evenings when she's not at premieres?"

"I wouldn't know," he said blandly. "That one was a figment of a tabloid reporter's imagination. I'm more interested in you," he said, ignoring her short laugh. "I think you're all kinds of an interesting puzzle. How did you wind up a sports trainer, for instance?"

Becka looked at him. "Twenty questions?"

"You were the one who wanted to change subjects," he reminded her.

Becka moved her shoulders. "I don't know. My dad coached basketball. I had five sisters. Hanging around the gym with him and being his gofer was the only way I could get any time alone with him. I guess I just got used to it."

"Turned you into a gym rat?"

"Track rat, more like."

"You ever compete?"

"For a while." She shrugged. "I made all-state in high school. Somewhere around my junior year in college I just stopped moving up. I guess you could say I hit my talent ceiling." She looked at the river that ran along across the field, staring across it to the ballpark that lay beyond. "I just wasn't top-tier at an international level. No Olympics."

The words still stung slightly, even after all these years. "You don't know what it's like, realizing that you just don't have the stuff to do the job."

"You'd be surprised." Bleakness shaded his words, then he shook his head. "So I don't get it. Why not just get out, leave it behind?" He stripped loose the Velcro of his tear-away warmup pants and tossed them next to his jacket as they circled the track.

Becka shrugged. "I love athletics. Maybe I didn't have the stuff, but I can still help someone who does."

"That's what Sammy thinks I can do." His tone clearly said he doubted it.

Becka stepped up her pace. "It means something to do that, to help the team excel. I guess I don't understand why you can't see the value in it. I mean, you had the good times. You were at the top for ten years. That's more than most people get their whole lives."

"We can't all be as evolved as you are." He cursed under his breath. "Sorry. That was a stupid thing to say."

"It's okay." They ran in silence for a few seconds, letting the conversation settle in. Finally, Becka spoke. "It wasn't easy for me at the time. It's still tough, and it's been years now. And I never had the big game to give up." She hesitated. "I guess I haven't really been thinking what it's like for you."

Maybe that was his problem, Mace thought. He'd had too much time to think about what he'd lost instead of going on with what he still had. Still, he didn't need her sympathy any more than he needed a sympathy job from the organization. "I'll live," he said briefly. A nice, simple affair was one thing. Letting someone inside his head was another. Instead, he changed the subject. "So why aren't you at a university?"

Becka laughed. "I should be so lucky. University spots

don't fall off trees, you know." She ran quietly for a few seconds. "Before I got this job, I was at an HMO working on weekend warriors and volunteering at Boston College in between. I'm hoping this will turn into bigger and better things."

"It's a little unusual, a woman trainer on a men's team."

"Why?" She brushed an errant strand of hair out of her eyes. "Women have the same qualifications as men in this field."

"You just don't see it very often. Maybe it's the whole thing of having a woman in the locker room."

She hooted. "Trust me, Duvall, there's no equipment dangling in that locker room that I haven't seen before."

"All those young studs covered in steam and wearing just a towel don't do it for you?"

"It takes more than young boys to do it for me."

"Me, I'm all man, sugar," he said with a broad grin.

"Thanks, I'll pass."

"So you keep saying, but I think you're warming up to me. You haven't told me to go to hell once today."

"The day's still young, Duvall."

They circled the track a few times in a surprisingly companionable silence. Gradually, Mace's pace began to slow.

"Hey, you're falling behind there," she chided with a sideways glance. "You don't want people to think you—" The words clogged up in her throat. For the first time, she noticed the ugly red tracery of scars that crisscrossed his left thigh, running up under his shorts. "Your accident," she breathed.

"Yeah." They ran on in silence for a few yards.

"What happened?"

"Surely as much as you've followed my personal life in the paper you must have read about it." Tight with effort, his voice didn't quite make it to flip.

"Car accident, right?"

"Semi truck, but you're more or less right."

"What happened?"

"Run off the road into a bridge." He said it as though it was something that he'd seen in a movie. "Worse than what's happened to some people, better than others."

The offhand tone hid warning signs in neon red. For the moment, she'd respect them, even though she wanted to know more. "Well, whatever happened, you've come back amazingly well."

"Outside of losing my career, yeah, I suppose you're right."

Becka slowed to a jog, then a walk. "It's a wonder you survived."

His lips twisted. "People usually tell me I'm lucky."

She glanced again at the scars. She couldn't imagine a more brainless response. But then she'd just been whining to him about not having Olympic-caliber stuff, when he'd had a brilliant career snatched from him by some idiot's irresponsibility. The sympathy from days before bloomed in her again, along with something more important. Respect. "I'd say you're a hell of a survivor."

Mace stopped as well and stared down at her. Long seconds ticked by. He brushed a strand of hair out of her face. "And I'd say I'm starting to realize what I find so intriguing about you."

Those whiskey-gold eyes delved into hers. She stared back and suddenly it was like diving down into a deep well until she was immersed in him, until sight, sound, and scent, there was nothing but Mace. He just stood there, and yet it was as though he was all around her. She felt warm, molten with a pulse of something that went beyond desire, something that she shied away from thinking about.

Off in the distance, a dog began barking. Becka stirred

and blinked. "Um," she said blankly. "Well, that's..." Her voice trailed off again and she started to walk slowly. "Time for the weight room."

Mace stared at her for another long moment, she could feel it, and then followed after her. "Wait a minute." He reached out and caught her arm to stop her. "You don't walk away from that."

"From what?" She wouldn't look at him, didn't want to risk a repeat.

He hesitated, then let go of her. "Never mind. Let's go lift."

THE OLD STEEL BRIDGE arced across the river. The trip across from the UMass track to LeChere ballpark didn't leave her nearly enough time for her system to settle. It seemed like one minute they were crossing over, the next they were in the gloom under the stadium grandstands, following the concrete walkway that led to the clubhouse entrance.

Mace leaned one hand against the door as Becka bent to pull a key from the Velcro pouch hooked to her shoelaces. "So how do you rate a key?"

Becka glanced up at him and took a breath. The shadows hooded his eyes and carved hollows in his cheeks. The lean, predatory look was back, she saw with a surge of adrenaline. Suddenly clumsy, she fumbled with the key.

"You want some help with that?"

She ignored him, concentrating on getting the key into the lock and opening the door. Inside, only the glow of the emergency lights illuminated the gloom. She brushed the wall, searching for the light switch.

"It's probably along here, somewhere by the door," Mace said, searching alongside her. The heat of his palm brushed her hand just as she found the toggle and flipped it on.

"No one's here, huh?" he asked.

Becka let a breath out slowly. The bright lighting didn't help nearly as much as she'd hoped it would. Instead, edgy awareness filled her. "Not this early. Any players who want to work out in the morning have to wait until the front office staff comes in at nine. For the time being, anyway, we've got it to ourselves."

They walked up to the darkened doorway of the weight room. When she snapped the switch, fluorescent lights flickered on and the walls of mirrors threw their reflections back at them, multiplied them tenfold. Becka and Mace. Mace and Becka. She'd known he was taller than she, but it surprised her to see that her head barely topped his shoulder. He looked deceptively lean; unless you'd seen him without a shirt, as she had, you'd never realize his strength. That outrageously sexy mouth and those hot eyes, though, you saw those coming a mile away.

"Nice equipment," he said, waving at the array of work-out gear, but his eyes met hers in the mirror.

She wouldn't jump to the bait. "Yeah, they redid it last year. It makes it easier to supervise workouts. Used to be the team had to go to a Gold's Gym across town. Now all I have to do is show up here and keep circling the room."

She walked over to the stereo and flipped it on. Talk radio filled the room with the sounds of a shock deejay she abhorred. Concentrating on changing it to a blues rock station, she didn't register the motion out of the corner of her eye. She jumped to find Mace standing behind her.

"Sorry, I was just looking for one of these," he said, gesturing to the stack of towels that sat on the table next to the stereo. He reached around her, leaning in until she could feel his breath on her shoulder and his arm curving around her body. She couldn't move away from his arm without backing into him. She wouldn't move away from his arm because she didn't want to give him the satisfaction.

After what seemed like an eternity, Mace stepped back and Becka took a deep breath. He crossed over to the quad machine and began to work his legs pitilessly, intensity and relentless drive etched into his face.

Becka sat down at the lat machine and reached up to grasp the wide bar that dangled from a cable over her head, pulling the bar down over and over.

Normally when she worked out, she focused on the movement, on making each muscle work to maximum effort. This time, her eyes kept straying to the mirrors, and Mace. He started doing cable flies. The muscles in his arm rippled and tensed, and Becka stared, mesmerized, holding onto the bar over her head. She'd seen his power the day he'd hit the homer at batting practice, but now there was no one around to distract her from the rigid definition of his body.

"Don't you have some weights to lift?"

She jumped, and saw Mace grinning at her in the mirror. He could see everything in the room, she realized, thanks to the myriad reflections. Including her staring at him, she thought with a flush. With renewed determination she went back to working her lats, staring determinedly at the tubular white frame of the weight machine. Behind her, the weight plates clanked as Mace finished working the other arm.

He moved to the bench press and began loading up the bar with weight plates. Becka stirred and stopped her exercise. "You shouldn't lift that kind of weight without a spotter."

"Do tell." He rolled his head to look at her as he put

his hands up to the bar. "Does that mean you're volunteering?"

She didn't answer, just crossed over to the head of the bench press and put her hands on the weight bar. Mace stared up at her, his eyes tawny and direct, his legs corded with muscle, hips lean and tight. He wrapped his fingers around the bar and gave a grunt as he lifted it out of the rack and lowered it to his chest, then pressed it up, straightening out his arms. As he lowered it, Becka held her palms under the bar, not carrying any weight, just shadowing the motion in case he needed help.

But clearly he didn't. The bar rose and sank, smooth and controlled, his muscles swelling with each lift. Each time, Becka leaned toward him, watching the intensity on his face as he moved the weight in a smooth line. He stopped after seven repetitions, his breathing quickening.

"You want to do one of your sets while I'm waiting for my next one?"

"Sure." Becka sat down on the chest press machine and moved the pin to select the weight plates.

"No free weights?"

"Not for chest press. I usually work out alone and I have an aversion to strangling myself with the weight bar." She sat upright on the padded seat of the weight machine and gripped the shoulder-high handles.

Mace walked up and stood in front of her. Taking a deep breath, she began to push out on the handles, breathing out as she did so. Mace curled his fingers around the square tubes of the weight machine, shadowing the motion of the bars as Becka pushed out to raise the weights, leaning in toward her each time she let the bars move in toward her body, lowering the weights. Mace leaned in and away, tracking the motion of the bars, a motion that was rhythmic, repetitive. Like sex, she thought suddenly. He leaned in again as though he was going to kiss her, and Becka stopped abruptly. "Your turn," she said, with only a slight tremor to her voice. Kissing him was definitely not on the program. In fact, *thinking* about kissing him wasn't even on the program.

Mace stayed put a moment, then turned to the bench press. "Whatever you say."

Becka watched as he lay back down on the bench and lifted the bar. There was something she'd always found enormously sexy about weight lifting. The process had always made her immensely aware of her body, its motions, its hungers. Suddenly Mace's eyes locked in on hers, his gaze intent, even as he pressed the weight up over and over. His eyes pinned her, held her until she forgot to move, forgot to breathe. Then he'd racked the bar and was sitting up again, raking his hair out of his eyes with a careless hand.

They moved to the military press bench and loaded up the bar, Mace sitting in the ruthlessly upright seat that faced the mirrors. Becka stood behind him, resting her hands on the bar. She stared at the tight sinew of his forearms, fascinated by the strength and power. Then his fingers brushed hers and she jumped.

"Becka?"

Her eyes met his in the mirror. "Yes, what?"

The look in them was knowing. "Can I lift now?"

"Knock yourself out," she muttered, her face flaming. It was that body, she thought as her hands shadowed the moving weight bar. That body and the fact that she hadn't had sex for three months. At least not with another person, anyway. Those were the only reasons she was getting distracted.

Mace lifted and the damp T-shirt caught on his back, inhibiting his movement. He put the bar down abruptly.

"This has got to go," he muttered and pulled off his T-shirt.

If it had been hard before to keep from getting distracted, now it was impossible. His body had stopped her cold the first time she'd seen him with a shirt off. Now, watching his muscles tighten and shift in the mirror, she was hard-pressed to keep herself together.

Mace finished his set and wiped the seat with the towel. "You doing any shoulder work?"

"Military press, same as you." She fastened bright red lifting straps around her wrists.

"I thought you didn't do free weights."

"Just not bench press." She loaded up the bar and sat down.

Mace stood behind her. She wrapped the lifting straps around the bar and clenched her hands on top to aid her grip. Then she took a breath and pressed the bar up. Instead of shadowing the bar with his fingers, he touched his hands under her elbows, following them as she pushed the weight bar up and her arms straightened. His touch sent tendrils of awareness curling through her muscles, tendrils she tried to ignore, focusing instead on her breathing. Three reps became four, then lifting the bar became an effort.

"Come on, you can do a couple more," Mace said, pushing lightly on her elbows to encourage her. Becka took a deep breath and began to press the bar up again, this time panting and concentrating on making the weight move. "Oh yeah, sugar, just like that," he said in that honey molasses drawl. "Oh yeah, that's good, don't stop." He was talking about weight lifting, but his voice...

His voice was talking about sex.

Muscles suddenly weak, Becka racked the bar and walked toward the squat rack without looking back, lifting straps still dangling from her wrists. She loaded the weight plates, then stepped into the frame to get the bar on her shoulders. Slowly, carefully she lowered. Concentrating on the movement let her keep from thinking about the man in the room. The first few reps were easy—they always were—but then she began to work. She saw Mace step in close behind her and waited for him to press his fingers on the weight bar.

Instead, he put his hands above her waist, high on her ribs and pushed up.

Becka caught her breath in a gasp. His hands slid under her cropped running T-shirt and burned into the skin like a brand. Becka tried to concentrate on her breathing without success. She should move to stop him, but it was hard because, she finally admitted, it was what she really wanted. As her endorphin buzz mounted, a growing part of her was whispering that having his hands all over her was all that mattered. "What are you doing?" she managed.

"Spotting you." His eyes were on hers in the mirror before them, intent as they rose up together until she was standing. "Again."

She sank down and he moved with her, his body curving against hers as she moved down to the floor, then brushing against her as they moved back up in tandem.

"Once more," he challenged her, his fingers moving infinitesimally upward. "Come on, sugar, I'll go with you. Give me one more." His hands pressed against her, his breath ruffled her hair, his eyes held hers in the mirror. Becka moved down through the rep and back up, her entire body humming. It was all she could do to rack the weight bar and step out from underneath it, her legs trembling with fatigue as she turned—

—only to find him closer than she'd thought. She started to brush past him, but then his hands snapped up to clamp around her waist even as her hands somehow flew in to clutch his shoulders. She opened her mouth to speak.

And he pulled her against him, his mouth taking hers hard and urgent.

There was no seduction; it was as primitive as the mastery of muscle over mass that they'd just fought through. His mouth tormented, making her want more even as he plundered. His flavor intoxicated, pulling her into a hot darkness that promised to set her afire. Every urge that she'd suppressed over the past days was alive, trembling through her, set loose at last.

His hands were warm on her skin, sliding up under her flimsy T-shirt, down over her hips. The touch made her twist herself against him to get even closer. The urge was insistent and insatiable as she ran her hands over his back, over the muscle that she'd seen flex and pull, feeling the defined ridges.

Mace ran his fingers over the stretchy fabric of her sports bra, then edged his fingers underneath to brush against the soft skin of her breast until she moaned. He opened his eyes and the mirrors reflected the two of them everywhere, replicating their images all around the room as he plundered her sweetness and tore a cry from her.

Finally, he edged her toward the lat pulldown machine, laying her back on the flat padded bench and pressing himself against her. He'd known she'd feel like this, soft and taut and tempting. He wanted to be on her and in her, but somehow he wanted more, driven toward some edge he couldn't name.

Becka shivered at the touch of his hands. It was like the times she'd tried body surfing, being bowled over, pulled under, tossed around until she was wholly disoriented and operating only on instinct. One moment, everything was a chaos formed of sensation. The next, Mace was leaning back from her, pulling her to stand up, stretching her hands toward the lat bar. His mouth on hers kept her mind clear of thought so that she only vaguely registered that he was wrapping the lifting strap of her left hand around the bar, then closing her fingers over it. ''Hold on tight,'' he whispered, and turned his attention to her other hand. When she opened her mouth to protest, he covered it with his and whirled her around with more of those mind-bending kisses, running his hands up and down her arms until she had goose bumps.

Brushing lightly, his fingertips slipped down onto her torso, slipping up under her shirt to tease her breasts, rubbing over the nipples through her bra until they were unbearably sensitive. Then he pulled the fabric up and his hands slid in to find her.

Becka gasped as his fingers stroked the soft flesh, slipping up until they touched a nipple. It jolted her entire system, the heat, the pressure, the friction. He rolled the nubbin of flesh between his fingers until she moaned, then slipped his whole hand around the firm globe of her breast.

She pressed herself toward him, toward the pressure of that hand. Need and desire had her twisting against him. It gave her a strange thrill to see them reflected in the wall of mirrors, her slender arms stretched apart, Mace's torso dark against the pale flesh of her body.

A slow, sexy blues song came out of the radio, the rhythm providing a counterpoint to their movement. Mace bent and put his mouth against her, stroking his tongue over her nipple, sucking and nipping it until she gave a strangled cry, then switching to the other side. His hands ran up and down her body until she wanted to scream.

Becka tried to move her hands on the bar, the lifting straps tightening against the pull as they were designed to do. Mace's mouth was sending her places she'd never been, even as his fingers stroked down over her hips and along the outside of her thighs, trailing up along the sensitive inner flesh until they just skimmed under her loose nylon running shorts. In a hypnotic circle, they ran up and down, even as the smooth stroke of his tongue and the scrape of his teeth on her nipples drove her mad. Then those clever fingers slid up under the shorts, swiftly, to find her hot and wet.

Becka stiffened and cried out at his touch. She moved against it. Mace stroked her slowly, teasingly, even as he traced a path over her quivering stomach with his tongue. Feeling her shudder against his hand wasn't enough. He wanted, needed to taste her. He moved to trail his lips up her thigh, then he was pulling her shorts to one side and finding her with his tongue.

She tasted like passion, and the flavor intoxicated him. He knew from her incoherent cries and the helpless motions of her hips that the swirling strokes of his tongue were pushing her to the edge. It wasn't enough, though. He wanted more, wanted to feel her move against him when she came, knowing that she couldn't stop herself from tumbling over the edge. And he licked and stroked, sucked and nipped to drive her there.

Becka gasped for air and tried to hold onto her sanity. She opened her eyes and saw herself and Mace, reflected in the mirrors all around the room. Saw herself, arms stretched out as though she were tied up, and Mace plundering her.

Suddenly, she realized the chance they were taking. Anyone could come walking in unexpectedly, she thought with dawning horror, to see her hands bound apart like some virgin sacrifice, breasts exposed while Mace sampled her. She tried to pull her hands away from the bar, but the lifting straps still held her in place. "Stop," she gasped. "Let go, let…'' She finally remembered the canvas around her wrists and fumbled to free them. But Mace had pulled away and was already unwinding them so her hands were loose.

Becka backed away from him, breathing hard. Slowly, clumsily, she slipped her bra back into place.

''Are you okay?''

''No I'm not okay,'' she replied. ''We were taking a crazy chance there. We're in the clubhouse.''

''Fine.'' He reached for his shirt. ''Let's go somewhere else and finish what we started.''

''I can't.''

''Don't lie to me. I know how you felt, I felt it, too.'' Mace pulled the gray fabric over his head and tucked it into his shorts.

Shorts that showed the outline of a world-class hard-on, Becka realized, still feeling the tension that bound her up.

''So you proved your point, you can get me turned on. Big deal. Put another notch in your belt if you want, but keep it buckled when you're around me.'' She walked toward the door and turned back to look at him. ''You're only here for a couple more days. It shouldn't be that hard.''

''This doesn't have anything to do with notches. And don't even try to tell me you're planning to walk away and ignore what just happened here.''

''That's *exactly* what I'm going to do,'' Becka said coolly, shutting the door behind her.

7

BECKA WALKED OUT of her apartment into the hall to the sound of a stream of curses. Below her, on the stairs, Mallory struggled with a half dozen grocery bags, one of which was slipping out of her fingers even as Becka hurried down to help.

"Here, let me get some of that," she said, rescuing some of the bags from Mallory's hands and carrying them to the landing. "You know, you could make more than one trip," Becka observed. "It'd be easier on your knees."

Mallory set down the bags to unlock her door. "I know, I know. I just hate doing that. I always wind up thinking I can do it and the next thing I know, I'm playing weight lifter on the stairs."

"So where do you shop around here?" Becka followed her into her kitchen and set the bags on the counter. "Is there an organic grocery store, or at least a Trader Joe's? You know, some place where you can get something besides junk foo..." her voice trailed off as she turned to see Mallory tossing frozen burritos and pizzas into the freezer.

Mallory stopped and gave Becka a suspicious stare. "You're not one of those health freaks, are you?"

Becka squinted at the bag of Cheetos in Mallory's hand. "More or less."

"Well, I would be of the other persuasion, so don't look too close at my groceries," Mallory said, pushing a pair of candy bars and a frozen steak to one side. "They're personal."

"I'll remember that," Becka said, pulling out canned soup.

Mallory reached past her to open up a cupboard. "So do my eyes deceive me or do I detect whisker burn on your chin?" She leaned a hip against the counter and looked at Becka. "Loverboy strikes again?"

"That obvious?"

"Yeah. What happened?"

"Nothing happened."

"Nothing?"

"I was running, he thought he'd be cute and show up, and then he tagged along to bug me when I was lifting weights. Nothing."

"You seem awfully irritated for just nothing."

"The guy just won't go away." Becka put the can onto the shelf. "I've told him I'm not interested. Most guys would back off and that would be that, but he has to try to prove to me he can change my mind."

"And of course when he started feeling you up and taking off your clothes you stayed calm and cool and gave him a blow job."

"He had my hands tied—" Becka shopped short and shot Mallory a dirty look.

Mallory raised an eyebrow. "Hands tied up? You have an interesting interpretation of not interested."

"I wasn't tied up. We were in the weight room and they were lifting straps and—" Becka stopped as Mallory burst out laughing.

"Nothing, huh? Sounds like my kinda nothing." She stuck a six-pack of soda in her refrigerator.

"I don't want to get involved with him."

"Just a guess, but you might want to try to be a little

more clear about that particular message,'' Mallory said, ''because it doesn't sound like you're all that hot on no either. Why not just have a fling? What does it matter?''

''Then he wins.''

''He wins what? You have a bet or something?''

''Of course not,'' Becka said impatiently. ''But ever since he got here he's been coming on to me. I keep telling him to take a hike and he keeps telling me he's going to convince me.''

''Ah,'' Mallory nodded and opened the crisper to add a bag of grapes. ''Point of honor.''

''I'm not so hard up that I'm ready to be the next willing candidate. Anyway, I don't have to hold out too much longer. He's leaving soon.''

Mallory stared at her like she'd grown a second head. ''Well if he's on his way out then just get over it and give the man a tumble. You're looking like you need one and he's volunteering. You get the good times without the games.''

Becka looked back at her, unconvinced.

Mallory finally shrugged and began gathering up empty bags. ''Well, good luck with it, whatever you decide. I do need to talk with you about something else, though. It's one of your players....'' she hesitated.

Becka looked at her sharply. ''What?''

''I don't know what his name is, but he comes in most nights. I took a good look at his license because he looks so young. Dark, good-looking. Cocky. Moretti? Morani?''

''Morelli,'' Becka filled in for her.

''Morelli. Yeah, that's it. He's been coming in a lot lately. Drinks like a fish, and last night he switched over from beer to bourbon. Got himself pretty toasted. What's his story?''

Becka listened with a sinking heart. "I don't know. He's got talent, but he's got an attitude to go with it."

"Yeah, well, he's also got himself a list of groupies that are just waiting to get all over him." Mallory shut her pantry door. "He almost got himself in some real trouble last night, though. He started up with some woman who was there with a date. A very big and very nasty-looking date who didn't take kindly to him coming on to her."

"Tell me he didn't do anything really stupid," Becka implored, closing her eyes.

"The girlfriend got the guy to leave without dislocating your boy's head from his skeleton, but it was a close one." Mallory pushed her hair back over her shoulders. "A bouncer friend of mine taught me some very nasty tricks for dealing with trouble. I've never had to use them before. I thought last night was going to be a first." She looked at Becka soberly.

Becka nodded. "Thanks for telling me. I'll take care of it. I'm not sure how, but we'll get a bead on him and keep track of what he's up to."

"Better you than me. He seems to have a pretty high opinion of himself."

Becka snorted. "Right now, he's a legend in his own mind. I just need to figure out how to keep him from blowing up before he ever gets out of the minors."

"It's because he's good-looking. It's always the gorgeous ones who give you trouble," Mallory said, shaking her head.

"Ain't that the truth."

LATER, BECKA LINGERED in the training room after most of the players had gone to dinner, putting off the inevitable for as long as possible. She'd debated about talking to Morelli herself, but came to the reluctant realization that only one person had a chance of getting through to Morelli.

Becka tapped on the open door of Mace's office. For a moment, he simply gave her a leisurely look. "Florence. To what do I owe this honor?"

"We need to talk."

She walked in and shut the door. A glint of amusement stole into his golden eyes.

"You changed your mind about this morning and you want to finish up where we started?"

"Let's forget about this morning," she said, struggling to suppress the image of them together in the weight room, reflected in mirror after mirror.

"You make it difficult. You're very distracting, you know. Watching you right now, for instance. It makes me wonder what you'd do if—"

He wasn't going to take her down that road again and turn her mind to mush. "Let's not go there right now, Duvall."

"Later?"

"Much later." Like after he was gone, she sincerely hoped.

"Well, grab a seat." He picked a pile of equipment off of the chair next to the desk and waved her over. "What's up?"

"It's Morelli." Becka perched on the edge of the chair, watching Mace lean back idly in his seat. "I ran into my neighbor Mallory today, the one who tends bar at Double Play."

"The sports hangout across the street?"

Becka nodded. "According to her, Morelli's a regular, and he's been stirring up trouble."

"What kind of trouble?"

"Getting mouthy. Spoiling for a fight. Making passes at other guys' girlfriends."

"That's a good way to get pasted. So what do you want me to do?" Mace tapped his fingers restlessly on the desk. "I'm here to teach batting, not manners."

"I was hoping maybe you could talk to him, straighten him out a little. He's at a really important point in his career right now. It'd be a shame to see him screw up."

"I barely know the guy. He's not going to listen to me."

"Are you kidding?" Becka gave a short laugh. "These guys worship you. Trust me, you'll make an impression."

"I doubt it."

"Will you at least try? Just stop by the bar and talk with him, that's all I'm asking." Even she could hear the pleading note that came into her voice.

Mace leaned forward to rest his arms on the desktop. "It really matters to you what happens to these kids, doesn't it?" he asked, staring at her searchingly.

She started to downplay it and then stopped. "Yes," she said slowly, "it does. I want to see all of them get to the majors and I'll do whatever I need to to make that happen."

The seconds passed, and then Mace blew a breath out. "Okay. I'll see if I can talk some sense into him."

"Thanks." She cleared her throat. "So I guess this means you're planning to stick around until your assignment's done?"

"I'm still holding out hope for you, Florence."

"You're either an incurable optimist or an egomaniac, Duvall. I can't figure out which." She laughed and stood up. "Let me know what happens with Morelli."

"Does that mean I don't get a rubdown after the game?"

"You're not going to have time for a rubdown. You'll be heading out for a hard night of partying." She started out the door then paused with her hand on the knob, wondering what she'd done, setting a playboy up to talk sense into a playboy in training. "Hey, Duvall?"

He looked up. "Hmm?"

"Don't teach him to be any worse than he already is."

8

ONE OF THE THINGS he'd never missed about the minor leagues was the traveling, Mace reflected as he tossed his overnight bag into the luggage compartment of what had once been a Greyhound bus, judging by the faint shadow of the running dog logo that showed through the new skin of blue paint. On the other hand, he doubted most of the players noticed the recycled bus. They were all either fresh out of high school or college. Compared to what they called team buses in his day, the motor coach was plush. Hell, it even had TV monitors.

He took a casual glance around for Becka. Given that she was the whole reason he'd stuck around, he'd be frustrated if she'd managed to somehow duck the four-hour bus ride to their first road stop. Although, he had to grudgingly admit that he'd gotten a kick out of the training sessions with the team. He'd enjoyed it even more when he saw the players use his tips to get hits. Maybe there was something to this after all, he mused just as Becka drove into the lot.

The breeze caught her swingy copper hair as she got out of the tiny Toyota. Slinging a duffel bag over her shoulder, she picked a sheaf of files out of the front seat and walked toward the bus. Shorts again today, though this time with a denim shirt thrown over a tank top. Even so, the loose shirt didn't quite camouflage the delicious body that he knew lay beneath the cloth. Before he left, he was damned well going to see it uncovered, and give them both the pleasure he knew was waiting for them.

"Okay, everybody on." Sammy stood by the door as they boarded one by one. "You got the paperwork, Florence?" He glanced over to where Becka was tossing her bag in the luggage compartment.

"Have a little faith, Sammy," Becka replied, brandishing her files as she climbed up into the bus.

Mace followed, snagging a bottle of water from the cooler up front and grabbing a seat. Sammy made a last-minute head count. When he was satisfied, he nodded to the driver and the door shut with a hiss.

Mace cracked the top off the water bottle as the bus lurched into motion and Sammy dropped into the seat beside him.

"How's it going, Duvall?"

"Not bad, Sammy, how 'bout yourself?"

"Three wins in a row, I can't complain."

"The team's looking good." Mace looked back behind Sammy's head to see Becka walking up the center aisle to the front of the bus carrying a thick envelope. She was looking pretty good herself, Mace thought.

"Okay everybody, listen up," she said briskly, holding on to the back of a seat to steady herself. "I've got your per diems here." She started working her way down the bus, handing each player an envelope with his name on it. "Five days and nights. The hotel has breakfast and there'll be sandwiches in the clubhouse before the games. Otherwise, you're on your own. If you use up what's in this envelope, your next meal is coming out of your own pocket." She held up a sheet of paper. "There's also a shuttle schedule. You know the gig, anyone who misses the bus gets himself to the stadium on his own nickel."

"And he'd better make it a cheap cab, because I'm going

to slap his sorry rear end with a whopper of a fine when he finally makes it to the clubhouse,'' Sammy added.

"Any questions?'' Becka asked. Taking the silence for a no, she wove her way down the aisle and back to her seat.

Sammy leaned over to Mace. "Makes a hell of a traveling secretary. Our old trainer couldn't keep a trip organized if his life depended on it.''

"She's a woman of many talents.''

"She's got what you need for a winning team.'' Sammy settled back in his seat. "Kinda like you. You're really getting this teaching thing down.''

Mace shrugged. "Getting good at faking it, more like.''

"Whatever you're doing, it's working. I'm gonna ask them to send you out here again.''

Time to nip this one in the bud, Mace thought uncomfortably. "Sammy, I was just trying this out here this week,'' he began.

"I know you were. You're good at this, Duvall. These kids are learning a lot from you.''

"Sammy, they stuck you with me. I know the score. You don't have to go overboard.''

Sammy blinked. "Sometimes I don't get you at all, Duvall. You're a good batting coach.''

"You can't tell that after just a couple of days,'' Mace argued.

"Hey, I've worked with lots of instructors in my time. Some guys know what they're doing but can't teach a lick. Some guys can't play worth a damn but they're good at teaching. Some guys got the gift for both. I think you're one of them.''

Mace tried to ignore the quick rush of pleasure. Sammy was probably just telling him what he wanted to hear. "Kind of a quick decision, isn't it, Sammy?''

"Hey, I'm paid for my judgment."

"I see." Mace worked to keep a straight face. "And would that be paid well?"

"We got four more hours to be on this bus. You keep cracking wise and see where it gets you."

Mace did grin then. "I'm too old to scare, Sammy. Save that for them." He tipped his head toward the back of the bus.

"I hear you took the guys out for pizza last night after the game."

"I got 'em back before curfew." Mace rubbed his jaw. "Seemed like a good idea at the time."

"'Preciate you doin' it. It means a lot to the guys that you took the time to hang out with them. Gives 'em someone to look up to."

Being a role model had never figured into his career plans. He wasn't at all sure how he felt about the paternal routine everyone suddenly expected of him. "I don't know if I want anyone looking up to me," Mace said.

"Too late, they already do."

The place had been a dive, with greasy pizza and cheap, cold beer. Clustered around scarred wooden tables they'd watched women, voted on their Hall of Fame fantasy team, and bitched about interleague play, wild card play-offs, and other aberrations of modern baseball. And it had been fun, he realized with a jolt. He'd missed the easy camaraderie of a team.

"Hey, tell me what you think," Sammy said, digging a piece of paper out of his shirt pocket. "I want to shift the batting order tonight. I think some of the stuff you've been teaching them has taken hold and we should work with it. Let me tell you what I've got in mind."

Mace couldn't resist at least taking a look. The notion was too tempting. As a player, he'd always had ideas about how things should be run. Now that Sammy was asking him, he couldn't help but have an opinion. He bent over to become absorbed in strategy, and the miles rolled away.

FOUR HOURS WAS a long time to be sitting on a bus, Becka thought as she looked up from her book to stare out the window. At least things were quiet for the time being. It might have been the middle of the day, but the torpor-inducing rush of engine noise and the soft sway of the bus on the road had lulled most of the players to sleep. Of course, the fact that they'd left at 7:00 a.m. might have had something to do with it, too.

She stared out at the flowing green hills of the Vermont landscape. It was nice, sometimes, getting to see the country you were traveling through instead of just skimming over clouds and appearing in another city.

A crackle sounded next to her and she jumped, turning to see Mace picking up her files to snag the seat next to her.

"I didn't mean to frighten you." He looked at her with interest. "You were pretty lost in your thoughts. Must have been thinking about something pretty fascinating."

"Did you want something specific? Strike that question," she interrupted before he could speak.

"Whatever you say. I just figured you might be getting bored about now and looking for some company." He craned his neck to read the title of the book that lay open in her lap. " '*Treatment For Repetitive Stress Injuries?*' Oh yeah, I've read that one. You're going to love the ending."

Becka could feel the heat of his jean-clad leg radiating across the inch that separated them. Nope, no touching, however much her muscles might want to relax so her leg fell toward his. Her mind knew that this was not a good idea. *Yeah, but he's leaving in two days,* the troublesome voice in her head spoke up. To quell it, Becka reached back to pull down the armrest between the seats and looked out the window.

The landscape rolling by was a quilt of fields, forests and rivers. Mace leaned back in his seat. "Pretty country. I didn't realize that they did any farming up this high."

"I don't know what grows here. Looks like they've got plenty of dairy. You know, Vermont cheddar and all that."

He opened his bottle of water and took a drink. "Hard way to make a living."

"That sounds like the voice of experience. Didn't you grow up on a farm?" She vaguely remembered hearing something about his rural past.

Mace nodded. "Hogs, mostly, some chickens, a couple of steers every year for eating. I've had a close personal acquaintance with more kinds of manure than any kid should ever encounter."

"Probably good training for the real world," Becka said dryly. "Where'd you live?"

"Georgia, over by the Carolina border."

"Did you ever get to a game in Atlanta?"

He shook his head. "We had a minor league team a few towns away, though. I used to drive my dad crazy dogging him to take us to a game. He didn't like to be gone often, but every so often we'd go."

"I never actually went to a minor league game until I came to work here, believe it or not. We were so close to Boston we always went to see the Sox."

"It's hard to compete with Fenway Park," he acknowledged. "Where I grew up, we didn't have a choice. We were a few hundred miles from the nearest major league club. Strictly farm teams for us."

"Is that where you got the baseball bug?"

His mouth curved. "I think I was born with the baseball

bug. Minor league ball was just a way to indulge it. We barely had enough kids in our town to get a couple of Little League teams going, but my dad tried to get me to baseball camp every year. He was great that way. There were a few times he had to scrape the bottom of the barrel, but he always managed it.''

''He must have been really proud of you,'' she murmured.

''He was killed before I ever got out of triple A,'' Mace said shortly. Even all these years later, it still hurt.

Impulsively, she put her hand over his. ''I'm so sorry to hear that.''

The quick, genuine compassion in her voice helped in a way all too many of the condolences hadn't. ''Thanks. I like to think that he knows, somehow, that I made it all the way.''

''It sounds as if he'd have liked that.''

They rode along in companionable silence for a few miles before Becka gradually became aware of the fact that her hand was still on his. The nerves in her palm became sensitized, telegraphing increasingly urgent signals to her brain, warning her to get away while there was still time.

She moved to pull her hand away but Mace caught it with his before she could succeed. ''Not so fast. Maybe I should read your palm. I'm sure your love line will show something interesting.''

Becka snatched her hand back. ''My love line is my business, thank you very much.'' She glanced around the neighboring rows, satisfied to see players either conked out and snoring or bobbing their heads to personal stereo systems. ''Speaking of business, did you talk to our friend last night?'' she asked in a low voice.

''Not exactly.''

Becka narrowed her eyes. ''What does that mean?''

"One of the guys walked by and heard us talking about going out and it sort of took on a life of its own."

"Group field trip?"

"Something like that."

"So you sat around and drank beer all night."

He shifted a bit. "I'll talk to him later."

It took work to keep her voice down. "Are you aware of the fact that you're leaving the day after tomorrow? Later would be a relative term."

"Yeah, but there's time between now and then."

"Don't knock yourself out, Duvall," she said sardonically, reaching out to pull a copy of *Runner's World* from the seat pocket.

"Hey, Sammy was just telling me what a stellar job I was doing with the training."

She flicked a glance at him. "Great. Maybe you've found your second calling." She opened the magazine and prepared to ignore him.

"Maybe I have." He put a hand over the page until she looked up at him. "It's been fun. Thanks for getting me to give it a chance."

Becka blinked. Oh, this wasn't fair. This wasn't fair at all. Bad enough the man was sexy as hell. Now he was threatening to turn nice on her. First he talked about his dad, now this. It was hard to have a defense for it. "Is that the lady-killer's secret weapon?"

"What?"

"Sincerity."

He shook his head at her in mock sorrow. "You know, Florence, you ought to start having just a little faith in me."

"Next week, Duvall," she promised, "next week."

TWO DAYS LATER, Becka stood at the edge of the dugout at the Troy Jackrabbits' stadium and watched the team mascot. The owners must have gone to the bargain basement when they bought the costume, she thought, because it looked nothing like a jackrabbit. She cocked her head, studying it. Actually, it sort of resembled a dyspeptic gopher, now that she thought about it.

Becka grinned as the top of the eighth inning began. With a five-run lead and their best hitters coming up, the Lowell Weavers were looking at sweeping their two-game series with the Jackrabbits and were feeling frisky.

"Toss me that rosin bag, will ya, Stats?" called Chico, who was next up at bat.

"You know, we win this one, we go into second place, y'all," Stats said.

Morelli whooped. "Time to go celebrate!"

"Keep your mind on the game. Don't count your chickens before they're hatched," Sammy scolded them.

Two innings later, the chickens had hatched and the ebullient Lowell Weavers exploded into the visitors' locker room.

"Next stop, number one!" Morelli shouted. "Let's hit a bar. First round's on me."

Steam billowed out into the locker room from the showers and the familiar cacophony rose, driven by the movements of twenty-some-odd men all showering and changing in very close proximity. Becka turned into the training room to wait it out.

Morelli came out of the shower room, a towel slung low around his hips. "Okay, party time, who's going out with me?"

"Ah man, I'm beat," Chico said, dropping onto a bench in front of his changing area. "Getting up at six-thirty did me in."

"You're turning into a candy-ass in your old age, Watson," Morelli jibed. "I don't believe you can't pull it together enough to go out and celebrate the fact that we just hit the number two spot in the league.''

"No Weavers team has been higher than third in the history of the team," Stats said. "I'll go with you, Morelli."

"That's more like it. What about the rest of you putzes?"

Sammy walked into the locker room and stood with his arms folded across his chest. "You got a curfew, Morelli," he said ominously.

"Hey, we got a couple hours between now and then to unwind, chief."

"Yeah, well, the bus leaves tomorrow morning at 6:30 a.m. sharp, and if your butt isn't on it, you're going to be one sorry customer."

"There's a place practically across the street." Morelli opened his locker to get his clothes.

Becka left the locker room as he dropped his towel, and stuck her head into the tiny coaches' office to find Mace at a desk. "You hearing this?"

"Yeah, I hear it."

"Should you go along to keep an eye on Morelli? If Mallory's right, he's headed toward trouble."

"Maybe. Of course Mallory could be wrong."

There was something she didn't trust about the glint in his eyes. "She's a bartender. I trust her judgment."

He finished up his notes on the game and rose to leave them for Sammy. "You barely know her."

No point in trying to explain the quick spark of friendship that had sprung up between them. "So maybe she's right, maybe she's wrong. The only way to know is to go along and find out." Irritation needled her. "Look, you said you'd talk to him a couple of days ago. You leave tomorrow, and you're quitting after that." She crossed her arms and gave him a hard stare. "Your follow-through sucks, Duvall."

"All right, all right, you've made your point. Any promise I make, I keep." He looked her up and down, only slowly, so she could feel her chin coming up in challenge.

He stepped closer to her. "However, maybe you should put your concern where your mouth is and join us?" Amusement flickered in his eyes. "As my date."

"Go to hell." She started to turn away.

"Who's the one who's always telling me to think about the team?" he said mockingly. "You talk a good schtick, but you're not even bothered enough about Morelli to make a small personal sacrifice?"

"This has nothing to do with Morelli and you know it."

Mace dropped into his chair and leaned back until it creaked, grinning with enjoyment.

It was on the tip of her tongue to tell him to stuff it, but she couldn't stop worrying about Morelli. The only person who had a hope of getting through to him was Mace. Morelli was the team's make-or-break player, and this was Morelli's make-or-break season. "Fine," she said shortly.

"Fine what?"

"Fine, I'll go to the bar with you guys."

He reached out to hook a finger in the hem of her shorts. "Not 'us guys,'" he corrected. "You'll go with me."

"Get real, Duvall. How do you think that's going to look?"

"I don't see the problem," he said blandly. "We're both staff, it's natural that we should hang with each other rather than the players. We go to keep an eye on them, but nothing says we can't have a little fun on our own. No avoiding me, no leaving early."

"I see."

"Oh, and wear something besides shorts if you've got it."

Becka's eyes snapped fire at him. "You can—"

"Ah, ah, ah," he waggled a finger at her. "Think of the team."

Becka walked out of the room fuming. He wanted her in something else besides shorts? Well, fine. One of her father's cardinal rules had been that whenever you went on a road trip with a team you brought one dress-up outfit, just in case something came up where you had to represent the team. She wouldn't exactly be representing the team this particular occasion, but she did have an outfit that would be quite sufficient for Mace Duvall.

Becka's mouth curved into a slow, wicked smile. He'd exhausted her patience. It was time he learned a lesson. She'd turn on the heat full bore, use everything she had to reel him in, bring him to his knees. And then, when he was begging for it, walk away and leave him wanting.

And she'd enjoy every minute of it.

9

MACE STOPPED at Becka's hotel room and knocked.

Long seconds passed, then the door opened. A whisper of scent flowed over him. And for just a moment, he forgot how to breathe.

She stood in a short, silky-looking dress in a bottle green. Buttons ran from the low neckline to the hem. Her arms were bare. It wasn't particularly snug, but somehow the fabric dipped in at all the right spots, hinting at the taut, lean body that lay beneath. He couldn't help but stare at the fragile bones at the base of her neck and imagine pressing his mouth to them. He couldn't help but imagine taking his time to flick open the glass buttons and fill his hands with her.

The hemline showed an outrageous expanse of leg. He'd seen more, he supposed, on the day they'd run together, but there was something about a short dress that tempted and aroused. Something about knowing that all he had to do was put his hands on that hem, push up the fabric and...

"Are you ready, or are you just going to stand here staring at me all night?" Her swingy red hair feathered around her face and she'd done something to her eyes that made them look deep and mysterious. Her full mouth was the color of the kind of wine that went straight to a man's head.

If they didn't leave now, they weren't going anywhere.

Mace cleared his throat. "Let's head out."

The pool hall was noisy, hot, and crowded. Shaded bulbs

dangled down over a dozen pool tables, illuminating expanses of green felt dotted with vividly colored balls. Overhead fans stirred the haze of cigarette smoke that twined up around the ceiling. George Thorogood blared from the jukebox, punctuated by the sharp cracks of pool balls smashing into one another and thudding into pockets.

"Hey, Duvall, over here." Morelli's shout carried across from the bar where the Lowell players were clustered. "Good to see you, man. Come on over here and introduce us to your lady frien…" Morelli stopped and took a closer look. "Florence? Is that you?" He whistled. "I think this's the first time I've seen you in anything but shorts. Wow." He'd obviously had more than a few drinks already and was swaying slightly on his feet.

"Take a seat, Morelli," she suggested as she locked eyes with Mace. "You're looking a little wobbly."

Mace stepped in closer to Morelli and leaned on the bar, flicking a glance at a couple of locals before turning back to the players. "How long have you been here?"

"Oh, 'n hour, maybe." Morelli reached for the shot of whiskey the bartender had just set on the bar behind him and downed it in a single gulp. "Oh yeah, making up for lost time," he said, thumping the glass down on the bar and pointing to it to indicate another.

"I keep telling you if you don't stop drinking that shit you're going to take all the enamel off your teeth, Morelli," Chico called from farther down the bar.

"And I keep telling you to quit that candy-ass beer and start drinking real drinks," Morelli yelled back, his slur becoming more pronounced. "Next time we should go somewhere that doesn't pour thish cheap crap."

A few local guys sitting near Morelli snapped their heads around to stare at him, then at the beer in front of them. The bigger one stirred. "You got a problem, buddy?"

Morelli swayed a little as he sucked down another shot and wiped his lips. ''Thass not beer, son, that there is a veterinary sample.''

One of the beefy guys stood up fast and got in Morelli's face. ''I've just about had it with your mouth. You've been a pain in the ass ever since you got here and I want you gone.''

''You tell 'im, Dix,'' his friend said with a belch and a hard stare toward the Lowell group.

''Get over yourself, Beavis, you doan know who you're messing with.'' Morelli was weaving even more now.

''All right, you little punk, that's it.'' Dix drew back a beefy fist and swung—

And a hand shot up to clamp around his wrist, stopping his fist before it reached Morelli. ''That'll do,'' Mace said, stepping between the two men. ''You'll have to excuse my friend,'' he said pleasantly to Dix without releasing his wrist. ''He's had a few too many and sometimes it turns him into a jackass.'' He watched the bigger man calculatingly. Bulky, but mostly gone to fat. With a bit of luck, they'd get out of this yet.

Dix tried to yank his arm loose. ''Don't mess with me.''

''I have no intention of it,'' Mace said, without emphasis.

''Get your hands off me right now or—''

''Hey, wait, you're that guy,'' his friend burst out suddenly.

''Shaddup, Leroy,'' Dix snarled.

''No, I know him. He's that guy played for the Braves, shortstop. The one who hit the grand slam off Pettit in that series game.'' He squinted at Mace. ''Aincha?''

''Yeah, he is,'' Chico said enthusiastically from behind Mace, where he'd been resigning himself to joining the brewing fight.

Dix rubbed his wrist, staring at Mace with a mixture of respect and anger. "Yeah, well you better teach that jackass," he jabbed a finger at Morelli, "to keep a lid on it or someone will do it for him."

"Doan need you 'pologizing for me," Morelli said from behind Mace, where Chico and Stats held him upright.

"Shut up, Morelli," Mace suggested evenly. "You're done for the night." He turned to the other players, now clustered around him. "Okay guys, the fun is over. Who's Morelli's roommate?"

Chico raised his hand and gave a disgusted grimace. "I'm the lucky guy."

Mace said, "Okay, get him back to the hotel, and put him to bed. Becka and I'll buy a drink for our friends here and smooth things over."

THE LINE BETWEEN good times and violence was so fine. How quickly a night out could cross from one side to the other, Becka thought with a little shiver, understanding for the first time how living nightmares began. The way Mace had stepped in to defuse the incident made her shiver a little, too. She'd never claimed to be the intellectual type. She was physical, and as much as she didn't want to be impressed by the way he'd handled the tense situation, at some visceral level she was.

Mace Duvall was a man who knew how to take care of himself, a man who protected others. She shuddered to think what might have happened without his intercession. Damn Morelli anyway. He was just out there looking for trouble and not caring who he dragged into it with him.

Still, the hullabaloo ended so quickly the bartender hadn't even noticed. With the whole Lowell team gone, you'd never have known anything had been amiss. Of course, Mace's celebrity status hadn't hurt. She sat quietly while he slapped Leroy on the shoulder, bought drinks for the duo, and told a few baseball stories. Finally, Mace turned back to her.

She raised an eyebrow. "Now do you believe that he has a problem?"

"Your friend definitely knows what she's talking about. I'll talk to him in the morning before you folks head out. He's going to be hurting, so I should be able to slap some sense into him."

"Get it through his idiot skull that he could have gotten a lot of people hurt tonight, and not just himself." She looked at him soberly. "I'm glad you were here."

"Skill and talent," he said modestly.

"It looked to me like all you needed was your famous face and your charm to win them over."

"I don't care about winning over Leroy and Dix. What I care about is what it takes to win you." He looked at her.

The bartender pushed a couple of beers in front of them. "Compliments of the guys at the end of the bar." They glanced down to where Dix and Leroy were talking with some buddies.

Becka pushed the beers back. "Oh, we're leav—"

Mace cut her off. "Tell them thanks." He saluted the group, who grinned and waved.

"I suppose we should drink it, huh?" she asked dubiously.

Mace shook his head and let his eyes linger on her. "Nope, as I recall, you're still my date." He took her hand.

Becka made a brief attempt to get her fingers loose, but met with no more success than Dix had. "I'm here, we're out. As far as I'm concerned, I came through with my part of the deal."

"Not even close. It's barely eleven. We've spent the last half hour dealing with Morelli's mess." He picked up her hand and brushed his lips over the knuckles. "Now's when we start our evening."

The icy bottle of beer felt cool against her hand, and she tried to focus on that.

In the background, someone called Mace's name over the intercom, and he released her fingers. "Looks like we're up."

"You got a table?"

"I figured it couldn't hurt. As long as we're here, we might as well shoot some stick."

Made of dark, polished wood, their pool table sat in the corner near a wooden ledge stained with the rings from countless beers.

Mace set the tray of balls down on the table and went to select a cue stick. "Want me to get one for you?" he asked.

Becka set her purse and beer on the ledge and shrugged him off. "I can get my own, thanks." Now that the adrenaline rush of the near-fight had abated, she was remembering her original plan to lure him along and then leave him wanting. He wouldn't take no for an answer, fine. She'd teach him a lesson, give him a little something to remember on his way home. She walked over to choose a cue, conscious of the swish of her dress.

She stood holding the cue stick and took a drink of her beer, watching Mace pack the balls in the triangular rack and pull it off, leaving them arranged just so. Casually, she walked around to the far end of the table, rolling the cue ball along with her. She leaned over the table to form a bridge and take aim at the cue ball. Then she glanced up at Mace. "Stripes and solids?"

"Whatever you like." The vivid light from the bare bulb above the table shadowed her eyes and made her cheekbones look exotically sharp. Her hair swung down over her cheeks in two glossy arcs. From his angle, he could see the smooth scoop of her neckline and the shadowed cleft of her cleavage as she stroked the cue to get the feel of it. Then, she slammed the cue ball to crack into the triangle of balls, sending them ricocheting around the table.

She straightened and shot him a challenging stare.

"I see you've played a little pool," he said, pacing around the table to check out his shots, but never taking his eyes from her for more than a moment. This was a very different woman from the one he encountered in the locker room. There was a confidence to her, almost an arrogance, one that demanded attention, admiration.

Becka picked up a blue cube of chalk and spun it on the tip of her cue. "My dad has a table in the basement. It's all we used to do in the summers when I was growing up. 'Course, I'm a little rusty now." She took a quick swig of her beer and watched as Mace sent a ball just brushing the edge of the pocket, then bouncing softly back into the center of the table. Slowly she circled the table, passing close behind him, close enough that she knew he could smell her scent. Then she doubled back and put her hand against his hip. "I just need you to move aside," she murmured, then leaned over to take her shot, putting in the two and the five in quick succession.

"I guess that makes you solids."

"I guess it does," Becka murmured, enjoying her effect on him as she set up to shoot. Then he lifted up his bottle to drink, his throat moving as he swallowed. Her mind flashed abruptly on how it had felt to kiss him there the day they'd been on her bed, the visceral memory running through her as she stroked the cue. Her ball went nowhere near the pocket.

Mace put down the beer and drifted around the table casually checking out his shots. Dressed in khakis and a polo shirt, he looked lean and powerful. No wonder Dix had backed off. When Mace leaned over the table to put the ten ball in, she found herself watching the muscles flex in his arms. The memory of having those powerful tendons and sinews moving under her fingers was impossible to dispel.

"Your shot."

"Huh?" Becka blinked.

"It's your shot." He took a long swallow of his beer, his eyes on her. "I scratched."

"Right." To buy herself time, she chalked her cue. It wouldn't do to forget why she was here. She was supposed to be the one seducing him, not vice versa. She pulled out the cue ball and set it on the green felt, lining it up perfectly to put the one ball in the pocket. One practice stroke and then she tapped it in, adding just enough backspin to keep the cue ball from rolling into the pocket after it.

"Nice finesse."

Even though she'd been hearing it for days, that warm molasses drawl still got to her, stirring something around in the pit of her stomach. Becka gave him a long, steady look, then stretched out over the table toward him for an intentionally difficult shot, putting in the seven. ball. Her next shot went wide, but she'd already had the satisfaction of watching Mace's eyes darken. As long as she could keep him off balance, she'd win the game.

She swallowed, suddenly thirsty. When she crossed to the ledge to pick up her beer, two more were sitting alongside. "Where'd those come from?"

Mace nodded toward the bar. "From our buddies."

Becka picked up a bottle and toasted to Dix and Leroy and they waved back. "This'll probably turn into some legendary story, you know."

He eyed her. "Why not? It seems like a legendary night.

Toss me the chalk, will you?" He caught the blue cube as it arced toward him and he chalked the tip of his cue. He prowled around the table, searching for the perfect shot. She watched his strong, capable hands slide over the polished wood of the cue and couldn't help imagining that touch on her skin.

Mace managed to put two balls in but muffed the third shot, an easy one. He cursed himself for sloppy play. Even if it was just for fun, he had an athlete's dislike of losing. He watched as Becka put in the six ball and then the three, setting herself up perfectly for the four.

There was an almost feline sensuality to her, with those cat eyes and that smooth way of moving. She stretched across the table toward him, her eyes slanted and exotic, her breasts covered only in shadow, and gave him a long, lazy, inviting look. There was something he didn't quite trust there, even as he was drawn to it.

She put her last ball in and circled the table, brushing his back with her body as she passed. He'd given away practically the whole game because he was too busy watching her. He'd played like an amateur, he thought.

And then a wicked thought popped into his mind.

"Eight ball in the corner pocket," Becka said. Unfortunately, she put a bit too much force on the cue ball and sent the eight ball caroming off the pads.

Mace lined up a shot carefully, making it look like it barely made it into the pocket. He deliberately missed the next one, giving the ball back to Becka so she could put in the eight ball and win the game.

"To the pool shark." He clinked bottles with her, then tilted his up for a long drink. "You're definitely a better player than I am, but I usually don't stink as badly as this. I think I need a goal." He glanced at the table. "I think we ought to make a little bet on the next game."

"I don't play for money, Duvall." She leaned back against the little shelf, resting her elbows on the edge.

He rested his palm on the wall beside her head. "No money. Something better." He took another swallow of beer and set the bottle down. "You win, the evening's over and I never bother you again." He traced a finger along her jawbone and up to her lips. "I win, we go to bed."

She opened her mouth with the express intention of telling him to go to hell, but stopped before the words got out. It was the perfect setup, she realized. He was basically offering her a chance to reel him in, to get him turned on and thinking he had her, then take the game from him and show him who was really in control. He'd been pushing for it since he'd arrived. He was asking for it now, walking right into it. And wouldn't it be sweet to teach him a lesson? What would the great Mace Duvall have to say about that when he was all hot and bothered at the end of the night?

"Well, what do you think?"

Her answer was a slow, smoky-eyed smile. "Mmm, I think that's a bet I can live with."

He leaned in and pressed his mouth to hers for a lingering kiss. The pool hall receded. Mace broke away first and gave her a wolfish grin. "That's a deposit," he said.

Becka began pulling balls out of the pockets and racking them, mostly to give herself time to recover from the jolt of his kiss. "Nine ball?" At his nod, she arranged the balls in a tight diamond shape. She'd do well to remember what his mouth could do to her, pumping up her adrenaline, muddying her thinking, shooting her coordination all to hell. Skirt around the edge of danger but don't step in, that was the thing to keep in mind. "I'll even let you break," she said. "Balls go in from lowest to highest. Player to pocket the nine ball wins."

Mace walked behind her, sliding a hand down her hip and she jolted. The heat lingered even after he was down at the other end of the table, looking up at her with those predator eyes. He leaned over the table, looking sexy, capable, and just a bit dangerous.

And suddenly Becka realized she'd made a very big mistake. "Wait," she blurted, just as the cue ball cracked into the balls, scattering them around the table and sending the one ball into the side pocket.

One corner of Mace's mouth turned up in an insolent smile. "Guess I'm still playing." He strolled around the table and put in the two.

Becka walked over to lift her beer with suddenly shaky hands, taking a drink to calm herself. Remember the plan. The important thing was to remember the plan. Taking a deep breath, she walked slowly over to the table across from where Mace was lining up a shot. She rolled the bottle against her cheeks so that the icy condensation rubbed off. Locking eyes with him, she slowly, deliberately stroked the water down her neck and into the shallow valley of her cleavage, then sucked the tip of her finger.

His next shot went wide.

Becka threw him a cool smile and swaggered to the far end of the table, sliding her hand idly up and down the cue stick as she studied the layout of the balls. Finally, she bent down, stroked the cue a few times, and neatly put in the three ball. She was lining up her next shot with the four when Mace walked behind her and leaned in.

"I love watching you bend over the table like that. It makes me think what it's going to be like to have you naked and on top of me when I'm inside you."

Her pulse jittered. She wanted to be offended, but the soft, drawling words just started a molten flow of desire deep inside of her. Her next shot was just a bit too aggres-

sive and the ball bounced off the cushion instead of going in.

He tsked at her. "Control is everything, Florence, you
should know that." Quickly, efficiently, he sank the four
ball. The five ball was going to be harder, he thought,
prowling around the table looking for the right angle. He
glanced up to see Becka wander over with her beer. Her
mouth curved, then she licked the rim of the bottle neck.
It was like a punch to his gut, seeing that lush mouth slide
around the tip of the glass column as she tilted the bottle
up. He watched, riveted, as she drank with indolent enjoyment, then lowered the bottle. She lingered even then, rubbing her lips against the glass to capture any stray drops,
staring at him with dark-eyed invitation.

"Are you still shooting?" she asked in a bored voice.

What ball was he on, Mace wondered blankly, then remembered. Still, his attempt at the five ball failed miserably
and gave Becka the shot.

She stepped forward, studying the balls on the table.
With swift decisiveness, she put in the five. Just a few more
balls and she'd have the game won, she noted with glee.
Run him up and shut him down. She focused on her shot
for the six ball.

"Game's almost over," Mace whispered in her ear. She
turned to find him too close to her, his eyes dark gold and
intent. He traced a fingertip down her arm, leaving nerve
endings shivering in its wake.

She scratched on her next shot, giving Mace the ball. He
put in the six easily, and the seven just as quickly. She
needed to get her turn back, Becka thought with a little
thrill of alarm, or she was going to lose the game.

Casually, she pulled a barstool over by the pocket he
was shooting toward and sat down on it, crossing one sleek
leg over the other in a lazy move. She pretended to rub an

itchy spot on her knee, then stroked her fingers slowly up her leg, sliding the silk skirt even higher.

Mace narrowed his eyes and straightened up. "Do you mind?"

"What?"

"Can you move so that you're not behind the pocket?"

She gave him a pouty look. "I'm four feet away, which is practically regulation playing distance. It's not my fault if you can't concentrate."

He shot toward the pocket but the ball carried so little momentum that it stopped on the rim of the pocket. He rounded the table toward her as she gave a low laugh of pleasure.

"It's not nice to laugh at your lover," he murmured into her ear.

"You're not my lover," she said, turning her head to him. It was a mistake. Her mouth brushed his. He took the kiss deeper, tangling his fingers in her hair and tasting her until he satisfied himself and felt her mouth soften.

"I will be," he said softly. "You know that. You're already wondering what it will be like, aren't you?"

For long seconds after he stepped away, she stayed absolutely still, then rose to circle the table. She did it twice. Almost, he mused, as though she couldn't quite concentrate. Her hand shook as she made a bridge with her fingers, then she took a deep breath and snapped the eight ball toward the pocket. It didn't quite make its destination.

Mace stepped forward, the taste of incipient victory sweet in his mouth. "Oh, you almost had it, you know," he said conversationally as he put in the eight ball. "Looks to me like maybe you want me to win. All I've got to do is knock in the nine ball."

Becka took a swallow of her beer and walked past, brushing her body against him, trailing her fingers across his back and hip. Mace stood stock-still for a second, struggling to control what had suddenly transformed into a raging hard-on. The firm, yielding flesh that had brushed against his arm only made him think of having her breasts in his hands, of having her under him hot and wanton.

She gave him a sly glance and sat on the bar stool, flicking her skirt to offer him a tantalizing glimpse of black lace. Then she did her best to still her nerves. All she needed was for him to miss and the game was hers.

"So what were the terms of the bet again?" Mace asked as he walked slowly over to line up his shot. "You win, I don't even go near you." He took a test stroke. "I win, we go to bed."

Becka stared at the cue, willing him to miss.

"Well," he said, turning to look at her, "it looks like I'd better win."

With a sharp, decisive crack, he slammed the nine ball into the pocket. Becka made a small involuntary sound of distress. Mace straightened up slowly, staring at her across the table. He put his cue in the rack and looked at her with relish.

"Your room or mine?"

10

SHE'D LET HERSELF get hustled, pure and simple, Becka fumed as she walked toward the hotel with Mace. She'd watched him play sloppily in the first game and had assumed that she could distract him into playing poorly and beat him, sending him off disappointed. Instead, she'd fallen for the oldest pool hustling trick in the book. And maybe the hardest thing to admit was that deep down, a little part of her wasn't really that upset that she'd lost.

In fact, a little part of her wasn't upset at all.

She stepped off the curb to cross the street and bobbled a bit.

"Careful." Mace curled his fingers under her elbow to steady her. "Those beers getting to you?"

"I'm perfectly sober," she said.

"I'm sure you are." He slid his hand down her arm to capture her fingers with a disconcerting heat.

Arousal thudded through her. She couldn't blame it on drink, not all of it. And it certainly didn't explain her current predicament. The reality of it was, she wouldn't have made the bet if she hadn't been willing to deal with the realities of losing. She wanted his touch, pure and simple.

"You're pretty quiet, Florence. In fact, I think it's an all-time record for you."

His mouth curved in a smile and she could practically taste it under hers. Anticipation jittered through her, that giddy feeling of knowing that in a few minutes she'd be

with a new lover, finding out for the first time how it felt
to have his naked body against her, what noises he made
when he was aroused.

How it felt when he was inside her.

She'd wanted him since the day she'd laid eyes on him.
Of course, he'd ticked her off from the day she'd laid eyes
on him, too, but tonight that didn't seem to matter. He made
her feel good.

And based on what had happened in the weight room,
she had a pretty good idea that he could do even better.

She wasn't about to give him the pleasure of thinking
that he'd hustled her into doing something she didn't want,
though. He definitely wasn't to think that he'd won their
little battle of wills. She knew what she wanted, and she'd
be the one making the first move. And move, she would.
She'd work him over until he was begging for her to take
him off the hook, she thought, as they reached the hotel
and walked across the lobby. At the elevator, they waited
until the doors opened, then stepped into the car. And the
minute the doors closed, Becka took two steps toward him,
speared her fingers through his hair and locked her mouth
over his.

Mace's arms came up around her instantly. Surprise and
desire slammed through his body as he pulled her to him.
He hadn't felt this kind of uncontrollable need since he'd
been a teenager, he thought as her mouth parted under his.
Before he could take them deeper, she was backing away
from him, a mocking smile on her lips. "Patience, Duvall.
Patience," she said with a husky laugh.

The elevator door opened on an empty hall. She walked
ahead of him, her skirt swishing sassily. Yep, about two
minutes after they got through the door of his room, that
dress would be off, he thought. She seemed a little uneasy
as he unlocked his door, her eyes feverishly bright, perhaps

with arousal, perhaps with danger of discovery. Then they were inside and he was crushing her to him.

He'd thought so long about having that firm, limber body against him. Her scent wound into his senses as he plundered her lush mouth, his hands roving over her body, sliding up under the thin fabric of her dress to find the silky smooth skin beneath. It was time to get her out of those clothes, definitely. Hunger rushed through him, and he pulled her head back to feast on her neck.

Becka's mouth parted and she made a soft sound that wasn't quite a moan. Her heart hammered in her chest, the excitement unbearable. She couldn't let herself give in to it, she thought dizzily, trying to keep from being overwhelmed by the sensations swamping her. His mouth traveled down her neck and across her jaw, traveling back to linger on her mouth. She couldn't keep control if she let him kiss her until her mind was mush. Still, it took all her resolve to push him away from her.

"Mmm. That's definitely a start." Becka swallowed, then twisted away as he reached for her again. "You know, we should have some water after all that beer or we're really going to be hurting tomorrow. Could you go get some ice?" She stared at him, her eyes heavy lidded.

"You're not serious."

"Just a little ice to cool things down." She leaned in and ran her fingers down his chest. "I'll be right here waiting."

Mace pulled away and gave her a narrow-eyed stare. "This wouldn't have anything to do with you doing a disappearing act, would it?"

Becka gave him a slow smile. "Oh no." She slid her hand up his chest and cupped the back of his neck to pull his head toward her. Nipping his lips, she closed her eyes against the drugging pleasure of his taste. "I wouldn't miss this for the world."

He stared at her a moment longer, then grabbed the ice bucket off the long, low dresser that sat opposite the bed. "I'll be back."

She set her purse on the dresser, staring at herself in the mirror on the wall above it. Okay, so she'd gotten distracted there for a bit. She was still confident she could stay in control of the situation. The important thing was that he not think he'd won.

An almost dizzying expectation shivered through her as she opened up her wallet and took out the condom she kept there. It had been too long since she'd really felt the touch of a lover. She stroked her fingertips slowly down the smooth skin of her chest, down toward the buttons of her dress.

Where was Mace, anyway? He'd had more than enough time to get down the hall to the ice machine and back.

Tossing the condom on the bedside table, she picked up the remote. She tugged the easy chair over to the bed and sank down in it, propping her feet up on the bedspread, knees akimbo. A click of the remote turned on the television that sat on the dresser next to the mirror. God only knew what was on at this hour, but she needed to rest her eyes on something. She flipped absently past QVC and ESPN, blinking at the flash of the channels.

Then stopped abruptly, eyes wide.

On the screen, fingers stroked the nipple of a bare—and very ample—breast. The camera pulled back to reveal a red-haired woman draped over a table, with a man rubbing oil over her naked body as she moved sinuously. Flavored oil, Becka thought, as he bent and licked the woman's breast. Candles flickered in the room, sending light glimmering over the skin of the lovers. Muscles flexed on the man's back as he leaned over the woman and gathered her up against him. Her hand moved down, obviously stroking him, though the camera angle coyly left that bit to the imagination.

That was all right—what it showed was more than enough to make Becka imagine the touch. The actor's hands were on the woman's breasts, rolling the nipples between his fingers. The actress slid around on the table to wrap her legs around his hips. As the camera filmed from behind him, he began to move rhythmically, obviously pumping himself in and out of her. The woman reached one hand up to tangle in his blond hair and pull his head down to hers. A soft sigh came from the television, mirroring Becka's own.

Sex, pure, raw and unadulterated. The images hit her like a series of sucker punches, making it hard to breathe. Watching the screen, she could feel every caress, every bit of it a preview of what could be next for her. She slid a hand from her bent knee along the inside of her thigh then back, reveling in the sensation.

Mallory was right. Give Mace a tumble and enjoy it. The bus left at the crack of dawn the next day, Mace was scheduled to fly back home to Florida, and it would be over. Why shouldn't she just enjoy herself? Months of celibacy were not normal. Her fingers slid up her flat belly to the sensitive skin of her breast. She'd been making a big deal out of principle, when it was just sex. Why not go with it?

MACE WALKED down the hall, shaking his head. Just his luck. All he wanted to do was get the damned ice and get back to his room. Instead, he'd spent fifteen minutes discussing swinging styles with a couple of players who'd waylaid him at the ice machine. It had been all he could do to discourage them from following him back to his room for an all-night session of ESPN Classic.

The ice was cool against his fingers as he fumbled with the card key. Unlocking the door, he stepped inside. And saw the naked bodies surging on the television, and Becka sprawled in the chair by the bed, legs cocked up on the bedspread.

He was hard, instantly.

Her dress lay open down to the middle of her taut belly, where a couple of crystal buttons made a pretense at modesty. The thin fabric gaped open to show tantalizing scraps of black lace over her breasts and at the vee between her legs. Somehow it was sexier than finding her naked would have been. The television screen opposite the bed was a shifting kaleidoscope of tanned flesh as a man stretched his lover back over a kitchen table. Becka's eyes were heavy-lidded, her full mouth tempting, hand resting on her hip, fingers dangling down between her legs as though he'd just interrupted her…

"Traffic at the ice machine?" She gave him a careless glance, her fingers stroking down her chest to brush the lace over her breasts. "I was beginning to think I'd have to make my own entertainment," she said mockingly.

The couple on the television moaned, their bodies moving in tandem. Mace tossed the ice carelessly on the bureau and took two steps over to the chair. He had time to see her eyes widen in surprise before he picked her up to pull her against him. It was her mouth he wanted first, he thought as he tangled his fingers in her hair. Ripe and hot and full of promise, it drove him to take more even as she moved against him, trying to get her feet on the floor. She was light, lithe as she molded against him.

He raised his head to look down into cat-green eyes hazy with passion. "Forget about the stuff on the screen. We can do better.'' He set her on her knees on the bed, and began kicking off his shoes and yanking his polo shirt off over his head. The need to taste her again drove him to lean in and savor her lips. He could feel Becka's fingers unfastening his belt, and he broke the kiss to step out of the khakis. Then he took her mouth with his, plunging deep until the addictive flavor of passion stripped away his control.

The warm, silky feel of her bare skin against his fingers sent adrenaline surging through Mace's system as he reached down to finish unfastening the buttons of her dress. He ran his hands over her smooth, pale flesh, pushing the fabric off her shoulders. He'd dreamed about how she'd feel, dreamed about having her against him naked, fevered and damp with arousal. Suddenly he was in a fever to get past the concealing scraps of lace under his hands.

Becka moved away, her mouth bruised and swollen from his. She reached back to unfasten her bra, the movement pushing her breasts forward until he had to taste them, running his tongue over the soft skin exposed by the demibra. Then the silky lace was falling into his hands as she shrugged off the straps.

Becka gasped at the friction as Mace's hands slid back up to cover her breasts. His palms were hot against her nipples, so that she pressed herself against them, against him. The drugging pleasure flowed over her, thick and fluid. She tasted the faint tang of sweat on his neck before he savaged her mouth with his. She'd take back control in just a minute, she thought hazily. Just for now, she wanted to sink into the sensation, to wallow in it.

Mace put first one, then the other knee on the bed, until they were both on the mattress, torso to torso. Her fingers skimmed over his chest and down the sensitive skin of his abs, then slid back to stroke his hips. Then her fingers curved around to torment the tops of his thighs, her teasing touch tearing a groan out of him. The couple onscreen moaned and he glanced up at the television, then groaned at what he saw in the mirror next to it.

The glass reflected Becka and him. He could see the sleek curves of her body, see her hand moving to find him rock hard and ready even as he felt it, and he groaned again.

"Look at it. Look at us," he muttered.

Becka tore herself away from his neck to glance toward the wall with the television and the mirror and saw what he had seen, their naked bodies together, the swollen staff of his erection. She watched in fascination as her hand ran up and down his hard cock, even as his hand curved around her breast and he leaned down to take it in his mouth. He closed his mouth over one nipple, then the other, sucking on them and nipping them lightly until she moaned help-lessly, feeling it. Watching it.

Mace hooked his fingers around the sides of the lacy scrap of silk she still wore and dragged it down her thighs until she could worm out of it. Then he moved around behind her, one arm curving up across her so he could hold her breast in his hand, the other slanting downward across her body to slide into the slippery cleft between her legs. She moved against him when he stroked his finger up and down, and the warm indentation between her buttocks rubbed against his cock until it pulled another groan from him.

Becka stared at the images in the mirror and on the tele-vision in fascination, watching Mace's hands rove over her body even as she felt his touch. She turned her head back and pulled his head down to hers for a kiss, but turned back to the mirror, unable to stop looking.

Now the couple in the film were spooning together over the table, the man stretching the woman across the polished wood as he drove himself into her from behind. Becka felt

Mace's hands bending her down until her hands hit the bedspread and she was braced on all fours, feeling the silky hard tip of his cock brushing against her. She gasped at the touch, then flung her head back with a sudden cry as he drove himself inside her. And then he was stroking, pumping, every sliding move taking her higher, exciting her more and more. She was in sensory overload, feeling him hard in her, his hands roving over her body and touching her in front, while she watched them in the mirror, watched the couple in the film. Tension built within her, an ache that focused everything on the exact center of her, the exact center where Mace was.

He tangled his fingers in her hair, his husky whispers punctuated only by the moans of the couple on the screen. Suddenly, the intensity and pleasure and imagery and sensation sent her rushing over the edge into a freefall of quaking glory. She felt Mace's shudder and heard his cry as he followed her.

SHE WOKE in the dark of the room, a thin line of pale light falling through the curtains and across her pillow. Next to her, Mace muttered into her hair and gathered her closer until she was spooned against him.

Memories of the last few hours came flooding back. The mirror and movie had been just the beginning, and all thoughts of control had been swept away in the revelation of what had truly been the most incredible sex she'd ever had.

With baseball's number one playboy.

She bit back a groan. Hadn't the weight room fiasco been bad enough? How could she have been such an idiot as to sleep with him? And during a road trip, when anyone could see her coming out of his room.

His body was warm and solid and she abandoned herself

for a moment to the luxury of bare skin against hers and sighed. No sense in going for the histrionics. She couldn't deny that she'd been just as hot for it the night before as he had been, and the experience had been even more amazing than she'd expected. If she could just get back to her own room without being spotted in the hall, it would be fine.

Holding her breath, Becka slipped out of the bed, easing off the mattress without making any sudden motions that might wake Mace. It had been the better part of a decade since she'd slept with someone who wasn't a boyfriend, but the awkward morning-after part of the proceedings hadn't changed.

The bedside clock blinked to 5:25. At least her ever-reliable body clock was still working, she thought as she picked up her purse and clothes and slipped into the bathroom to dress. In an hour, she'd be getting on the team bus and rolling on out of there. Mace's assignment was officially over, so it wasn't like she was going to have to deal with him anymore. With a bit of luck, she could sneak out quietly and close this chapter.

Becka stared at herself again in the mirror. He was going to be congratulating himself on this one, she knew it. After all her big talk, he was going to think that he'd seduced her, convinced her to do something she didn't want to. He was going to be notching his belt, making a check mark on his list next to her name. She opened her purse to get out her key card, saw her lipstick and stopped.

Check marks.

A wicked smile spread across her face. It wouldn't do to just slip out without a backward glance. She'd give Casanova a little something to think about. Pulling out her lipstick, she twisted up the narrow column of color and wrote a few words on the mirror. Then she flicked off the light and padded silently out into the room toward the door. With the bus leaving at 6:30, the slim chance of getting down the hall without running into someone made her gulp a little.

Almost noiselessly, she made her way toward the door, glancing in the mirror. And stopped, staring at the reflection of a sleeping Mace. She thought of what she'd done in the bathroom. One more small gesture would drive the point home. In for a penny, in for a pound. Adrenaline surged through her as she turned to tiptoe stealthily over to the bed. Holding her breath, she reached out toward him and the deed was done in a second. Mace gave a murmur and rolled toward her. Becka froze, her heart hammering against her ribs, but he rolled back and began breathing deeply again.

She slipped quietly out the door and hurried down the hall, listening to the noises in the rooms as she walked past. Of course she'd had the bright idea of putting Mace's room as far from hers as possible as a deterrent. Well, it hadn't deterred her from doing anything, only left her with the greatest possible risk of discovery.

Becka shook her head and broke into a light jog. Forget about winning power points over Mace. A good reason not to sleep with him would have been to keep from jeopardizing her job. She had enough of an uphill battle as a woman in the clubhouse. The last thing she needed to do was have Sammy worrying that she was going to sleep with his players, she thought, fitting her key card into the door lock just as a door latch clacked up the hall.

Her heart tried to vault out of her chest as she wrenched the door open and pushed inside. Breathing a sigh of relief, she slumped back against the wall next to the door.

Suspense over, she was free to notice the pounding headache that the drinks the night before had earned her. Water was what she chiefly needed, though a handful of ibuprofen wouldn't hurt. And toothpaste and a shower, she thought, rubbing her tongue over her teeth and heading for the bathroom.

By the time she stepped aboard the team bus forty minutes later, she was feeling alert enough to be nervous about Mace. All it took was for someone's slamming door to wake him. Who knew what he'd do? The players drifted onto the bus as she sat, edgily watching the lobby door. Time to go, it was long past time to go.

Finally, the bus doors slammed shut and the vehicle pulled away from the curb. Becka let out the breath she'd been holding and relaxed infinitesimally. It was over, it was done, and she was home free.

MACE WOKE to the sound of a chirping alarm in the room next door. The first thing he registered was the pile driver headache slamming through his head. The second was that he was alone. The third, was that it was 7:30 and the team bus was long gone.

Becka was long gone.

He sat up and groped for the glass of water he noticed on the bedside table, downing it in a gulp. He blinked at the clock. The display flicked to 7:36. He stared at it stupidly, wondering why something nibbling at the back of his brain was telling him that time was important. Nothing was important except getting rid of this headache, he thought, rolling back over and closing his eyes. Then awareness washed over him.

He had a flight back to Boston at 10:00 a.m. to pick up his truck and head south. It was 7:36, he hadn't showered or packed, and he had a ten o'clock flight. He was out of bed and into the bathroom before his brain fully registered the fact that he was vertical.

He turned the shower taps to hot, then turned back to the sink to brush his teeth while the water heated. Clean teeth might not cure a hangover, but they'd at least help, he thought as he glanced at himself in the mirror to see how bad the damage was.

And saw the writing on it.

You were the notch on my belt this time. The red letters marched across the glass surface, which was beginning to steam up around the edges. Then he looked beyond the letters and his eyes widened in fury.

On his forehead was a red X.

11

As much as she loved her job, it definitely cut into having a personal life, Becka thought as she biked toward downtown Lowell. She'd gotten out of the weight training session late, and now she was reduced to biking like mad so she could arrive on time, if a bit disheveled. A smart person would have driven that day, but parking in downtown was awful, and after the recent road trip, she needed all the work she could get.

The breeze felt good as she walked into the courtyard restaurant and looked for the brightest color she could find. A flash of magenta caught her eye even before the dark-haired woman wearing it waved her over.

"Why haven't you called me?" Ryan chided her, even as she wrapped her in a hug. "I've been calling you for weeks."

Becka gazed at her childhood friend. "What are you talking about? I called you to set up lunch."

"That doesn't count." Ryan waved it off. "That's not conversation, that's social planning, and you only talked to my answering machine, anyway."

Becka swept her bangs out of her eyes and ordered an iced tea from the waitress. "So how are the wedding plans going?"

A smile spread across Ryan's face like sunlight. "Amazing. Becka, I never knew I could be this happy."

"God, you're dysfunctional," Becka said in mock disgust. "Normal people are miserable planning weddings. It's like it's this special sort of hell. How can you be enjoying yourself?"

Ryan giggled delightedly. "I can't help it. Nothing could get to me right now. Anyway, we haven't had too many headaches. I suppose it helps that I'm not seventeen and fighting with my parents over every detail."

"I don't even want to tell you about the battles my mother had with Nellie over her wedding," Becka said, rolling her eyes. "Two control freaks. They fought over dyeing the bridesmaids' shoes, if you can believe that. It was like a holy war for my mother."

"It probably helps that Cade and I are the ones paying for it, so we can pretty much suit ourselves," Ryan acknowledged.

Becka waved it off as the waitress brought their tea. "Your parents are saints. They wouldn't give you a hard time even if they were paying for the whole thing."

Ryan laughed. "I think my parents are just thrilled that I'm getting married, period."

"Oh, what, like you were on the verge of turning into an old maid?" Becka leaned back and looked at her best friend, admiring the rich dark hair, the bloom on her cheeks. "I swear, you're even more gorgeous than the last time I saw you."

"True love," Ryan grinned.

"How's Cade?"

If possible, Ryan's smile became even more luminous. "He's wonderful. I don't know how I got so lucky. It's so bizarre. I mean, this time last year I didn't even know he existed. Now I can't imagine life without him." She took a sip of her tea. "At the same time, I don't believe it. I keep making all the arrangements like I think it's going to happen, but in all honesty it doesn't seem like it's real.

Three weeks from now we're going to be married and on our honeymoon." Her eyes widened. "I keep thinking someone's going to jump out and say 'surprise, it's all a joke, this wasn't supposed to happen to you.'"

"Of course it's supposed to happen to you," Becka said impatiently. "If anyone deserves a fairy tale, it's you."

The waitress appeared and they ordered quickly, eager to get back to their conversation.

"So what about you?" Ryan asked, pushing her hair back over her shoulders. "How's the new apartment, by the way?"

"Great, and thanks again for the bed. It's wonderful."

"Good." Ryan nodded in satisfaction. "That bed's good luck. It's been charmed with amazing sex."

"It does give me a little buzz when I sit down on it, now that you mention it." What gave her the buzz was remembering the feel of Mace's body on top of hers, but that was a topic best relegated to the past. "What I can't get over is the fact that your parents stood for you moving in with Cade before the wedding without having you excommunicated."

Ryan waved it away. "Given that it's a week and a half to the wedding, it's sort of a moot point. Besides, officially I'm sleeping in the new house and Cade's at his place."

"They don't buy that, do they?"

"Of course not, but it gives them something to tell Father Ramsay."

"I also can't believe you guys got that incredible house."

Ryan shook her head in amazement. "Cade's dad wanted to do it. Said Cade had never let him give him anything after he'd turned sixteen. What I can't believe is that they're actually talking. Not a lot, and they're probably never going to be Ward Cleaver and the Beav, but it's a start.'' She blinked back sudden tears. ''God, I can't believe this. I've turned into the most appallingly sentimental person in the past month. Weddings.'' She swiped at her eyes.

''You've *always* been appallingly sentimental, Ryan.''

''Well, take my mind off it and tell me what's going on with you. It's been three months since you broke up with Scott. Are you seeing anyone?''

''I'm not sure seeing is the right word for it.'' Becka tried to keep a straight face.

''Oh really?'' Ryan looked at her more closely. ''And just what is the right word for it?''

''What? There's nothing going on.''

''Nothing going on my foot.'' Ryan leaned forward, elbows on the table. ''Fess up, or I'll tell your mother about the time you flicked paste into Sister Magdalena's hair during art class.''

Becka stared at her, aghast. ''You wouldn't.'' The statute of limitations didn't exist for Becka's mother when it came to parochial school crimes.

''Try me,'' Ryan invited.

''But you swore to secrecy on the blood oath,'' Becka said aggrievedly.

''I only pretended to cut my finger.''

''You violated the blood pact?'' Becka yelped in betrayal. ''I can't believe it. It took two weeks for my cut to heal.''

''Pain makes me faint. Anyway the oath's invalid. So tell me.''

''Okay, I give,'' Becka said in defeat. ''There's this guy at work.''

''Not one of the players?'' Ryan's eyes widened in shock.

''Give me some credit, will you?''

''Who, then?''

"He's an instructor. Was," Becka corrected herself. "Was an instructor. The team has a whole roster of them who come through on a rotating basis."

"What's his name?"

Becka blew out a breath. "Mace Duvall."

"What kind of a name is—" Ryan stopped. "Oh, wait. You mean the guy who plays baseball?"

"Played baseball. He's retired now."

"The one who was named Sexiest Man Alive by *People?*"

Becka's expression became grim.

"I can see you've come up in the world," Ryan said admiringly.

"Hardly. He was in town, he got bored. I was the nearest target."

"So what happened? Somehow I don't see you and him together."

Becka waved away a gnat that spiraled in toward her face. "I told him I wasn't interested and he wanted another answer. And let me tell you, when a guy like that decides to go after something, he can be very convincing." She began at their first meeting, telling every detail she could remember while Ryan listened avidly, hissing and cheering in the appropriate places, and looking predictably horrified by the ending.

The waitress dropped their salads at the table, along with a basket of bread. Becka nibbled on a whole wheat roll. "So that's it. Maybe I didn't leave him tied up like certain people I know, but I gave him something to remember me by."

"He'll remember it, all right." Ryan picked an olive out of her salad and popped it in her mouth. "Just watch out. Remember what happened to me."

"Yeah, you fell madly in love and got engaged. Trust

me, it won't happen here." Becka forked up some salad. "It was undeniably great and is now undeniably over. The only thing that really bugs me is that I wound up tumbling for him just like everyone else."

"Oh yeah, 'everybody else,'" Ryan said mischievously. "You mean like Megan Barnes and Lara Portman, those actress/supermodel everybody elses?"

Becka grinned. "Yeah, well, I wanted to be different. And I don't like to make a fool of myself by drawing a line in the sand and then crossing it. I'd be humiliated if I hadn't had such a good time. And if he weren't long gone and hard to find." She bit into the lettuce and chewed.

"Don't be so sure. You might hear from him."

Becka rolled her eyes. "Ryan, give me a break. This guy is the original Casanova. Compared to the crowd he runs with, I'm small time. He was just keeping limber, like a concert pianist doing finger exercises."

"You know, there might be more to him than you think. I read a profile on him last year. He sounded like a pretty interesting guy, actually. Real, you know? Not pretentious. Not a word about the whole Hollywood shuffle."

Becka glowered at her. "Don't get started on the nice thing. He's already hit me with that."

"All I'm saying is that for a playing the field kind of jerk he was cool," Ryan said innocently. "So are you going to see him again?"

"You don't seem to hear what I'm saying. He's a G-boy. He's had people telling him he was beautiful and talented all his life."

"Yeah, so?"

Becka let out a breath and searched for patience. "Ryan, you're hooked up with the perfect man, probably the only one on the planet except for your dad. For your information, most gorgeous guys are creeps, interested only in themselves. Look at Scott.'' She sighed. ''Trust me, Cade is one in a million. Most men who are beautiful know it, and play it like it's collateral. I mean, women aren't people to Duvall, they're arm candy. The only reason he was even interested in me was because he was stuck in a backwater and he needed something to do.''

''You looked in the mirror lately?'' Ryan asked mildly.

''Look, I'm not pretending I'm Cinderella's ugly stepsister or anything. I know I'm okay. But looking good and looking like Giselle Bundchen are two different things. I didn't make it into the Most Beautiful People issue. This guy's out of my league.''

''Well, that's probably a good thing since you think he's such an idiot.''

''He's not an—'' Becka stopped and narrowed her eyes, studying Ryan. ''Oh no.''

''What?''

''Oh no.'' She shook her head. ''No.''

''What?''

''You've got that look.''

''What look?''

''That look that says I'm in bliss and I want everybody I know to find the same thing.''

''I don't know what you're talking about,'' Ryan said blandly. ''By the way, I've got you RSVP'd to the wedding with a date.''

''Don't you start matchmaking,'' Becka warned her.

''I'm not.''

''Because he's gone.''

''I'm sure.''

''He's history.''

''Definitely.''

''The guy can't even commit to a three-month job.''

"Hard to believe." Ryan kept her face suspiciously deadpan.

Becka took a swallow of her tea. "But he was amazing in bed."

"What a manipulator," Ryan said, sticking her tongue firmly in her cheek.

Becka burst out laughing. "I sound like an idiot, don't I?"

"No, just like a woman who's had herself a good time and doesn't want to admit it. I've been there, remember."

"Yeah, but at least you could blame Cade for playing you," Becka said. "The only person I can blame is myself. Thank God he's gone, at least. I'd hate to have to face that smirk every day."

BECKA LOCKED HER BIKE and walked into the clubhouse, glancing at her watch. It was absurd to feel guilty for showing up at the official reporting time. Granted, she was usually in her office several hours ahead, but it wasn't like the whole organization was going to crumble because she wasn't early for once. Only a compulsive nudge like her would still feel like ducking her head when she walked through the front office and into the crowded locker room.

Which was currently full of half-naked or nearly naked men.

If she were the cradle-robbing type, there were some amazing bodies standing around the locker room in little more than jockstraps, Becka thought idly.

"He won the Gold Glove three years in a row," Stats was saying to Chico as she walked past. "It makes sense that they'd bring him back for infield instruction." Stats pulled his pants up, covering a marble hard-set of buns. Not nearly as enticing as Duvall's though, she thought.

Nope, Duvall had a world-class ass, to say nothing of the rest of him. Too bad she'd never have her hands on it again.

"Hey, I'm not complaining about having him back," Chico threw back, buttoning up his jersey. "I learned more from him than I've learned from the other coaches combined."

Obviously the new instructor had arrived, Becka thought, wondering briefly who they were talking about. It had to be someone who'd been through previously, not that any of them had been all that impressive, with the exception of… She rounded the corner to Sammy's office and froze.

He was talking with Mace Duvall.

"Hey, Becka, look who's back," Sammy bawled, seemingly oblivious to the horrified look she was sure was plastered all over her face. "We get him for another week."

"Another week?" she asked faintly, unable to stop staring at Mace. He was tall and golden and definitely but definitely there. "You're here for another week?"

"Yep." Whiskey eyes glinted with challenge. "Back for round two."

12

WHEN THEY'D BEEN tearing up the clubs in her college days, Becka and her friends had had one immutable rule—never change your mind about sleeping with a guy after 10:00 p.m. The punishment for a known offender had been dire, involving, she seemed to recall, public humiliation and drinking designed to induce catastrophic hangovers. Of course, the group had been known to do any outlandish thing they could to keep a friend from breaking the rule, because they always predicted heinous repercussions, the least of which were galloping regrets.

She was older now, Becka thought as she walked to the training room without a backward glance, but apparently not wiser. If she'd started the evening saying no and had changed it to yes by the end, she had only herself to blame for the consequences, which in this case might make a two-day hangover look mild. She knew the rules. Now, the one time she'd let herself lapse, she was…well, she didn't know what she was, but it couldn't be good if it had her facing down a guy who'd scored points on her. No, she thought immediately, he hadn't scored points on her, she'd scored on him. That was the thing to remember. She'd done the seducing, she'd changed her mind and chosen to sleep with him, for better or worse.

Now she had to deal with baseball's playboy as her lover. Ex-lover. One-night stand. What on earth the man was doing back in Lowell when he'd said he was quitting, she hadn't a clue. If she didn't know better, she'd say it was just to annoy her. Now he could run around grinning at her, telling himself that he'd seduced her. Becka felt a telltale heat in her face that she knew meant she was blushing. Hell, he knew things about her body all of her other lovers combined didn't know.

Having it out with him didn't scare her—she could give as good as she got. What did scare her was word of their night together getting around the locker room. Now, that would be awkward. Still, he didn't strike her as the type to kiss and tell. She'd just have to rely on his discretion.

Of course, after the lipstick incident, that discretion was more than likely negligible.

He hadn't looked all that ticked when she'd seen him moments before, she thought, holding out a faint sliver of hope that the lipstick had rubbed off on the pillow. Or if it hadn't, that maybe she could take him to bed and work him over to take his mind off it. Of course, that would only compound the problem, not that it wouldn't be diverting.

An image of Mace naked bloomed in her mind. Diverting was an understatement. Oh, the things that they'd done, she thought with a mixture of glee and mild dismay. The mirror thing had just been the beginning, she recalled. Then there'd been the part when she'd been leaning up against the pillows and he'd straddled her and…

Becka cursed and shook her head. She'd changed her mind. Once. And now she'd changed it back, that was all there was to it. Perhaps she'd felt like being a little uninhibited, but that was an isolated evening, as far as Duvall was concerned. Whatever her body thought it wanted, she didn't need any more complications in her life. And Mace Duvall was the biggest complication she'd ever seen.

THIS WAS GOING TO BE entertaining, Mace thought as he walked down the hall. He wasn't sure what he was going to enjoy more, teaching Becka a lesson or having her as a lover again. Because if there was one thing he was certain of, it was that they were going to be lovers. The lipstick thing, that had ticked him off for a few minutes, but only as long as it took him to savor the image of teaching her just who was in control.

Of course, he'd spent the past week with memory flashes of the night they'd spent together dancing through his head. Becka was not the kind of woman a man walked away from. Even if he hadn't already decided to commit to the job, he'd have come back for her. Having the two things together as a package was well nigh irresistible.

His mouth turned up in a grin as he rounded the corner to the training room and stood out of sight for a moment, watching her work. That lithe body, those cool, capable hands, that sulky mouth had been haunting his dreams for days. When he taught, he heard her talking about helping others to excel. When he relaxed in his room at night, he amused himself by deciding just how he was going to make her eat her words. A notch on her belt his ass. The day he got taken to bed by a woman without wanting to be there was the day he lost his mind. Becka Landon needed to be shown a thing or two, and he was just the man to do it.

He cleared his throat. "So how does a guy get a rubdown around here?"

She gave an almost imperceptible jerk, then spared him a glance. "Players only, this close to game time."

"I count."

"You're not a player."

"I know how to play the game." He walked into the training room and sat on the edge of the desk.

"Unless the game is baseball, we've got nothing to talk about," Becka said, turning the taps to fill the whirlpool.

"Oh, I don't think that's the case at all," he countered. "I'd say we've got plenty to talk about."

"I'm on the job, Duvall. This discussion can wait."

She wasn't getting off the hook that easy, he thought. "Name the time and place."

"How about—"

Cacophony broke out behind him. "Hey, Duvall, welcome back."

"Duvall, I hear you're infield this time."

Becka threw him a triumphant smirk over her shoulder.

"HEY, FLORENCE, can you give my shoulder a rubdown before I hit the field?" Morelli asked.

Becka frowned. "You know, you wouldn't have so much trouble with your muscles if you'd train harder in the weight room and focus more on stretching."

"Hey, I do all the focusing I need when the ball's coming my way." He lay down on the massage table. Becka gave a small sigh and began working on his arm. The rest of the players drifted off. Chico stayed to talk with Mace, who apparently was staying to talk with her.

"This isn't high school, Morelli. If you concentrated more on the basics, your performance would improve." She was one to talk about concentration, she thought, fighting the urge to look at Mace.

"I knock myself out on the diamond," Morelli said hotly. "I don't know why everybody's always on me about it."

"I'm not talking about the diamond," she said, pressing his muscle slightly to emphasize her point. "Training's about more than playing. It's all the off-diamond hours, too."

Mace stirred. "She's right. Every Hall-of-Famer I ever

knew spent more time training off the diamond than on. You've got to, it's the foundation of your game.''

Morelli raised his head to give Mace a man of the world grin. "Oh sure, like you did that? That's not what I read."

"Listen to what the man's saying," Chico said. "Why don't you stop partying like it's 1999 and start concentrating on the game?''

"Nobody listens to Prince anymore, Watson," Morelli scoffed. "That's what you get for being an old married man.''

"Put a lid on it and focus on your game, Morelli," Chico said intensely.

Morelli raised his head and gave him a hard stare. "You got a problem with me, Watson? 'Cause I don't see anyone's saying anything about my performance on that field." He put his chin back down on his hands. "Maybe you should be the one lifting weights or doing extra batting practice. How long's it been, five, six games since your last hit?''

"Four." Chico flushed a dull red as the jibe hit home. "Four games, Morelli. You got a problem with that, buddy?''

"I'd say you're the one with the problem. Buddy."

"Stop it, both of you," Mace said. "You're still on the same team and you're supposed to be after the same thing."

The two men were silent for a moment.

"Yeah, whatever," Morelli said.

"I gotta go change," Chico muttered and walked out of the room.

"You know," Mace said casually a few moments later, "he has a point. What you're doing isn't good for the team and it isn't good for you. You've got the talent, Morelli, but you're not using it.''

"I'm just getting out and having some fun. I mean, we're

lucky if we get two days off a month. I just like letting off a little steam sometimes.''

Becka worked at his shoulder. ''Yeah, well, you'd have more energy for doing your workouts and stretching if you didn't party so much.''

''Partying relaxes me. Otherwise I'm wired and I can't sleep. Working out, shit, the last thing I need is something else to do.''

''We all work a long day,'' Becka reminded him.

''Hey what is this, tag team Morelli day?'' he asked hotly. ''There's working a long day and then there's busting your ass out on the diamond for five hours. You try doing batting practice sometimes and see how you feel after.''

''If it would make you show up for your training session, I would.'' Becka concentrated on working out a knot in Morelli's shoulder.

He rose up on his elbows to glare at her. ''Yeah, well, you knock a few out and I'll think about showing up for weight training.''

''Name the day, Morelli,'' Becka said evenly. When he laughed and put his head back down, she stepped away from the table and put a hand on her hip. ''You think I'm joking, don't you?''

''I think you're dreaming.''

''Name the day. We go head to head and I bet I'll come out better than you.''

He raised up again and gave a patronizing laugh. ''Don't embarrass yourself, Florence. I could beat you batting left handed.''

''Yeah?'' She crossed her arms. ''Then let's see you do it.''

''Yeah, right.'' He lay back down.

''No, I mean it, Morelli. Let's do it, you and me.''

"Oh, come on," he backpedaled. "You know I was just—"

"Then you shouldn't have shot off your mouth," she pointed out coolly. "That's how you get in trouble, in case you haven't noticed. Anyway, what's wrong with making the bet? According to you, there's no chance you'll lose, so what does it matter?" She glanced toward Mace, who appeared to be fighting a smile. "We've got a witness, let's make it official. End of this week, in the batting cage. You get more hits than me, batting left handed, and I won't say another word about it. I beat you, and you start showing up for weight training."

"What?" Morelli yelped.

"It was your idea," Becka reminded him calmly.

"But I..." He stuttered into uncertain silence. Becka watched him, and it was like a transformation. The attitude trickled back, the confidence bloomed into swagger. "Yeah, okay, sure," he said, a cocky smirk ghosting around the corners of his mouth. "Hell, you beat me and I'll do whatever you want."

Becka looked at Mace again. "Duvall, you're my witness, so when I paste his butt, he can't weasel out of it."

"You can count on me," Mace said. He grinned at Morelli, who shot Becka a quick, uneasy glance.

"Well, I guess that's it. You're done, Morelli, go get dressed," she said, slapping his shoulder and turning away.

The interchange had amused and diverted her. In a way, she was sorry it was over, because now all she had to think about was Mace, who still sat on the edge of her desk. She could feel his gaze burning into her back as she concentrated on gathering the kit of supplies that she usually took to the dugout.

"You do seem to get yourself into trouble with this betting habit you've got,'' Mace said idly. ''I'd think you'd learn after a while not to make bets you're going to lose.''

Becka gave him a brief glance. ''I'm going to win this one, Duvall, rest assured.''

''Oh yeah?'' He looked at her with interest.

''I was on the softball team in high school and college. I was all-State twice, and my batting average was about .340.'' She shrugged unconcernedly. ''I know how to hit. I just need to spend some time in the batting cages for a couple of days to get my timing back. The worst that happens is I don't make it, in which case I sic Sammy on Morelli and force him to show.''

''Why not do it that way to begin with?''

''I was hoping to avoid having Sammy bawl him out.''

Mace looked at her curiously. ''Why? He's got it coming.''

''Yeah, I know. It won't help, though. It'll only get his back up. He's just a kid, Duvall.''

''You going soft on me, Florence?'' he asked, studying her with those unsettling gold eyes.

''Of course not. I just keep thinking there's a way to get him to straighten out before he throws everything away. Maybe losing a bet in front of his teammates will make him think. And if I lose, I lose,'' she said with a shrug.

''You don't always get off so lightly with bets.''

Didn't she know it. ''Practice is starting, Duvall. I've got to get out to the field.''

''Don't think you're off the hook.''

''I couldn't possibly be that lucky,'' Becka said with a coolness she didn't feel.

BECKA YAWNED as she walked out of the clubhouse, letting the door slam behind her. She shivered a little in the cool night air. Good old New England, chilly even in the heart of summer. She walked to the rack where her bike stood. Too bad she couldn't lock up her problems with Mace as easily as she'd snapped the lock on the chain that afternoon, she thought, leaning down to twist the dial through its combination. A mixture of luck and skill had allowed her to avoid Mace during practice and the game that followed. The players had helped, especially when they'd spirited him off to the dorms after they'd won their game against the Batavia Beavers. She couldn't have asked for anything more, save his complete absence.

She squinted to see the dial in the dim lighting.

"What do you think you're doing?"

Becka jerked and smacked her elbow on the unyielding steel of the bike rack. She straightened to glare at Mace, rubbing the joint to ease the ache. "Will you stop sneaking up on me like that?"

"I could have done worse if I'd a mind to," he said testily. "It's 11:30 on a Friday night and I hope you're unlocking your bike so you can put it on your car and drive home."

"I don't have my car here, not that it's any of your business. I rode today."

"And you're out of your mind to think about cycling home."

"If I'm out of my mind, you're the one who's putting me there," she said grimly and bent back over to unfasten her lock. "I thought you were quitting." Successful, she pulled the chain out of her tires and wound it around the stem of her seat.

Mace shrugged. "I thought it over and I decided to keep with it. You only have yourself to blame, you know. You were the one who guilted me into staying." His voice turned lightly mocking. "I thought you wanted me to."

"Hardly," she snapped, jerking the wheel out of the bike

rack. "The team can do just fine without you. Sammy's talking about getting into the play-offs. Who knows, maybe he'll even take them to the championships."

Mace picked the bike neatly out of her hands and began walking toward where his Bronco was parked. It was demeaning to try to pull the bike away from him, Becka decided, trying to look as if she were voluntarily walking with him rather than chasing her property. He was right, she supposed, they had to hash things out sooner or later. Besides, she was more tired than she wanted to admit. Biking home had definitely lost its luster. So, she'd let him drive her home, they'd have a little chat on the porch, and that would be that.

When he parked his truck at her house, though, she wasn't so sure.

"Where does the bike go?" he asked shortly.

"Upstairs in my work room. I can get it," Becka said, reaching unsuccessfully for the bike.

"Oh no, we offer a full service operation," he said, neatly evading her groping hands and heading toward the porch with the bike on his shoulder. When she unlocked the front door, he just walked right into the hall and up the stairs. Short of having it out with him in the hall, she didn't have a lot of choice about letting him into her flat, Becka thought.

That didn't mean she had to like it.

Mace set the bike down in her hallway and followed her into the kitchen. Because she needed to keep her hands busy, Becka reached into the refrigerator for a couple of iced teas and set them on the counter. "So what exactly are you doing back here?" she asked. "I assumed you were heading back to Florida." She leaned against the kitchen counter and tipped her head back to take a drink.

"I don't believe in unfinished business."

"You finished your assignment with the Weavers."

"I don't mean the Weavers. I'm talking about you and me."

"There is no you and me," she corrected.

He studied her, taking his time. She refused to back down, but she could feel the telltale heating of her cheeks that meant she was giving in to the redhead's curse and flushing.

"So what is it that really gets you? That I made you want me, or that I made you like it?"

"You didn't make me do anything, Duvall. I did what I wanted to. You just happened to be the equipment I did it with," she said, and took another drink of iced tea with studied carelessness.

"You're funny when you try to be tough, Florence." When Mace moved closer, she would have edged away, but she was trapped against a corner of the U-shaped counter. He stroked a fingertip along her collarbone and she shivered.

"You know," he began conversationally, "there's something I don't understand. If you're the one who seduced me, then why is it you start trembling every time I touch you?"

"You're just bent out of shape about the lipstick," she said lightly.

"I'm amused about the lipstick," he corrected, brushing his fingers through the ends of her hair, letting the strands spill over his fingertips. "In my experience, when people protest too much, it's usually because the opposite of what they say is true."

"Meaning?" She didn't notice when he took her drink from her hand.

"Meaning you didn't seduce me."

"Oh really? Then just what did go on?"

"I seduced you." Then his hands were on her and his mouth was dragging her down like an undertow into a dark current of passion that left her powerless and gasping for breath. Blindly, she clutched at him, found her hands running up and down his back, reminding herself of the body hidden beneath the clothes and how much she wanted it. When it felt this good, did it really matter who was in control, who was running the show? She heard his groan even as it vibrated against her lips, felt the thud of his heart against her. When it felt this good, was either of them really running things?

Mace slid his hands down over her hips and then back up to pull her shirt out. Her mouth worked magic on him and he fought to keep his focus. Her scent tantalized him, the slow twist of her body against him pulled him in. More. He only wanted more, wanted to take them both to that place, that red-tinted physical place where sensation alone ruled.

For the past week and a half she'd slipped into his dreams, driving him to twist and turn through the night to wake in a haze of arousal. The quick, cheap release he could bring himself hadn't even dulled the knife edge of need that scraped at him.

He could have her now, the thought drummed through his brain and tempted him to just keep going, to get her heedless and naked and half-mad with need so that he could bury himself in her. Instead, he clawed his way back to sanity and pulled away.

Becka's eyes gradually cleared. "Let go of me," she said venomously.

"Not on your life." He pulled her closer to him and rubbed his lips over hers. "It really fries you, doesn't it?"

"What fries me?" Becka struggled to free herself unsuccessfully.

"The fact that I can seduce you. The fact that even though you don't want to want me to touch you," he leaned in to suckle her earlobe, "you want it. The way you wanted it in the hotel." He licked at her lips and felt her soften against him. "The way you want it right now."

"You caught me in a weak moment, Duvall," she managed. "It's not going to happen again."

He smiled dangerously. "Oh, I think it will. Want me to demonstrate?"

His hands slid under her shirt, roaming over the sensitive skin until she shuddered. She felt as much as heard the clasp of her bra unsnap, and then his hands were on her, making her gasp at the friction and warmth. Helplessly, she heard herself moan. His lips on her throat, he gave a soft laugh at her surrender, but she couldn't make herself care anymore. All she could do was want him.

He was harder than he could remember, Mace thought feverishly. That was what came of spending a week fantasizing about the memory of making love with a woman. And now that he could feel that pliant body in his arms, it was unbelievably difficult to think about anything but getting her out of those clothes and onto the bed.

And then she was on fire in his arms, kissing him feverishly, yanking his shirt from his pants to get her hands on the skin beneath. Her touch was like witchcraft, making everything else meaningless except having her naked against him, crying out her pleasure in his arms. And he'd do that, he thought, clawing his way back from the madness. After he'd taught her a lesson.

Mace pulled her up until her legs were wrapped around his waist and walked out of the kitchen and toward the bedroom. Twining her arms around his neck, Becka pressed kisses on every part of his face and neck and hair she could reach. "Forget about the bedroom," she whispered into his ear, her voice ragged, tight with urgency. "Here. Now. On the floor if we have to."

Mace shook his head. "Some things are worth waiting for," he murmured, walking into her bedroom and laying her back on the coverlet. "There's something I really like about this bed."

He dropped down on the springy surface and leaned in for another of those mind-bending kisses.

"Get your clothes off," Becka managed. "I want you."

"And you'll have me," he whispered, pressing his body against hers for a tempting moment. "When I decide." He stood up and looked at her sprawled on the bed, staring back at him with dazed eyes, her mouth red and swollen from his. "Sugar," he said, leaning in to give her a quick peck. "I do believe the score is now even."

And he turned and walked out.

13

BECKA WALKED BACK up the stairs to her apartment, sweat-soaked, legs trembling with exhaustion. The morning run had been just what she'd needed to burn off the irritation that still surged through her from the events of the night before. She aimed her key at the lock just as the door opposite rattled and Mallory stepped out into the hall.

Stunning, she couldn't get used to the fact that the woman was simply stunning. That was the sort of woman Mace should be out with, Becka thought, although now that she considered it, he hadn't given Mallory more than a glance the day he'd met her.

Mallory studied her. "Let me guess. Your car broke down and you got chased by feral dogs into the river."

"Cute." Becka rolled her eyes. "You know my car didn't break down."

Mallory sighed and shook her head in mock concern. "Are you sure you don't have a fever or something? I just find it so hard to believe that anyone would voluntarily abuse themselves like this."

"If I don't abuse myself, I'll wind up abusing someone else," Becka said grimly, jamming her key into the lock.

"Uh-oh. Guess you ran into Loverboy again, huh?"

Becka opened the door and threw a glance over her shoulder. "You don't know the half of it."

Mallory's eyes brightened. "This I gotta hear," she said, crowding behind Becka. Inside, she pointedly made for a chair at the kitchen table. "So what happened? I thought when I saw you the other day you said he was supposed to be gone."

"I thought he was." Becka set bottles of iced tea on the tabletop and dropped exhaustedly into a chair. "I was wrong. He's back."

"Mmm-hmm. So I guess he's ticked off about the lipstick thing?"

"Forget about the lipstick thing. This has escalated into all-out war."

"What happened?"

Becka told her, feeling the fury afresh as she watched Mallory's eyes widen and her jaw drop.

"He did what?"

"He stood up, tucked in his shirt, and walked out."

"But what did he say?"

Becka set her jaw. "Are you ready for this? He said 'I do believe the score is now even.'"

Mallory sucked in a breath between her teeth. "That's bad."

Becka nodded. "Evil."

"Truly evil," Mallory agreed. "Of course the lipstick thing was evil, as well."

Becka did a double take. "Whose side are you on, anyway?"

"Yours, of course. I'm just saying."

"I was trying to make a point," Becka said with dignity.

Mallory nodded, something that looked suspiciously like a grin hovering around the corners of her mouth. "Judging by what he did last night, I'd say you did."

"He had it coming to him."

"I bet that's what he'd say, too. The problem is that men just want the easy labels, good girls, bad girls. They never know what to do with you when you're real." She stood up to pace around the kitchen. "And they definitely don't know what to do with someone who knows what she wants and isn't afraid to go after it. What you need to do is give it back to him." She peered out the window, watching their neighbor weed his garden. "Act like nothing happened, come on to him with everything you've got. When you've got him completely wound up and right on the edge, that's when *you* teach *him* a lesson by walking away."

"How do **you** think I got in this mess in the first place?"

Mallory smiled at her like a benevolent aunt. "When you're out for revenge, sweet pea, you've got to keep your wits about you. This is warfare. You're supposed to be seducing him, not yourself. And definitely not letting him seduce you."

"I didn't get seduced by anyone," Becka said hotly.

"Then why are you so annoyed?" Mallory sat back down at the table, her short skirt rucked up over her knees. "Sounds like you need to figure out what you want. If you just want to give him a tumble, that's easy enough. But if you just want to prove something to him, you've got to stay in control." She drained her tea. "Well, I've got to git. I'm driving down to Newport for the day."

"What for?"

"I don't know." Mallory gave a careless shrug and stood up. "I might move there. Who knows, maybe I'll go into business for myself." She gave a wave as she headed toward Becka's front door. "Good luck with Baseball Boy. Oh, before I forget, that guy from the team was in again last night."

"Morelli?"

Mallory nodded.

"I thought he was easing off."

"He was for about a week, but he got himself pretty toasted last night."

Becka shook her head and sighed. "I don't know what to do about him. I've tried talking, but it goes in one ear and out the other."

"Yeah, well, if he goes on like this too long, he's not going to need to get knifed in a bar fight. His liver will give out long before that."

"Thanks for the tip. I owe you."

"Well, why don't you come by one of these nights and have a drink with me?" Mallory waved again and walked out the door.

Becka drifted back into the kitchen to put the tea bottles in the recycling bin. What *did* she want to do with Mace, she wondered idly. Say they were even, as he'd said, what would she want then?

The image bloomed in her mind in Technicolor. Mace as a lover, that was what she wanted. If they both agreed right up front that no one was running the show, then maybe it could work. Just a week of good, hot sex.

Of course, he'd have to die first as punishment for the night before, but after that she thought they might just be able to negotiate something.

Right now, though, she had something more important to think about, which was a certain bet. She was just itching to wipe the smirk off Morelli's face, and the only way to make that happen was to make contact with the ball.

BECKA SHUT THE DOOR of the chain link batting cage that sat under the grandstand of the deserted Lowell Weavers ballpark. It took a moment to get herself set at the plate, to dredge up the long-forgotten motions. She swished the bat through the air, testing it. Slowly at first, then faster, she swung, putting the full motion of her body into the movement until the polished wood whistled through the air. She filled the pitching machine with the bucket of scuffed balls that sat to one side and switched it on, hustling up to the front of the batting cage so she could get there before she was in danger of life and limb from flying baseballs.

Before she could even get set in her batting stance, the first ball shot out of the machine, making her jump. She took a quick look around, but there was no one to see her. No one on the grounds, period, she imagined. Everybody was probably long gone and hard to find, thrilled to have a day off.

She raised the bat over her right shoulder and waited. This time, when the ball shot out, she swung at it, but the result was just a swish of air. The result was the same for the next half dozen. By the ninth ball, though, she'd gotten her timing to the point that she could actually put wood onto the ball, even if it did foul up over behind her head.

"Your foot's in the bucket." The drawled words came from behind her. This time, she didn't even jump. It figured he'd be here.

She turned slowly to face him. "What?"

Mace Duvall stood outside the batting cage, where sunlight met shadow on the ground. The sun coming from behind him gilded his hair with a halo; his eyes were shadowed and unreadable. "Your foot's in the bucket. Don't step back when you swing, step toward the pitcher."

"Why don't you get out there and I'll use you as a target, Duvall," she invited.

"You don't really want to do that, do you?" he asked, rounding the back of the cage to the door.

"Buddy, you don't want to know the half of what I want to do to you." The rhythmic "thoof" of balls shooting out of the pitching machine punctuated their conversation.

Mace swung open the door to the enclosure and stepped

inside. "I can think of a few things I want to do to you, too."

"Mine involve murder and mayhem," Becka said silkily, "what about yours?"

Humor crept into his eyes. "This is a special moment in our relationship, you know. We're sharing our fantasies."

"Let's make 'em reality, Duvall."

"You're not still ticked about last night, are you? The way I figure it, we're even."

"Oh, you think so? I'll tell you what I think," she started.

"Oh, I'm sure you will."

Becka stopped and narrowed her eyes. "What are you doing here? Everybody's supposed to be off today. I was hoping to get some privacy." Behind her, the pitching machine switched to idle.

"There's plenty of that around. Trust me, the few players that are here are either sleeping or over at the pool."

"So why aren't you?"

"I kind of figured this is where you'd be. I thought I'd come help out."

"I don't need your help," she said shortly.

He gave her a mocking grin. "Sugar, from what I've seen, it looks like you need all the help you can get. Assuming you want to teach Morelli a thing or two, and I think you do."

It was tempting, she had to admit. She'd seen the difference in the performance of the players after Mace had worked with them for a couple of days. Still, after what he'd done to her... Becka raised her chin. "I'm doing fine on my own, thanks."

"Come on. You talked me into sticking around to teach. Seems only fair that you should let me practice on you a little." Mace picked up the bucket and started tossing balls into it, the long lines of muscle in his back showing through his T-shirt as he bent over.

It made her mouth water, until she thought of the night before. "You never did tell me why you were here. I thought you were going back to Florida."

Balls landed in the bucket with metallic pocking sounds. "Let's just say this teaching stuff grew on me. I flew back up here and got in my truck to head for Florida, to just quit like I'd been talking about. But I couldn't do it."

"Why?" Becka asked curiously.

"I don't know." Mace looked at her, then straightened up and hefted the bucket. "It felt wrong." What had felt right was having a purpose, a reason to get up in the morning. Something more than skin diving or golf or pounding nails on his half-built deck. It had felt like something that made a difference. "I was working with the guys at batting practice yesterday and I saw Stats swing. It was part of my swing, I could see it. And he got a hit. I taught him how to do that." He smiled. "And it felt really, really good."

Becka stared at him, her mouth ajar just a bit, as though he'd surprised her. *Good*, he thought as he walked down to the pitching machine and loaded the balls into the hopper. A woman like Becka needed surprising now and again. "Anyway, I owe you a thank you." He left the machine on standby.

She blinked. "Why?"

He walked back up to her. "Because you talked me into giving it a try at the beginning, when I was ready to cut out. And you did it even when you wanted me gone worse than anything."

"Temporary insanity," she muttered, glancing away, but not before he'd caught the flicker of pleasure in her eyes.

"Maybe. And maybe it was because you were thinking of something besides yourself." He pushed the hair out of his eyes with an impatient hand. "When you get torn up, it's easy to turn in on yourself. You got so many people worrying about how you feel all the time that you start thinking that's all that matters. I needed to be reminded that it wasn't." He picked up the bat and handed it to her, pretending he didn't see the look of blank surprise on her face. "Now let's see you swing," he ordered, stepping in front of her where he could study her motion.

Becka took up her stance at the plate, bending slightly at the waist, and sent the bat whistling through the air. He watched her appreciatively. There was something about the way that her body looked, especially when she was moving, that purely made his mouth go dry. "Again." The bat swished and she made a soft noise of effort. The kind of noise she made when she was making love, he remembered, when he was inside her and she was straddling him, riding him.

Mace walked over to stand behind her, staring at the loose, turquoise running shorts that covered her taut haunches. It would be so easy to just hook his finger in them, pull them to one side, bend her over and... "Get your legs a little wider," he instructed, sliding one hand along the inside of her thigh.

She jerked around to glare at him. "Cut it out, Duvall."

"Do you want to beat Morelli?" he challenged her. At her reluctant nod, he put a hand back on the silky smooth skin of her thigh. "Then do what I tell you."

"YOU NEED TO GET your whole body into the swing, not just your arms." Mace put his hands on her hips. "These should rotate along with your torso." Heat bloomed from where his palms rested on her. "When you swing, your hips should turn, just like this." The heat disappeared for a moment as he reached up with one hand to pull the bat away from her, then held her hips again. "Now swing," he ordered. She mimed a swing, and his hands rotated her hips. "Again," he ordered, rotating her with such force that she spun around to face him.

His eyes flashed with surprise, then darkened as he took a step closer. His hands on her hips pulled her in against him. "Well, you seem to have the rotation part down," he said softly. "Now the key part is making contact. You've got to get wood on the sweet spot."

Getting wood on the sweet spot indeed, Becka thought, feeling the beginnings of his erection against her belly. She wasn't going to make it that easy for him, she thought, remembering Mallory's advice. Maybe he was right about them being even, but that didn't mean she was ready to sleep with him again.

At least not right then. First, she had to show him that two could play at the game of walking away. She slid her hands down his arms—God, biceps like rocks—and over his hard, sinewy forearms, and down where his hands now rested on her ass. "Mmm, I see your point," she said throatily, bringing her lips closer to his. "Especially about the sweet spot."

Mace leaned down to kiss her just as she twisted away. "But I still have a bet to do in a couple of days, so let's get to it."

He gave her a narrow-eyed look, then pushed the wall switch that started the pitching machine going. "Fine, let's get to it. Okay, *swing*," he ordered, as the first ball shot out toward her.

Becka snapped the bat around and sent the ball fouling up back behind her.

"You're starting your swing too late. Go a tick earlier than you think."

Obediently, she swung again. The ball tipped off the bat, flying up to bounce off the ceiling.

Mace switched the pitching machine to standby. Becka straightened up and turned to look at him as he walked toward her. "You're holding the bat too low," he said. "You want it up higher. Let me show you." He stepped up behind her, wrapping his arms around her to get his hands on top of hers on the bat. "First, you want a tight grip on the wood." He curled his fingers around hers. "See? Now raise the bat up higher above your shoulder, and when you swing," he slowly moved the bat in an arc, "you want to keep it up here."

His chest was hard against her back, his thighs pressed against hers. It was like they were in bed, spooning. Becka struggled briefly to bring her mind back to the present. "I've never seen you use this technique with the players," she managed, trying for dry.

She sensed, rather than saw his grin. "I save this technique for a very select clientele." He released her and stepped back to switch on the pitching machine. "Now let's try it again."

This time, when the ball came at her she made solid contact, the vibration singing up her arms and drawing a surprised laugh from her.

Mace clapped. "Good job. That's the way, now let's see it again." She stuck with it for another half hour, making contact with plenty of the balls, Mace offering advice and approval.

Finally, he turned off the pitching machine. "You were hitting about .300 there. Another day or two like that and you'll be ready to take on Morelli."

Without thinking about it, Becka grabbed him and gave him a smacking kiss. "Thanks for the lesson."

His arms came around her automatically. "No problem,"

he said. "I'll take payment like that any day. Of course, you're going to need some more instruction," he continued blandly. "Maybe you'd like to put down a deposit on future lessons."

She did think about it then, calculating the best way to get revenge on him for the night before. Becka laughed low in her throat. "Sounds more like you're the one who'd like to leave a deposit."

He pulled her up close to him. "Your mama ever wash your mouth out with soap?" He kissed her experimentally. "Mmm, nope, no soap there."

"Maybe you'd better check again," Becka whispered, wriggling closer to him. Her hand slipped down to slide over his hip and butt, and curve around in front to his crotch. It was only to teach him a lesson. Not because she wanted to touch him or kiss him or anything. At least not much, she thought feverishly.

Becka's hands tugged at his belt, fumbling with the buckle, and Mace reached down to help her, wanting to free himself of the ache that ran through him. He kissed her open mouth, his tongue darting in to duel with hers. Nope, no sharp tang of soap, just sweet, a mind-melting smoky sweetness that took over his thoughts. So that he almost didn't feel the delicious curves of her breasts nestled against his chest. So that he almost didn't feel the heat of her hand through his jeans until she… He stifled a groan.

"You seem to have a bit of a swelling there," Becka breathed against his neck as her hands deftly unzipped his jeans. "Maybe I should give it a massage to get some of the stiffness out."

This time he did groan, as she pulled him out and held him, pulsing in her hand. Her smooth fingertips danced along the length of him from root to tip, leaving a trail of sensitized nerve endings in their wake.

"Of course, I seem to remember you telling me earlier to get a firm grip on the wood and stroke." She tightened her fingers around him and began to slide up and down on him. The rush of sensation sent need surging through him and he cradled her neck in his hand and kissed her hard, trying not to concentrate on the touch that threatened to send him over the edge.

Becka fought to keep her head clear, even as those mind-bending kisses threatened to take control. The feel of him hard and leaping in her hand made her dizzy with desire. His fingers edging under her shorts tantalized her beyond all reason. It would be so easy to just wrap her legs around him then and there and go where she knew he could take her.

But she needed to prove something to herself. And to him. She needed to prove that she could walk away, too. His breathing sounded harsher and harsher in her ear. She broke the kiss, leaning her forehead against his chest, then she stilled her hand.

"Well," she gave him a light kiss, "thanks for the batting tips. I should probably get going now, though, I've got some unpacking to do." She released him and stepped back. "Don't hurt yourself putting that thing away." She turned to the door.

She missed the gathering determination in his eyes.

He caught her and whirled her around, pressing her up against the chain link fence. His hands pinned her wrists to the wire, and he pressed his body lightly against hers. A thrill shot through her, and arrowed down into the pit of her stomach.

And lower.

"No games," he said softly. "No more one-upsmanship. We're even, okay? Let's make it official, here and now.

Drop the control stuff for a minute and just go with how you feel.'' His lips were at her ear, the words like a spell.

"Stop trying to seduce me," she managed.

"I'm not. This isn't about you or me, Becka, it's about us, being lovers." He nipped at her lower lip, the brief smart of sensation quickly blanketed by the outrageous softness and warmth of his mouth on hers. "You remember how good it was. You can't tell me you don't want it, because I know better." His fingers stole under the edge of her shorts and panties, finding her slick and hot. "I can feel it."

The brush of his fingers tore a moan out of her. The surge of her hips against him took both of them by surprise. The liquid pleasure seeped into her bones, throughout her flesh, and slowly, slowly her temperature began to rise.

"Don't think you're seducing me," she whispered against his neck as she kissed him passionately.

"No, ma'am." The steady slide of his fingers was driving her mad, little licks and curls of pleasure flickering through her body like flames as the heat and tension built.

"Because you're not," she managed. "I'm doing this because I want to."

"Hallelujah," he murmured.

"If anything, I'd say I'm seducing you," she said breathlessly, reaching down for him.

"I'd say you worry too much about the wrong stuff." His words cut off in a groan as he felt her fingers rub against his cock. Need flooded through him, overriding any other concern. He had to have her, hot, tight and wrapped around him, now.

Mace's hands slid round her hips to the tops of her thighs. When Becka raised one leg to wrap it around his hip, he slid a hand underneath her. She curled her fingers into the wire mesh of the fence and raised the other leg to wrap it around his waist.

"If you stop this now to prove a point, I'm going to be the one thinking about murder and mayhem," he said raggedly.

She felt the silky tip of his cock brush against her leg. A breath of cool air hit her as he hooked her shorts and lace out of the way.

Then he drove up into her and Becka cried out. The sensation burst through her in a rush, sweeping her up and over the edge of sanity as her body convulsed until she could only cling to him, shaking with the force of her contractions.

The blind pleasure in her eyes as she tightened him pulled him closer to the edge, but he fought to continue. In and out, he surged against her body, the friction rocketing through both of them. Though he wanted to spill himself, he held on, trying to prolong the feeling.

Becka tightened her arms and legs around him. "I'm going to come again," she whispered in amazement just as her body tighened around him. Mace managed only a stroke or two before the clutching spasms of her muscles drove him beyond control and he burst out in a jolt of pleasure.

14

THE SECONDS TICKED BY while they caught their breath. Finally, the sharp stab of chain links digging into her back drove Becka to move. Her pulse still hammered, but the temporary insanity was over. And as she drifted back to reality, alarm came creeping in. "Tell me we didn't just do that," she groaned, dropping her feet back to the ground.

"Oh, we definitely did." Mace stepped away from her and slipped himself back into his jeans.

"I am such an idiot," she raged. "I must be out of my mind."

"No one's around, if that's what you're worried about."

"That's not what I'm worried about," she snapped.

"Okay, what is?" he asked, tucking in his T-shirt.

She opened her mouth and stopped. Welcome to life in the brave new world, she thought. "Did it occur to you that we didn't use any protection during that little go 'round?"

He gave her a level look. "Did it occur to you?"

"Obviously not soon enough."

"It wasn't your fault. You were being seduced." He caught her gaze before she could reply. "It's a *joke,* sugar," he emphasized. "We both got carried away and you know it."

"Well, I hope it won't bruise your feelings too much if I say that with your history, the idea of unprotected sex makes me really uncomfortable," she said tartly.

She heard his quick intake of breath, and shame

swamped her. "Look, I shouldn't have said it like that. What I mean is—"

"I know what you mean. I should have seen that one coming," Mace said aridly. He looked at the ground as though searching for the answers there. "I was hospitalized for most of last fall, remember?" He raised his head and gave her a level stare. "They gave me transfusions, cut me open, sewed me up, took samples...they tested me for every damned thing, including HIV. I'm clean."

She swallowed. "Well, that's good news," she said brightly. "But what about the people you've been with since then?"

He spun and kicked the chain link in a sudden surge of violence. "Listen, will you?" There was an edge to his voice she hadn't heard before. "I haven't been with anybody since I got out of the hospital except you, okay? I'm clean."

Relief washed through her, contrition on its heels. "I'm sorry to have asked you about it like that. It's just with your reputation..."

"Jesus, let go of it, will you?" His voice rose as he stalked away in frustration. "All that newspaper stuff was pure fantasy. I never even met half of those women. If I shook hands with them they had me dating, if I dated them, they had me engaged." He rounded on her. "I hosted a charity auction with Megan Barnes one year and when I ran into her in a parking lot a few months later, *US Magazine* ran a two-page story on it, complete with photos. It was a five-minute conversation in a *parking* lot, for Christ's sake." He raked a hand through his hair and dropped his hands to his sides. Abruptly, the fury seemed to abate, leaving him simply shaking his head. "You know, if you're not worrying about who's in the driver's seat, you're worrying about my reputation. Maybe if you'd start worrying about what we're doing we'd have a chance.''

The silence stretched out for a beat, then two.

''A chance of what?''

''Of—'' He stopped. ''I don't know. And we never will know because you're too busy worrying about all the stuff that doesn't matter. And while we're on the topic, we've established that I'm clean, but what about you? Didn't I hear something about an ex-boyfriend?''

''You're asking me if—''

''I'm asking you if I should be concerned.'' He watched her reaction sardonically. ''Not a very pleasant feeling, is it?''

Becka recovered quickly. ''I'm a health professional. I get tested on a monthly basis. As of my most recent results, I'm clean.''

''And birth control?''

She stared at him. ''I'm on the pill.''

Mace gave her a long look, and nodded. ''Well I guess we know something, then. We could say it's over, walk away right now, and it's no harm, no foul.''

We could walk away right now, his words echoed through her head. She stared into his golden eyes, eyes that were suddenly unfathomable.

Mace hooked a thumb in his front pocket and leaned against the chain link. ''Calling it over is one option. Is that what you want to do?''

What did she want to do, Becka wondered. He was offering to let it go, just forget about everything that had happened between them. Except that she didn't want to forget about everything that had happened, she discovered with sudden certainty. She didn't want to call it over.

She wanted more.

Becka walked up to Mace and pressed a kiss on his

mouth, lingering until his lips softened and he began to kiss her back. Then she took his hand and pulled on it, heading toward the batting cage door. "Give me a ride back to my apartment, Duvall, and I'll show you what I want."

His mouth quirked. "Does it involve your Chinese sex book?"

"Guess you'll have to come along and find out."

THE REST OF THE WEEK settled into a pattern: working out in the morning with Mace, followed by an hour in the batting cages, practice, the game, and back to her apartment with him at night. The workouts were a revelation to her. More than a year might have passed since his accident, but he still fought grimly every day for a fraction of the endurance and strength that he'd once taken for granted.

"What actually happened to you?" she asked one day toward the end of their run, when the pain had obviously set in.

"The truck crushed part of my hip when it hit me. They needed to do surgery, but I was in a coma and they couldn't risk anesthesia. By the time I woke up, it was too late." He kept running alongside her, his face set in the look of stoic endurance that she'd come to know. "They had to put in an artificial hip. No chance of playing. None."

Shock robbed her of the ability to speak. He wouldn't want sympathy, she thought, not for this.

"No chance of playing, maybe, but you're still able to teach. Coaching, managing. You're good at it."

He mustered up a smile. "So you say. I don't know, sounds to me like you just want help in the batting cages so you can win your bet with Morelli."

"Oh, that's not for my bet. I'm just doing it to help you practice your teaching skills."

"Is that what that is?"

She slowed to a walk, grinning at him.

"COME ON, FLORENCE, knock 'em silly."

It was the moment of truth, Mace thought. Becka stood at the plate, swinging the bat to warm up. The players crowded around the batting cage, shouting encouragement to her. Earlier, they'd heckled Morelli unmercifully, catcalling when he only managed to hit .240. Now, every time Becka made a hit, a cheer ran around the group.

"Nobody bothered to cheer me." Morelli stood a little away from the cage, next to Mace.

He sounded a little wounded and Mace gave him a sideways glance. "You make it pretty clear that the team is less important than partying, Morelli. Why should the team give a damn about you?"

"Hey, I care about this team," he said petulantly.

Time for some hard facts, Mace thought. "Listen, every one of these guys here is busting his behind to make himself better. Then there's you, who seems to think that just showing up and using the stuff you were born with is enough. Is it really a surprise that they don't like your attitude?"

Morelli gave a laugh. "That's pretty rich coming from the original party animal."

Mace stared at him until his laugh faltered into a throat clearing. "Are you finished? Every guy on my team knew that I was there in the weight room, there for extra batting practice, there for extra fielding drills. They saw it. Just like your teammates see that you're never around any more than you have to be."

"I do my job," he muttered sullenly.

"Morelli, really doing your job means doing more than just your job. You want to know why Becka is kicking your ass out there?"

"She's not kicking my ass. I'm not going to get beat by a girl."

"Yeah, well, that *girl*—and I sure wouldn't let her hear you call her that—has been in this batting cage every day this week for a couple of hours of practice. She refused to consider the idea of losing." He watched Becka tense herself, eye on the pitching machine as she'd practiced so many times. The ball shot out at her and she swung, launching it to the back of the cage. Hours of practice, she'd put in. And every time he thought she'd be done, she'd ask to do one more bucket of balls. Not that watching her move was any hardship. Having an excuse to watch her body for hours a day was only slightly less entertaining than having an excuse to touch it.

The last ball in the bucket cracked off her bat for a final hit, triggering wild applause from her audience.

Becka turned around to bow modestly, then gave Stats an inquiring look. "So what does the official scorekeeper say?"

Stats furiously scratched numbers on his pad, then looked up. "Congratulations, Florence, you hit .275. You're our winner."

The players cheered her.

Mace gave Morelli a fraternal pat on the shoulder. "Congratulations, buddy, looks like you just got beat by a girl."

He headed toward the door to the batting cages where Becka was coming out and swept her up in a hug. "You were great." Then the rest of the players crowded around and he backed off and watched her enjoy her moment.

The group morphed into a riot of celebration, the high fives, head rubs and hugs circulating around. Then Mace saw one of the players give Becka the ritual butt pat and he tensed for an instant. *Hands off my woman,* the thought leaped into his head before he could suppress it.

One of the players made a joke and Becka laughed in delight, the high flush on her cheeks making her look fresh and alive. Suddenly, with a singular fierceness, Mace wanted all the other players gone. The need to be alone with her suffused him. He was to leave the following day for another assignment, and already he could hear the clock ticking in his head. The preceding days had only sharpened his craving for her. He needed her, now.

The group started to move off toward the dorms to kick back for an hour or two before practice started. Mace tapped Becka's shoulder.

"I won!" she said, her eyes bright with excitement.

"You didn't just win, you hammered him."

"I guess it pays to have a former major league batting champion as your private tutor."

Mace stopped, letting the other players go on ahead. "You were the one who did all the work. Two hours a day practicing in a cage. It's a wonder it didn't make you crazy."

"It did make me crazy, but mostly because I was thinking of what we did Monday. For the rest of my life, chain link fence is going to turn me on," she laughed.

"IT'S A GOOD THING you don't live around here all the time," Becka said lazily as she lay in bed with her head on his stomach. "We'd never get anything done. I haven't gotten one thing unpacked since you came back."

"Orgasms are so time-consuming."

"Aren't they, though?" She eeled around so she lay next to him. "My parents gave me their Polaroid to take pictures of the place and I haven't even managed to do that."

"I was wondering why you had that on the bedside table," he said, giving her a bawdy look.

"Down, boy," she scolded smilingly and leaned in for a kiss. "Mmm. So you leave tomorrow?"

"Yeah, unfortunately. Only for a five-day assignment, though. Sammy requested me again, so I'll be back here in less than a week."

"Where are you going?"

"Georgia."

"That's a lot of driving in only a few days."

He skimmed a hand over her belly. "God, I love your body," he murmured, leaning down to kiss her flat stomach. "I won't be driving. I figured I'd just fly down and leave my truck here. It's faster that way."

Illogically, it gave her a little warm glow to think that he was leaving something behind, some demonstration of his intent to return. She hadn't expected the idea of him being gone to bother her so much. "Is it tough for you, always being on the road like this?"

"It's not all that much different than when I was playing."

"Except that then you had a home base that you kept coming back to," she pointed out.

Somehow, in a very short time, Lowell had come to feel like home. "I can always go home at the end of the season. It's only another month."

"What, you're not going to spend winter working the Mexican leagues?" she teased.

Mace considered it. "I don't know. I have to get used to the idea of this coaching thing. I mean, I like it, a lot, but life's been changing pretty suddenly over the past year. I just want things to settle down, you know? Get some time to think about what I want to do next year. What about you?"

Becka threw an arm over her head and looked at the ceiling. She hadn't thought about it much, but Mace was right, the end of the season was all too near. And she supposed that meant she really needed to figure out just exactly how she was going to make a living until spring training started again. Assuming she still had a job with the team. "I'll probably try to find something at a local HMO or hospital, I guess. Sammy's talked about keeping me on for next year, but nothing's set yet."

"He talks about you like he expects you to be around for the duration."

"In my dreams." Her life was nearly perfect at the moment. Unfortunately, holding onto it was about as feasible as holding water in her fist. The job was going to end—if not for good, at least for the season. Mace would leave and go on with his life. The thought stabbed at her. It wasn't like she'd thought for a minute that there was any possibility of a future. He had a history of coming and going with women, if the papers were to be believed.

And if they weren't? What then? Did she really think they had a chance at a future? "I wish I could just freeze everything right now just the way it is," she said aloud.

"You'd probably want to have more clothes on, in that case."

Becka giggled. "I adore you," she said without thinking. "I love the way you make me laugh." Leaning close, she pressed a smacking kiss on him.

Mace caught the back of her neck and held her there, and suddenly the intensity and passion were back.

"How does this happen?" Becka asked, running her hands over that amazing body and feeling the arousal start afresh.

"What?"

"We can be completely intense, then laughing like a couple of loons, and then it all goes back to wanting you so much I feel like I would die if your hands weren't on me right now," she whispered. "Is it like that for everyone? I've never had so much fun in bed before."

"Obviously you haven't been doing it right," he murmured, kissing his way down her stomach. "Did you check the instruction book?" he asked, tracing his tongue along the vee between her legs.

"I was hoping for private tutoring, remember," Becka said, her voice strained.

Mace shifted so he was laying between her legs. "Then I'm your man." His mouth was hot and avid against her. The feel of his fingers against her bare nipples made her gasp. What an incredible feeling, the silky heat of his tongue as he drove her up, the jolts of sensation from his hands on her breasts. Suddenly, abruptly, she craved him in her mouth. She slid away from him.

Mace raised his head inquiringly. "What's wrong?"

Becka smiled. "Nothing's wrong. I just think you should be on your back so that I can suck on you."

"I want to do something for you."

"You had your chance earlier. Now it's my turn," she said in satisfaction as she pushed on his shoulder to lay him flat. Finding him hard sent a burst of extra arousal through her. Knowing she was going to make him even harder was intoxicating.

Mace groaned as she slid him into her warm, wet mouth. Becka moved her head, feeling the fragile skin shift over the thick length of him. There was an immediacy about the act that was unbearably exciting. She could feel the effect of each slide of her lips, each stroke of her tongue, each driving instant that made him that much harder, that much closer to orgasm.

Her hands roved over the heated skin of his chest, until his breath hissed in. No coarse hair, just silky, sculptured flesh. Her fingers traced the dips and rises of his abs even as the muscles tensed. Then she increased the speed of her motion and brought her hand back down to curl around his stiff shaft and stroke.

Mace wove his fingers through the silky spill of her hair as his hips rose and fell in an erotic cadence. He moaned as Becka swirled her tongue around him in a caress that drove him nearly mad. Her mouth was hot and insistent, stroking, sucking, driving him relentlessly with an excruciating intensity of sensation, drawing him inexorably to the point of no return. Suddenly, he was hit by the overwhelming need to feel her pleasure, feel her convulsing around him even as he went over the edge. He curled his fingers around her arms and stilled her motion. "I want to be inside you," he managed through the blur of sensation. "I need to be in you."

He pulled her up to straddle him, then tensed as she slid him into her damp heat. It tore a cry from him, but he held onto the barest thread of control as she began to move up and down. He traced a finger down her belly and into the slick cleft between her legs, finding the hard bud of her clitoris, stroking it every time she rose.

He watched Becka's face tighten with a purity of pleasure as she neared her orgasm. "Touch yourself," he whispered. Her eyes widened, then she raised her hands to her breasts, cupping them, caressing them. A wave of arousal swept through him at the sight of her voluptuous enjoyment, carrying him closer to the edge.

"I want this to last forever," he said in wonder, fighting to wait for her. "I don't ever want to lose this."

Then it was his turn for surprise as Becka reached out to the bedside table and handed him the camera.

That was almost the end for him right there, but he managed to hold on. "Are you sure?" he asked, and with her eyes closed, Becka nodded. Then her breath began hitching and she got that otherworldly look on her face as though she were listening to magical chimes that only she could hear.

And as the orgasm burst through her, he snapped the shutter and captured her glory.

15

IT WAS A WRENCHING SURPRISE to her how much she missed Mace in the days that followed. Her runs, a time she'd always considered solo and precious, felt empty somehow without the companionship. She'd look for him during practice, during games, only to remember a split second later that he was gone.

And she missed him after the games most of all.

Maybe that was why she found herself at eleven o'clock at night walking through the door of Double Play instead of going home to sleep. The long, polished wood bar stretched along a mirror-covered wall dotted with lighted beer signs and clocks. A couple on what looked like their first date shot pool in the back as Aerosmith played on the jukebox. But it was the televisions that were the draw for the clientele. They were everywhere, showing every sports channel a satellite dish could offer.

Becka eased onto a stool. Down the bar, Mallory talked breezily with a pair of city leaguers still in their team jerseys. A cropped white T-shirt showed off her smooth, tanned belly where a gold ring glinted at her navel. Low-cut black jeans clung to her hips, accented by a fringed suede sash that she had knotted around them. Silver beads glinted on the dangling suede thongs, clicking together as she moved. She set beers in front of them, laughed at what might have been a joke, and began to walk down toward Becka.

"Hey, neighbor. To what do I owe this honor?" She pushed her tumble of dark hair back over one shoulder. At the end of the bar, the city league duo watched her with wistful adoration.

"You've got a fan club there," Becka said with a nod in their direction.

"Don't encourage them. I'll never get them out of here." She wiped the bar in front of Becka. "What can I get you?"

"Sam Adams."

Mallory moved away to draw the beer. "I hear the team won tonight."

"Oh yeah? How'd—" Becka looked at her. "Morelli's here?"

Mallory nodded and pointed to a corner where he slumped at a table watching soccer, empty bottles lined up in front of him.

Annoyance surged through Becka. The guy just wouldn't learn. "How long's he been here?"

Mallory glanced at the clock. "Oh, a half hour, forty-five minutes. Not that long."

"Long enough to suck down four beers." Becka shook her head in frustration.

"I'd cut him a little slack tonight," Mallory said quietly. "He's having a hard time."

Becka turned back to her. "What do you mean?"

"He was up at the bar talking to me earlier." Mallory leaned toward Becka. "It's his birthday."

"Well, why didn't he tell us?" she asked, baffled. "He should be out celebrating with the guys."

"He tried," Mallory enunciated softly. "They all told him to take a hike. It sounds like he's not real popular in the locker room these days." She set the beer in front of Becka. "I think he's feeling a little hard done by."

Becka turned around to stare at the silent and solitary Morelli. He was just a kid, she thought. She'd been so focused on his screwups that she'd forgotten that he was maybe twenty-two or twenty-three if he was lucky.

"That's tough," she murmured. "No one should be alone on their birthday."

Mallory nodded. "I talked with him for a little bit, but he seemed to want to brood."

"I might just have to go interrupt that."

Mallory winked. "I thought you might."

Morelli had isolated himself at a table off to one side and sat staring at a television, his back to the room in a way that screamed "No Trespassing." The fact that he'd lost the bet to her a few days before wasn't likely to make her his favorite person. Still, nothing ventured, nothing gained.

Becka walked up to the table. "Hey, Morelli, how's it going?" She pulled up a chair and sat down straddling it, setting her beer on the table.

He barely gave her a glance, just took another drink. "Don't start with the lectures, okay? I'm really not in the mood for it. Just go back over to the park and do your team thing."

"Game's over, remember? I figured I'd come over here and take it easy for once."

"Careful, you don't want people to think you're not living up to your potential." His tone was flat, hostile, full of the humiliation of losing to her.

"Nah, I figure I'll hang out for a while."

"Hey, it's a free country. It's not like you've got someone breathing down your neck about a curfew, so why not?" He gave her an opaque look before taking a deliberate swallow of beer.

"I hear that congratulations are in order. Happy birthday." She held her beer up to toast with his.

Morelli's eyes flicked from the beer to her face and back. Finally, after what seemed like ages, he clinked his glass with hers. "How'd you find out?"

"The bartender's my neighbor. She mentioned it. How old?"

"Twenty-two." His voice turned bitter. "Twenty-two and still in A ball."

Becka circled her glass on the Formica tabletop, creating a glossy ring of water. "How long have you been in the minors?"

"Since last year. They signed me mid-season out of junior college."

Twenty-one was old for junior college, she couldn't help thinking. "I thought you went to the University of Michigan for football or something."

"At first." He took a drink. "Let's just say the coach and I didn't see eye to eye. I changed to the junior college by home. That's when I got signed."

"Where's home?"

"Wisconsin." Morelli scowled. "Kenosha, Wisconsin. A little town you've never heard of."

It was all coming clear now. The U of M was practically a city and the coaching staff had a reputation for toughness. Morelli would have been lost there, going from a small town where he was worshipped as a sports star to the enormous university where no one knew his name, and no one had any patience for homesickness. "Big family?"

"I got three little brothers."

He must have been used to being a big fish in a very little pond, she thought. His first try in a new environment had probably been a disaster, judging by the fact that he'd been bumped from a scholarship. Morelli was used to moving through the world like he owned it. Now he was finding out the hard way that he wasn't as important as he thought he was. It couldn't be an easy lesson.

"Why don't you go back to the dorms and call your family? It's only 9:30 out there. It'll make you feel better."

"What would have made me feel better would have been to go out for a few laughs. But my teammates decided they had better things to do."

"Are they giving you a rough time?"

He snorted. "Compared to you and Duvall, they're amateurs. Why's everybody on me all of a sudden?"

"It's because we know you've got the potential to go somewhere."

He gave her a bitter look. "Twenty-two and still in A ball? Looks to me like I'm going nowhere. I might as well have some fun, at least."

"I think you can go as far as you want to. You just have to want it bad enough."

"I want it." His voice was suddenly intense.

"Then stop partying and work for it. Think about how it's going to feel the first time you step up to the plate in a major league park and hit one out."

Morelli stared moodily at his beer and didn't answer. The seconds ticked by.

"It's almost curfew. Go home, Paul," she said softly. "Get some sleep and get to the ballpark tomorrow. Your teammates aren't bad guys, they just want the team to win."

"I want the team to win, too."

"Maybe if you show them that, it'll make a difference."

He nodded slowly and stared into space some more. Then abruptly he stood up. "I'm outta here. See you tomorrow, Florence."

"Sleep well, and happy birthday."

He snorted. "Yeah, right."

Becka watched Morelli head out the door, then she returned to the bar.

"How'd it go?" Mallory asked.

Becka shrugged. "About as well as it could. He's 2000 miles away from home and all of a sudden he doesn't matter anymore. Not to the fans here, not to his teammates. He's a very lonely kid, is our Morelli."

"It makes a lot more sense, what he's been doing lately."

Becka nodded. "Act up, you get attention. I doubt he's thinking it through that way, but that's what it amounts to." She slid back onto the barstool.

"Work never stops for you in this job, huh? Want something else to drink?"

"Just water, thanks." Becka glanced around the rest of the bar. "It's pretty quiet."

"Actually, your timing is perfect. I can talk instead of running around serving the whole time."

At 11:30 on a Wednesday night, only a half-dozen patrons still remained in the bar. "How can you stay in business if this is all the draw you get on a weeknight?" Becka asked curiously.

"Trust me, earlier tonight this place was hopping. We've got a whole league that makes this their regular stop after their games are over, so it's usually standing room only until they start drifting off about nine."

"Except for your fans," Becka said, nodding again toward the end of the bar, where the city-leaguer, now solo, was waving for service.

Mallory rolled her eyes. "Except for them. Keep yourself busy," she said, putting a dish of pretzels on the bar in front of Becka and walking down to her customer. His buddy must have gone to see a man about a dog, Becka thought idly, watching the interchange with interest. Mallory laughed at something the guy said and apparently gave him the wrong answer. His voice rose. "Oh come on, who's going to know?"

"I will," Mallory said sharply, her voice carrying down the bar. She turned her back on him with finality.

"What did he want?" Becka asked curiously when she returned.

"My phone number." She put a glass on the counter and filled it with club soda.

"You probably get that a lot."

"Often enough," Mallory said dismissively. "I just tell them we're not supposed to date customers."

"Didn't seem to work with him."

"Everybody thinks they should be an exception."

"And are there any?" Becka asked curiously, watching Mallory add a lime to her drink.

"Here?" She gave a laugh. "Trust me, I've got better taste than to get involved with some guy who walks into my bar and thinks he can order me up like a drink. I'm not on the menu." She took a long drink of the club soda and thumped the glass down.

At the end of the bar, the city leaguer's friend had come back from the bathroom and the two made for the door. She raised her glass to him as he passed. "You have a good night, now."

He threw her a dirty look and stomped out.

She turned to Becka with a wink. "Somehow, I don't think I'm missing out on anything." She picked up the remote that controlled the television over the bar and flipped the channel. On screen, David Letterman laughed with a guest.

"Well how about outside of work?" Becka persisted. "It

seems like we're always talking about my man problems and I never hear about yours.''

"That's because yours are more interesting than mine,'' Mallory said lightly. "Anyway, I'm not sure that any of them are worth having, Loverboy notwithstanding.''

"They do have their moments, though.''

"For the occasional fling, I suppose,'' Mallory allowed. "It just seems like as soon as I get involved with a guy, he immediately wants me to stop doing all the stuff that got us together to begin with.''

"You should move to Boston and go to work in one of the chi-chi bars there. You'd be the toast of the town.''

Mallory topped off Becka's water. "Newport's actually looking more likely.''

"Your visit there worked out?''

"Maybe.'' Mallory moved her head noncommittally. "I've seen a couple of places that could work. Now I just have to talk my big brother into coming into it with me. It costs too much to go it alone in that town.''

"Yeah, but just think, you could meet yourself some rich Newport guy and do it up in style.''

"I'd rather get rich on my own and pick a boy toy, thanks,'' Mallory laughed. "Anyway, fill me in on the latest with Baseball Boy.''

"He's gone again.''

"For good?''

"Just for five days. He has an assignment down in Georgia, then he comes back up here.''

Mallory looked at her assessingly. "You're not gritting your teeth when you talk about him. Does that mean that you two have worked something out?''

"I suppose. I mean, what we've got now is working,'' she said offhandedly. At Mallory's amused look, Becka gave a sigh. "Okay, it's great, really. Maybe too great.''

"What's that supposed to mean?" Mallory took another drink of her club soda.

"I don't want to get hooked on something I can't have. I mean, the season ends in a few weeks and he's off to Florida. I live up here. It's not like we've got a lot of chance for happily ever after. Not that that's what I'm looking for," she added hastily.

"Oh, no, I'm sure it's not," Mallory said, deadpan.

"It would be nice to be able to just sit back and ride with it, see where it goes. Like a normal relationship."

Mallory snorted. "Honey, there *are* no normal relationships."

"You know what I mean," Becka continued. "One where we didn't have to have a 'define the relationship' conversation a month into it, where we could just let it happen until it made sense to make a decision."

"What does Mace say? Okay, dumb question," she said quickly as Becka's eyes rolled skyward. "Here's a better one: what do you want?"

Becka sighed and propped her chin on one hand. "More of this, except that it's impossible. When the season ends, everything changes. We'll be living in different states, I'll have to find a new job. It raises the stakes from 'let's keep seeing each other' to 'let's uproot our lives to be together based on a one-month affair.'" She blew out an impatient breath. "It's impossible. We hardly know each other. It's ridiculous to even think about making that kind of a jump. It's too soon."

"What is soon? Weren't you telling me about your girlfriend whose parents married in two weeks?"

"Married?" Becka stared at her appalled. "Who said anything about married? Get a grip, Mallory."

"I'm just saying, soon is relative," Mallory said, unperturbed.

"This is coming from the woman who won't even date?"

"We're not talking about me, we're talking about you."

"And I'm not talking about marriage," Becka said emphatically.

"You like him, though." It wasn't stated as a question, but as a fact.

Becka leaned her head against her hands, then raised her face to peer at Mallory between her fingers. "Yeah," she sighed, dropping her hands. "I like him a lot. He gets under your skin, you know? He was only here for a few days, and now I keep finding myself looking for him. I miss him," she said simply.

"So what are you going to do about it?"

"If I had the answer to that one, girlfriend, I wouldn't be here crying the blues."

MACE OPENED the bathroom door and walked out into the hotel room in a cloud of steam, a towel still slung around his shoulders. It was a typical road motel: worn shag rug in a dispirited beige, mottled tan wallpaper, cheap wall-mounted lamps with plastic shades. A polyester bedspread in muted tones of green and brown covered the king-size bed. The furniture was vintage seventies veneer ornamented with the odd cigarette burn, and a chrome rail hanging on one wall substituted for a closet.

When he'd been in the minors, he'd been so enamored of the opportunity and so focused on the goal that he'd never minded. He'd lived for the ballpark; everything else was just a waste of time. Now, things were different. He was different. Thanks to Stan and Becka, he'd found a job that meant something to him again. He'd found a way to wind up at the end of the day tired and satisfied. Unfortunately, being on the road in cheesy motels went with the territory.

Mace sat back on the bed and stared around the room. Did it bother him, the idea of staying in the tacky motels with bad mattresses, living on the road for months at a time? The alternative was a leisurely lifestyle, a beachfront home, all the relaxation and comforts he could stand. Did he miss it?

No, he thought slowly, he didn't. What he missed was baseball. Being in a ballpark, having something to do in life, those were the types of things that he missed. He missed feeling like he'd accomplished something with his day besides surf fishing.

And he missed Becka.

The sharp longing ran through him. She was addictive— a week of daily doses had left him with a craving impossible to assuage.

It didn't do him any good to want her when he was a thousand miles away, though. He looked on his bedside table where he'd tossed the manila envelope Sammy had given him the week before. The envelope that contained a roving instructor contract for the following year.

Mace picked up the envelope and pulled out the contract, flipping through it idly. He'd been sitting on it for days, wanting to be certain about his decision. It seemed like a big commitment to tie himself down to a job he'd only been doing a month. So what if he enjoyed it, it was probably still foolish to make such a sudden decision. Mace tapped the paper. When he was ready, he'd know.

He tried to slide the papers back into the envelope, but they caught on other things tucked inside. He tipped it upside down impatiently. In the past days, the envelope had become a catchall for schedules, per diem envelopes, airline tickets, and…

And a plain white envelope that held the Polaroids he and Becka had taken days before. Desire flowed through him, thick and hot at the sight of her naked body, of the two of them together. He flipped through the stack and swept back in time as though it were happening even then.

He couldn't wait. He had to talk to her now, no matter what time it was. He needed to hear her voice, needed it with a singular intensity that he didn't question. When something felt right, you just knew it.

BECKA WALKED into her apartment to hear the mechanical clunking sound of her answering machine picking up a call.

"Hey, darlin', are you up?" She'd recognize that molasses drawl anywhere. A flush of warmth ran through her. "I thought I'd take a chance—"

She picked up the phone. "Mace? Where are you?"

"Some town in Georgia. I couldn't sleep and I thought I might catch you up."

"I just walked in from Mallory's bar."

"Oh, I get it, I leave town and Becka's wild side comes out," he said, making her smile. "So how's Mallory?"

"Wrong question. Ask another, like how's Morelli?"

"Ah. And how is our boy?"

"Oh, right about now feeling pretty sorry for himself," she answered. "It's his birthday and all the guys blew it off."

Mace was silent for a moment. "That's a drag."

"It's a drag when your teammates couldn't care less about you."

"Be fair, it's mostly because he acts like he couldn't care less about them."

"I'm not sure he gets that, though." Becka picked up the phone and walked into her kitchen to get a glass of wine. "He doesn't seem to understand that it's his own behavior that's put everyone off. I think I've figured out why. Do you know anything about his background?''

''Not really.''

She filled him in on the details.

''I'll make a point of talking to Morelli when I get back. Anything else going on? I didn't think you were much for the nightlife.''

''I don't know, I just had an urge to go out.'' Becka stroked a finger along the side of the phone. ''I've been promising Mallory to stop in for weeks now. I figured it was about time.''

''That urge didn't have anything to do with missing me, did it? Because I've definitely been missing you.''

The sarcastic response she'd been about to make died in her throat. Her lips curved into a foolish grin. ''Really?''

''Yeah, really,'' he said softly. ''I wish I were there with you. I know what we'd be doing right now.''

''Oh really?'' Becka lay back on the couch and closed her eyes. ''And just what is that?''

''Well, for starters, by now I'd have you naked.''

''You think so?'' she purred.

''I know so,'' Mace said easily. ''Guess what I found in my things here?''

''What?'' Becka asked, propping a pillow behind her back.

''That photo of you. You look amazing, darlin'.''

''Uh-huh.''

''You should look like that now.''

''Meaning?''

''Unzip your shorts. Take them off.''

''And why should I do that?'' she asked him smoothly even as her fingers strayed to the waistband.

''Because I can't reach you from here,'' he growled.

"Don't play hard to get with me because I can hear your zipper over the phone."

Becka squirmed out of her shorts and lay back on the couch. "All right, they're off, but only because you insisted."

"I wish I were there to see it," he whispered. "Slide your hand down your leg and up the inside of your thigh, just barely touching the skin." His voice was husky, hypnotic in her ear, and she did what she was told. "Now tell me how it feels."

"Sexy," she breathed at the soft brush of her fingers, "smooth."

"Now keep stroking, and imagine it's my hand touching you."

"Mmm."

"Are you wearing those lacy things you usually have on?"

"You mean a thong?"

"Oh yeah." She could hear him draw a breath. "Roll on your side. Your hand is my hand, and I'm running it over your thigh, up along the side, then rubbing over that sexy ass of yours. I love the way it feels, so firm in my hand. Can you feel that? Are you touching yourself?"

"Uh-huh," she breathed, transfixed.

"Now slide your hand up under your shirt. Oh yeah, I love running my hand up your side, feeling how silky the skin is, feeling your ribs, knowing I'm getting closer to your breasts. In fact, I think we need to have your shirt come off, now."

As though mesmerized, she did what she was told, then lay back on the couch in just her thong and bra.

"What color is your lingerie?"

"Black."

"Black what? Slide your hand over it and tell me how it feels."

She'd never been so outrageously aware of sensation before, so outrageously tactile. "Smooth satin on top."

"God, the feeling's incredible when I'm naked and you lay against me in just your lingerie. Your skin's so warm and soft, it looks like it glows, like you could see right through it. So delicate," he whispered. "I know how sensitive it is. Run your fingertips down your neck, slide them over your collarbone and down. Imagine it's my hand. I'm sliding my hand down, feeling how the skin turns so incredibly thin and soft where your breasts begin. Curve your hand around your breast, slide your fingertips under your bra. That's me, babe, close your eyes and imagine that's me touching you." He gave a little groan. "You feel so good. Now unfasten your bra."

Becka flicked open the clasp on the front of her bra. Just the friction of the material against her nipples as she pulled the cups off was enough to make her gasp.

"Is it off? I'm looking at this picture of you naked and I can imagine being next to you right now, licking your nipples, sliding my hand over your breasts, down your waist and hip, running my fingers up your thigh to touch you. You know where I'm touching you. Can you feel me now? Can you feel me?"

Becka gave a soft moan at the heat of her fingers. With her eyes closed, with Mace's voice whispering hypnotically in her ear, she could almost believe that the touch was him.

"Oh yeah honey, up and down, slide it against yourself. That's me. That's my mouth on you, my tongue licking you over and over, rubbing against your clit."

The tension coiled tighter and tighter in her as she felt the hypnotic stroking, those husky words hot in her ear, turning her on more than just touch alone could have done.

It drove her higher and higher, though who was doing the driving she no longer knew, just that the urgency, the intensity and exquisite sensation had tightened to a point that she could no longer bear.

"Come on, baby, come to me," he whispered, "come to me...." and she did, in a blazing burst that had her shuddering and crying out mindlessly. The receiver fell away as she shuddered until the sensation died away to aftershocks.

With an arm that felt boneless, Becka picked the receiver back up, laughing a little. She lay for a moment, panting, waiting for her heart rate to subside. "That was amazing. It was like you were here."

"I wish I had been. You have no idea how hard that got me listening to you."

"Really?" she asked, sliding down on the couch. "And are you naked?"

His soft laugh came over the phone. "Just what did you have in mind?"

Becka smiled and ran her fingers down her neck. "I thought we could try a little therapeutic massage."

16

THE HIGH GREEN WALL of Boston's Fenway Park spread against the purpling sky of twilight as Becka and Mace walked into the ballpark. Hot dogs scented the air. Kids waved pink and blue cotton candy. Becka watched as a peanut vendor barked out his wares, tossing bags unerringly to fans ten feet away.

"Tell me who we're meeting again?" Becka asked as Mace led her up steep concrete stairs.

"Stan Angelo. He was on the Atlanta team when I was just starting out. He kind of took me under his wing."

"What's he doing now?"

"He's up in the Red Sox organization. Does a lot of traveling to coordinate trades and stuff with the other clubs. He was the one—" Mace turned his head at the sound of a whistle.

"Hey, Duvall, over here." A burly man in a Red Sox cap shouted and waved to them. They threaded their way between rows to get to the empty seats beside him, Becka leading the way.

"Hey, Stan, good to see you." The two men shook as Mace and Becka dropped into their seats.

"'Bout time you got here, Duvall. What, now that you're not playing you figure you don't have to show up for the start?"

"Hey, I got a job, in case you forgot," Mace said good-naturedly. "Our day game went into extra innings. We got here as quick as we could."

Stan leaned over to Becka. "Always excuses with this guy," he said, jerking a thumb at Mace. "He give you this routine, too?"

"Not so far, but I'll keep an eye out for it," Becka promised gravely.

Stan's eyes crinkled as he grinned. "I'm Stan Angelo, since this bum hasn't bothered to introduce us."

Becka found her hand enveloped in a hairy-knuckled paw. "Becka Landon," she said in amusement.

Mace looked down to where his knees were stuck up against the seat in front of him. "Couldn't you get any better seats than this, Stan? I thought you had clout with the organization."

"Oh, Duvall, you're breaking my heart," Stan shot back, with a wink for Becka. "You want to see a ball game right, you got to sit in the stands, not up in some luxury joint with a fancy buffet. You know you can't even get a hot dog in the 600 Club until after the game starts?" he asked aggrievedly.

"What kind of a sick world do we live in?" Becka asked.

"My thoughts exactly. So how's our boy doing out there in the minors, anyway?"

"We've moved up two spots in the standings since he came on board. You tell me."

Stan laughed. "See, Duvall? Aren't you glad I play such a good game of pool?"

Becka's mouth curved into a smile as the light dawned. "You're the one that hustled him into it."

Stan buffed his nails on his shirt. "It was nothing," he

said modestly. "I knew he didn't have any money I could win so I settled for a moral victory."

"You piker," Mace said. "You set me up and you know it."

"And I see you hated it so much you stuck around, huh? I'm hearing good stuff about you from the organization. They like your style." A hot dog vendor started up the steps of the aisle, barking his wares. "Hey, you guys eat?" Stan asked. "You want a dog?" Becka hesitated and he gave her a suspicious stare. "What's the problem? You're not one of those that pretends she doesn't eat, are you?"

"She's a health food nut," Mace said. "I'll take a couple if you're buying, though."

"None for the lady? Oh come on, you're at a baseball game. Everybody eats hot dogs at a game. It's un-American not to."

Becka grinned and gave in. "Okay, one."

"Good girl," Stan said approvingly and whistled to the vendor, waving five fingers.

"So you work for the Red Sox, too, Stan?"

"Yep. I'm sort of a fancy gofer. Spend a lot of time running around the country on recruiting missions and things," he said, pulling a twenty out of his wallet and handing it to Mace to pass down to the aisle. "I'm in town for some meetings next week. I figured I'd come in early and harass Duvall, here."

The hot dogs and change made their way hand to hand back from the aisle to Mace and Stan. With a crack, the ball sailed off the bat of a Boston player on a trajectory headed over the Green Monster and the crowd erupted in an orgy of joy as the home team took the lead.

"So why the Sox?" Becka asked a few minutes later, trying not to think about the contents of the Fenway Frank she was eating and appalled to realize that she was enjoying every bite.

"You got to go where the jobs are in this business." Stan swallowed. "Speaking of which, I hear there's an opening for a batting coach at the Trenton club."

"New Jersey?" Mace hooked a peanut from a bag Stan handed him. "That's the double A team, right?"

"Yep. If you like what you're doing, you oughtta put your name in the hat."

Mace cracked open the goober shell and popped a peanut into his mouth. "Oh yeah, I've always wanted to live in Jersey for half the year."

"As long as you're in a ballpark, who cares where it is? Don't be such a prima donna." Stan crumpled up his hot dog wrapper. "Anyway, we can talk about all this later. Let's watch the game and get dinner after. You up for it?"

"Wouldn't miss it for the world," Becka replied.

THEY SAT at a table in the bar of a local microbrewery that featured mid-1960s space-age decor in the form of tall, flowing room dividers, tables in swooping abstract shapes, and a freeform bar that Austin Powers would have found shagadelic. It was too hip for Becka's taste, but it was one of the few places still serving dinner.

The detritus of dinner had been cleared away, leaving only beer samplers, half-full cups of cappuccino, and dessert plates on the table.

"So it's about time you got yourself a woman, Duvall." Stan leaned toward Becka. "For years, we used to have to read about the ladykiller, here, bagging all the babes."

"You can stop any time, Stan," Mace said with a frown.

"You kidding? I haven't even gotten started yet. We see him on the news, all over the papers, Mr. Heartbreaker.

And you know what? He's doing nothing to earn it, nothing,'' he said in disgust, one eye on Mace to gauge the effect of his razzing. ''I was the one doing the hard work, going out to the parties and stuff. All Duvall did was work out and watch game tapes, but the minute he did a walk-on at a charity auction, they'd have him engaged to some gorgeous model or something.''

Becka raised an eyebrow at Mace, who gave her an innocent shrug. ''And here I was congratulating myself for trapping the playboy of western civilization,'' she said in mock chagrin.

Stan broke into laughter. ''Him? He's just got a good press agent. I'm the one you want, sweetie pie.''

''Stop horning in on my date, you bandit.'' Mace rose. ''I'll be back in a minute, and you'd better not have run off with her while I'm gone.''

Becka watched him walk toward the rest rooms.

''I don't know, Becka, what do you think? You want to run off to Bermuda with me?''

''Gee, Stan, what's today?'' She pretended to think. ''Nope, can't do it. I've got to wash my hair later,'' she said, shaking her head in regret.

''Just my luck, when Duvall finally gets involved he steals my one true love right out from under my nose.''

''Or maybe he saved you from the wrong woman so that when Ms. Right comes along you'll be available.''

Stan squinted at her. ''You think?''

Becka nodded, fighting a smile.

''Yeah, that Duvall, he's one of the good ones,'' Stan said, tapping his fingers to a rhythm only he could hear. ''He came up about two years before I retired. He's...I don't know, he's wired right. Solid. I really think he can go all the way with this coaching thing. He sees what's going on under the surface with guys, understands how they work.''

''He's doing really well as a batting coach, Stan. Do you think he'll try for the New Jersey job?'' She struggled not to dwell on the fact that Trenton was five or six hours away from Lowell. It wasn't like they had a future together. It wasn't like they'd even seriously talked about the idea. Still, she couldn't help worrying at the notion in her mind.

''The Jersey job would be something permanent, and it's a step up the ladder.'' Stan shrugged. ''Tough to say. I hope he at least thinks about it.''

He looked up at the same time as Becka to see Mace walking out of the bathrooms and past the boomerang-like point of the space-age bar.

Becka watched him come across the room. God, he was a beautiful man. It was no wonder the rumors flew about him, whether he'd earned the reputation or not. Certainly if Stan was to be believed, he hadn't. Maybe what he'd told her all along was true, Becka thought.

''Excuse me, are you by any chance Mace Duvall, the baseball player?'' A woman stepped away from the bar to stop Mace a few feet away from their table.

''What do you need?'' he asked briefly.

The woman unloaded a dazzlingly white smile. ''I'm Amber. Amber Stewart.'' She tossed her spill of long blond hair over one shoulder and put out her hand. Her dress was gold, one of those short, skimpy dresses that had always made Becka's tomboy nature simultaneously envious and impatient.

''Becka,'' Stan said softly. ''Ignore it. It doesn't even register with him. I've seen it happen a hundred times. He just pats them on the head and sends them on their way.''

She paid no heed to Stan, straining to hear what the woman said to Mace.

"I thought it was you. I read that article about you last year in *People*. You've had a pretty interesting life." Her smile invited him to tell her more.

"It hasn't been dull. Look, it was nice meeting you, but I need to get back to my friends."

"Wait," she said a little desperately. "Are you in town for a visit? I can show you around. Just give me a call. We can go out for a drink." With a bold stare, she licked her lips and tucked a slip of paper into his pocket.

"Watch what happens now," Stan said softly.

Mace pulled the scrap of paper out of his pocket. "Amber, is it?"

"Yes," she said eagerly.

"That's a nice name. Thanks for the invitation, but I'm going to have to pass on it." He handed her the paper. "Have a good night, now." He touched her on the shoulder and gave her a smile that had her melting, then he walked away without a backward glance.

Becka let out a breath she didn't know she'd been holding.

"Perfect technique, Duvall," Stan said as Mace sat back down. "You poleax her and still leave her thinking you're the nicest guy around. How do you do that, anyway?"

"It's a gift, Stan," Mace said blandly. "It's a gift."

SHE THOUGHT ABOUT IT the rest of the evening, waited to ask him about it until they were on the highway headed for home. "Those newspaper stories about you being involved with the beautiful people," she said without preamble, "they're really not true, are they?"

Mace raised a hand in the air. "Hallelujah, brothers and sisters, she's seen the light."

Becka made a face. "You don't have to get smart about it."

"Hey, I'm just amazed, is all. You're a hard one to convince."

"Cut me some slack, here. You know your reputation. It can't be all that much of a shock to you that people believe it."

"No, but it's kind of nice when my lover doesn't." The brightly lit Charles River Bridge was a fairyland tracery of gleaming cables on their left. Mace rested his hand on her thigh.

Becka turned in her seat to see him. "So how did it happen? I mean, the rumors had to start somewhere."

He stared at the road, the highway lights strobing over his face. "It's kind of a long story."

"We've got an hour's drive. Tell me."

He reached out to adjust the air-conditioning and sighed. "Well, I went into the minors straight out of high school, and moved up pretty quick my first season. My parents were still farming, and my twin sisters were about twelve. Next year, I got invited to show up at spring training for the Atlanta club. They still started me out in the minors, at the triple A team in Richmond, but it meant they were taking a good, hard look at me. That was the season the major league club was having its worst year ever. I figured if I kept playing well, I might get a chance to get sent up to Atlanta at the end of the season, since they were so far out of contention.

"Then I got a call one afternoon telling me about my dad."

Becka put a hand to his shoulder. "I'm so sorry," she

whispered, searching to see his face in the shadows. "I know you still miss him."

Mace squeezed her thigh. "Yes, I do," he said simply. "It kills me that he never saw me play. I'd have given anything for him to see me in the majors, just once. All the times he found a way to practice with me or to send me to baseball camps..." his voice trailed off. "I'd never have gone so far so fast without him."

"So what happened when you found out?"

"I drove home. The team gave me a week off so I could help sort things out." It was etched in his brain, that week. He'd faced merciless pitchers and batters who wanted to drill the ball right through his chest, but nothing had ever prepared him for the wild grief in his mother's eyes, or for the news that the farm was in debt so deep that selling it would still leave them in the hole. Sitting in their attorney's office, he had grown up in a matter of hours.

"My sisters were still in junior high. My mom had never had a career beyond working on the farm. I figured I had to find a way to support us all."

"What did you do?"

He blew out a breath. "Put the farm on the block. Got them in a house in town. Took draws on my credit cards and crossed my fingers that I'd get into the majors before the collectors came looking for me. Spent a lot of nights staring at the ceiling." He drummed his fingers on the steering wheel. "The worst part was, I couldn't really be there for them, you know? I had to play, at that point I *had* to, or we'd all have been sunk."

"What then?"

"I got really lucky was what happened. They sent me up to the majors early in the season, right around the time

I'd maxed out my credit cards. I even talked my agent into giving me a loan.''

''And the happy ending?''

He shook his head. ''It still wasn't enough. I had to pay for their place, my place. I could barely cover the interest on the farm debt.'' He slowed down to take the interchange ramp onto the highway that ringed Boston. ''I called Wally, my agent, and told him I needed a way to double or triple what I was making, and I needed it soon. He said it was easy—play my butt off, make rookie of the year, and he'd get me endorsements.''

''Piece of cake,'' she said dryly.

Mace gave a short laugh. ''Yeah.''

''So what did you do?''

She could see the gleam of his teeth as he grinned. ''Played my ass off, made rookie of the year and went after the endorsements. Wally said I needed to be a household name, so when the off-season hit, he started setting me up as a walker. I remember the first one, some B-list starlet that I've never heard of since. Man, I'd never seen so many flashbulbs go off, not even when we won the Series that year. I guess agents liked the idea of their clients being seen with an athlete on their arm—looks good, but no competition, you know? So I started doing it a lot.''

''And the reputation was born,'' she said slowly.

''Oh yeah. It wasn't an accident. I worked for that tag,'' he offered. ''At least for a couple of years,'' he added and lapsed into silence.

''Why'd you stop?''

''Huh? Oh, nothing much.'' He shrugged. ''Just one of those relationship things that told me I was way out of my league. By that time, I was on a new contract and I didn't need the money anymore.''

"But you'd created a monster."

"Yeah, but you know, I put a roof over the heads of my mom and my sisters. That was the important thing. What the papers say about me rolls off my back. My family knows not to believe it. The people that are important to me know not to believe it. Except you."

She flushed.

"You were a damned hard sell. I wanted you from the moment I saw you, but every time I turned around, you were throwing headlines at me."

"How was I supposed to know? I figured you were just looking to stay in practice while you were in Lowell."

"Oh, I don't know." He flicked on his blinker to change lanes. "I suppose you could have asked."

"Well, I'm asking now."

"What?"

"Am I just the flavor of the month?"

The corner of his mouth curved up. "You are pretty tasty, now that you mention it."

Becka punched him in the shoulder.

"Hey, don't take it so seriously." He rubbed his shoulder as he drove. "I told you a couple of weeks ago, you're the only woman I'm seeing. I like it that way. I like you." He reached out to take her hand and held it in his lap.

After a few moments, Becka stirred. "Are you willing to put your money where your mouth is?"

"What, another bet?"

"No." Becka laughed. "Are you going to be around next Sunday?"

"Unofficially, yeah. I get back that day. Why?"

"A very dear friend of mine is getting married. I'm her maid of honor and I need an escort."

"And?"

"And I figured with all your experience escorting the stars, you'd fit the bill."

He gave her a quick, sidelong glance. "Well, I'll do it, but there is a price, you know. I don't take on walker duties for free these days."

"Well, I'm a little strapped for cash," Becka said, sliding her hand up his denimed thigh. "I don't suppose you'd consider taking it out in trade, would you?" Her fingers danced up to unbuckle his belt.

"Depends on what you have in mind."

She unbuttoned his jeans and found him already hard. "I thought an oral I.O.U. might do the trick," she murmured as she bent over him.

17

THERE WAS SOMETHING magical about an outdoor wedding, Becka thought as she and Mace looked out at the grounds where Ryan and Cade's vows would be held. A stately baroque palace lay nestled in the midst of immaculate formal gardens where flowers bloomed in a rainbow of colors to accent emerald green lawns and hedges. In the distance lay the skyline of Boston.

"What is this place?" Mace asked.

Becka turned to get her garment bag out of the Bronco. "It's a private museum. The wedding's in a sculpture garden out back. It's beautiful, isn't it?" The sun shone benevolently out of an impossibly blue sky, dotted with puffs of clouds. Long pastel ribbons streamed from the line of tall stakes that led to the wedding area, evoking a feel of pageantry. "It's perfect, everything's perfect." She leaned in to press an exuberant kiss on Mace. For long moments the grounds receded and she was only aware of his mouth on hers.

Finally, she pulled away. "I've got to go in and find Ryan. Can you grab the cooler?"

"Tell your friend she really did a nice job," Mace said as they walked toward the museum building. "It looks great."

Becka nodded. "I'm sure her mother wishes it were a church wedding, but she's learned to let it go. Mine, now, mine would be pitching a fit like you would not believe."

Becka rolled her eyes to the sky. "She drove my sister nuts when they were planning her wedding." Their feet crunched in the gravel of the parking lot.

"That explains it," Mace said, nodding to himself.

Becka gave him a suspicious glance. "Are you by any chance trying to say I'm a control freak?"

"Not at all. It's just that you have a certain very pronounced reaction to anyone else trying to call the shots."

"Well, when you grow up with it, it gets kind of old. Not that I don't love my mom, but she can be like a velvet-covered tank. You'll meet her today, you'll see."

"Maybe she's just trying to look out for what's best for you," he said reasonably. "Mothers do that, you know." They stepped onto the walkway that led to the entrance.

"I'm sure she means well, but I'm an adult now. If I don't want to do something, I usually have a good reason."

Mace reached out an arm to scoop her in close. "A person could observe that you don't always know what's best for you," he said casually, nipping at her lower lip.

"A person could, but if they valued their health, they might avoid it." She pushed to get away from him.

"A person could demonstrate it," he countered, pulling her closer to press soft kisses on her temple.

Becka squirmed against him and laughed. "Quit it or you'll wrinkle my dress," she said, holding the garment bag away from her. Mace didn't respond, just nibbled his way across her jaw and under her chin. "I need to go inside," she said with less conviction, but he merely continued. "I need...mmm," she broke off, letting the magic of his touch take her away.

"What was it you were going to say?" Mace asked, sucking on her earlobe.

"Kiss me," she sighed, curving her free hand around his neck. Pleasure seeped into her bones as he pressed his mouth on hers. What was she going to do when he left? She hadn't a clue. His touch had become something she needed to live, like food, like water. Like air. For long minutes, her world was bounded by the pressure of his lips, the feel of his body, the clean crispness of his scent.

"Becka?"

The voice came from behind them. Becka jumped and turned to see Cade Douglas walking toward them.

"Sorry to interrupt you, but could you go up and see Ryan? I think she's a little nervous."

Actually, it was Cade who looked a wee bit nervous to Becka's eagle eye as he bounced restlessly on his toes. Dressed in his tux, boutonniere blooming on his lapel, he looked like a model in some *GQ* spread on grooms.

"Cade, this is Mace Duvall. Mace, this is Cade Douglas, the groom." If Cade was *GQ*, Mace was more *Esquire* in cream linen slacks and a soft blue silk shirt under a wheat-colored jacket. Not as polished, Becka thought, but just her type.

The two men shook hands. "You're the baseball player, right?" Cade asked. "A buddy of mine is into fantasy baseball. He used to love having you on his team."

Mace grinned. "Happy to please."

Restlessly bumping his hands together, Cade looked back to Becka. "Ryan's in the room at the top of the stairs getting primped, I guess. You can just go on up. I have to go put out the flower stands." He gestured toward a flower truck that sat at the edge of the pavement.

"Let me get Becka inside and I'll come help," Mace said. He walked her to the room at the top of the stairs and set the cooler down, then pulled her close for a hot, hard, utterly possessive kiss that went all the way through her. She melted against him, feeling the strength of his body against hers, the impossibly soft feel of his mouth. When he pulled away, she blinked at him, half dazed.

"Mmm. What was that for?"

"Because I know that I'm going to want to have you all night," he said lightly, "and I'm only going to be able to look."

"Not necessarily."

Mace grinned. "Sugar, if your daddy is on the premises, a peck or two is all you get."

"Give me a break, Duvall," she laughed. "My daddy's not like that."

Mace grinned and patted her behind as she turned to the door. "Sweetheart, every woman's daddy is like that. Have fun," he called as he walked down the stairs.

SUNLIGHT STREAMED IN from enormous windows. Ryan's dress hung from a door, an elegant column of white. With lingerie strewn across the comfortable-looking couch and cosmetics dotting the dressing table, the room looked soft and feminine.

Becka made an impromptu buffet of the cheese and fruit she'd brought, then handed Ryan a mimosa. "To you and Cade," she toasted. "Here's to health, happiness, long life and wild sex on a daily basis."

"Now, that I'll toast to." Ryan clinked glasses with her and sank down on the couch.

"Are you nervous?" Becka asked, watching her drink.

"Hmm?" Ryan considered. "No, I don't think so. I was worried about the weather, but it's turned out to be beautiful. I think it'll be great." Ryan picked up a cracker as Becka pulled up a chair at the dressing table to put on her makeup. "This is like the sleepovers we used to have. Remember?"

"I remember your mom always coming in about one in

the morning and telling us to go to sleep.'' They'd really tried, she recalled, only to be seized with fits of giggles just at the edge of sleep.

"I remember staying up to watch *Love Boat* reruns. And playing Barbies all night and eating Pop-Tarts.''

Becka giggled as she stroked on mascara. "Remember making Barbie and Ken have sex?''

"Oh God,'' Ryan clutched her arm. "What about the night we had the orgy with GI Joe and Skipper and Malibu Barbie?''

"And your brother came in and found us and washed GI Joe in the bathtub to get rid of the cooties?'' They shrieked with laughter at the memory.

"Any more of that champagne?'' Ryan asked, waving an empty glass.

"Just be careful,'' Becka warned. "We don't want Cade thinking he married a lush.''

"Just one more,'' Ryan promised as she took the fresh drink. "I'll be good.'' She rose and walked to the window that looked out over the sculpture garden in back, watching the wedding preparations. "So did you see Cade when you were coming in?'' she asked offhandedly.

Becka grinned. "We ran into him out front when we drove up. He looks fabulous. And a little nervous.''

"Nervous like cold feet nervous?'' Ryan asked, her voice elaborately casual.

Becka shook her head. "Nervous like something really exciting is going to happen and I can't wait, nervous. I left Mace with him. He'll take care of him.''

Ryan looked back out the window. "Oh my, is that Mace in the tan and cream?''

Becka walked up to peer over her shoulder. Amazing. Even from where she stood, just the sight of him gave her butterflies. "Yep, that's him.''

"He's gorgeous. No wonder you got tired of saying no."

"Down, girl." Becka pushed her shoulder affectionately. "You've already bagged your limit."

"Well that doesn't mean I can't—oh my God," she clutched Becka's forearm. "There's Cade!" The words ended in a squeak. "Look at him, he's really down there, and…" she broke off, her voice unsteady. "This is really going to happen." She put a shaking hand to her face.

"Are you okay?" Becka asked anxiously. "Breathe, please."

"I'm fine, I'm fine, I just need to sit down," she said, beginning to tremble.

"You want some water?" Becka asked anxiously.

"No." She sat on the couch, looking pale. "No," she said, more calmly. "It's just, this whole time, none of this has felt real, you know? I've been going through the motions like it was all going to happen, but it didn't really feel like it was happening to me. And just now, when I saw Cade—"

"You realized it was true."

Ryan turned to her, her eyes huge. "He wants me for life, Becka. We're going to stand in front of all these people and he's going to say forever. I love him so much I feel like my heart's going to explode."

Becka pulled Ryan close, close enough to feel her body shaking. "Hey, you're not going to pass out, are you?"

Ryan shook her head and blew out a breath. "It just hit me all at once there."

"That's because you've been in denial for five months. An hour and a half more, and you're done for. Now finish your makeup," Becka ordered as she reached for the champagne bottle.

"What happened to all the warnings about getting drunk?"

"I'm a trained EMT," Becka said blandly. "This is for medicinal purposes only."

WHERE HAD THE YEARS GONE, Becka wondered as she walked down the aisle toward Cade, listening to the strains of the harp player. Flowers and ribbons lined the aisle, daisies dotted the grass at her feet. It seemed like only minutes earlier she and Ryan had been playing hopscotch. Now, they were going down the aisle to her wedding ceremony.

As Becka neared the seats, one face only caught her eye: Mace, staring at her as if she were some magical creature that might disappear. Then he blew her a kiss and something shifted so that she blinked. Everything around them seemed unchanged, but something was different. It was as though every line and plane of his face was underscored by some special importance, and even when she knew she should look forward, she couldn't stop gazing at him.

She didn't have time to do more than wonder because then she was standing at the front, looking on as Ryan approached with her father. Becka watched Cade's face light up, watched Ryan become absolutely incandescent with joy. With the blooms of the bouquet cool against her fingers, she heard them recite their vows, listened as they pledged their lives to one another. And the words she'd heard so many times became new again as they joined hands, exchanged rings, and became husband and wife. And somewhere along the line, when she wasn't noticing, tears dampened her cheeks.

MACE WATCHED BECKA walk down the aisle after the wedding, hand on the best man's arm. The skirt of her gauzy peach dress fluttered around her calves, making her look like some woods nymph.

Becka stepped away from her escort, surreptitiously wiping her eyes. Something twisted inside Mace, as he looked at her, and he walked over without thinking. "You okay?" he asked.

Becka blinked and nodded. "Sure."

"Why is it that weddings always make women cry?" he wondered aloud, shaking out his handkerchief and pressing it into her hand.

Becka gave him a bashful look and wiped at her eyes. "I know, it's such a girl thing to do. But when it's someone I love, like Ryan, and everything's so wonderful, it just…fills me up and I can't keep it all inside." She blinked and sniffed again. "That probably sounds dumb."

"No." He pulled her close and kissed the top of her head. "It sounds nice. They're going to be good together, I think. She was all he could talk about before the ceremony."

A throat cleared. Mace looked up to see an older couple standing before him. Becka pulled away hastily.

"Mom, Dad, hi." Becka cleared her throat, looking a little nervous, he thought. "This is Mace Duvall, from the Lowell team. Mace, these are my parents, Nola and Dale Landon." She stepped in to hug them. Her father dutifully pulled her close, but never took his eyes off Mace.

The look swept him back to high school, taking Lucinda McFarr to senior prom. He'd pinned on her corsage in the doorway, her father glowering at him the whole time. Here it was, nearly fifteen years later, but he felt an absurd urge to reassure Becka's father that he'd have her home by ten.

"Mr. Landon." Mace shook hands with her father, one corner of his mouth quirking up as he felt the older man's grip testing him.

"Call me Dale," her father said.

"Nice wedding, huh?" Becka asked.

"It was lovely," her mother said, picking a stray bit of fluff off of Becka's shoulder. "But I can't think what Sonia was thinking, not making them get married in the church."

Dale gave Mace an assessing look. "I was sorry to hear you had to retire. You were a fine player."

"Thank you, sir," Mace said. Funny how the Southern manners came back. Next thing he knew, he was going to start telling the man what he had planned for his and Becka's date.

"So you're trying coaching on for size now? It's a job worth doing."

"You're a basketball coach, right?"

Dale nodded. "There's nothing like watching a team win and knowing that you were part of it." He glanced idly across to the pavilion. "Looks like the bar's open. Why don't you and I go get these ladies a couple of drinks?"

"Daddy!" Becka hissed, widening her eyes at him.

"You stay here and talk with your mama, honey," Dale said, unperturbed. "Mace here won't mind ferrying some drinks with me, will you?" He gave him a bland look.

"Not at all," Mace said.

Becka sent him a grateful smile. "White wine, then, please."

"Fine. Mrs. Landon?"

Nola looked thoughtful for a moment. "I'll have a spritzer, please." A breath of wind pulled her hat loose and Becka stepped in to help her get it pinned back on.

"Pretty girl, my daughter," Dale said as he and Mace walked away.

"She's a beauty, sir. You and your wife did a fine job." Squirrels chittered at them from the trees.

"We like to think so. She's a trusting young lady. Hasn't always expected as much from her gentleman friends as she should have." His tone was conversational. "You can

understand that as her father I like to see her treated right."
They drifted over to the bar set up under the tent.

"Yes sir." The man certainly didn't beat around the
bush, Mace thought with amusement. He tried to imagine
how he'd feel if he had a baby girl, a beauty like Becka
that he'd watched bloom from a child.

And decided he didn't blame Dale Landon one bit.

Just what was going to happen with Becka, Mace wondered, watching the breeze molding the thin fabric of her
dress against her as she talked with her mother. One more
week wasn't enough. He had no answer for the question
her father had obliquely been asking because he didn't
know what he wanted. More, he definitely wanted more,
but it seemed too soon.

Except when he thought about walking away, it didn't
just feel too soon.

It felt impossible.

THE LAST RAYS of the setting sun shone in through the
ballroom, turning the gold leafed scrollwork on the walls
to fire. Chandeliers glimmered overhead, white and soft
green swathed the tables and chairs. Flowers spilled out of
the centerpieces and dotted the room, filling it with scent
and the sense of extravagant celebration.

A jazz trio at the back of the room played light after-
dinner tunes as Ryan and Cade moved around the tables to
greet their guests and accept congratulations.

"I'll be right back," Mace said, brushing his lips over
hers. Becka watched him walk into the crowd, still trying
to understand what had happened during the ceremony. It
was nothing she could put her finger on, but she had the
feeling it was somehow critical.

Out in the room, someone clinked a knife against a water

glass. Around them, others took it up until the room was filled with the clinking demand for bride and groom to kiss.

"If you insist," Cade said and put his arms around Ryan to dip her back so low that her veil brushed the floor, kissing her until people began whooping. He raised her back up and accepted the applause with extravagant bows. "You'll excuse me, but I think it's time that I dance with my bride," he said, and pulled Ryan onto the floor.

Becka rose and walked over to watch. Ryan and Cade moved together as though they were connected. They didn't seem aware that anyone else was watching them, or indeed, that there was anyone else in the room. They were different, somehow part of a whole in a way they'd never been before. There was something about the wedding ceremony, Becka thought, something about making those pledges aloud. The vows were just words, the commitment already made long since, but saying them to each other in front of witnesses somehow made it real.

For good or for ill, she wondered. Nellie and Joe, and her mother and father, they all made her want to shake her head. Yes, they were marriages and part of a unit, but they took each other for granted. Becka had watched Ryan plan the wedding from afar, wondering how she could take the chance that the magic of her relationship with Cade might be supplanted by complacency. The tie that became obligation, she knew from her parents' marriage. No fire, just teamwork. Somehow Ryan and Cade's love seemed too fragile to subject to that.

Then Ryan's parents stepped out on the floor to the opening strains of "I Only Have Eyes For You," and Becka caught her breath. If Ryan and Cade moved like they were connected, Phil and Sonia Donnelly moved as one, flowing across the floor in a private world of their own. Phil looked into his wife's eyes as though she were a rare and precious gift, and he leaned in and kissed her gently on the forehead. He guided her into a slow, graceful turn, and she laughed aloud, then reached in to hold him.

This was love, Becka thought, blinking suddenly damp eyes. True love, lasting love. Suddenly, it made sense that Ryan would think marriage natural, because where there was this kind of love, complacency could never enter. Where there was this kind of love, the only thing that mattered was that the two people were together. She watched them move around the floor and her eyes looked beyond, to where Mace was skirting the edge of the dance floor, coming to her.

And abruptly it was as it had been in the ceremony. Everything else was backdrop, all sounds and sights receded except him. As he walked toward her, his face held all the meaning of her life. Becka stared, barely breathing.

As though mesmerized by a sudden purpose, Mace passed the table and walked directly to her. He caught up her hand to lead her onto the floor, his fingers curled around hers, and her heart began to race. And with sudden shock, she realized the truth.

She was in love with him.

18

BECKA HURRIED from the team bus to the New York hotel lobby, fighting through a torrential downpour. It was hard to decide which was worse, the rain or the relentless humidity that had preceded the storm. All evening, she'd felt sticky and sweaty, now all she wanted was a real shower.

"And people bitch about the storms in Florida," Mace said disgustedly, as they joined the group of sodden players standing in front of the elevators. Morelli raked his wet hair back with his fingers and looked around. "Anybody want to go out after we get cleaned up?"

Chico gave him a hard stare. "What, you want to celebrate? In case you didn't notice, Morelli, we lost."

Morelli shrugged and offered a half grin. "That's okay, we can go out and cheer up."

The other players didn't bother to answer, merely loaded up on the elevator when it arrived.

Upstairs, Becka watched the colored lights on the card lock blink as she let herself into her room. It was a typical traveling motel: bed, dresser, television, chair. And a connecting door on one wall that led to the room on the other side.

She pulled it open. One of the great benefits of being the traveling secretary, she reflected, was being able to choose room assignments. With Mace assigned to the room on the other side, it was easy to open the connecting doors and sleep together with no one the wiser.

She heard the snick of the dead bolt as Mace opened his door. In two steps, he had her against him. For a moment, he didn't even kiss her, just held her, his cheek against her hair. Becka closed her eyes and absorbed his presence. More so than ever before, her moments with him had become precious, because lurking underneath it all was the knowledge that in five days he would be gone. And then she had to figure out what to do. She sighed and squeezed him to her. Their wet clothing squelched.

Mace laughed and stepped back from her. "You look like a drowned rat."

"You're looking a little humid yourself," she said, eyeing him.

He traced a finger down from her shoulder to the peak of one breast, where the nipple stood out through the damp fabric. "I have to say I like what soaking wet clothes do for you."

"You think they look good on me?"

"I think they'd look even better off," he said, reaching for her.

Becka put a hand against his chest. "I have a better idea. How about a hot shower?"

"Your place or mine?"

"Mine. I've got better shampoo."

He grinned and turned toward the bathroom.

"You go ahead," she called. "I'll be with you in a second. I just want to check to see what the Weather Channel is predicting for tomorrow."

He pulled her close for a lingering kiss. "Okay, but don't take too long."

As the shower started up in the background, Becka sank down on the bed. She still hadn't truly processed the realization that she was in love with Mace. She knew how to take a lover and how to leave one, how to kiss, how to have sex, how to give the ultimate sensual massage.

She hadn't a clue how to be in love.

Waking up the morning after Ryan's wedding to go on a road trip hadn't helped. She was out of her depth, unsure of her moves, and every day she was that much more conscious that the end of the season was drawing nearer. He'd spend the final weeks with teams in Florida and Georgia. And after that, who knew?

That was the frustrating part. Instead of it being a normal relationship, after barely a month as his lover, her choice was either leap into the void and ask if he wanted to keep it going, or let it end. Compared to that, her anxieties over whether she'd get a contract for the next year or whether she'd find a job to pay for rent and food during the off-season were minor.

The question she wrestled with, the one that kept her up nights staring at the ceiling long after Mace had fallen asleep, was whether to tell him she was in love with him. He had feelings for her, that was clear. What was impossible was finding a realistic way to have any sort of long-term relationship. Long-distance arrangements worked only in the movies. In reality, there were times you just had to say maybe love wouldn't conquer all.

During the season, a week here or there, the very rare day off was all they might manage, and that, only if he stayed as a roving instructor. If he took the New Jersey job, they'd never see each other at all. And the off-season was even more impossible—he lived in Florida, she lived in Massachusetts. She had to be out of her mind trying to think of a way they could have anything even resembling a real relationship, even assuming that that was something Mace wanted.

And yet, when she thought of telling him goodbye at the end of the week, she wanted to weep.

It was needing him that was the hardest. With all of her previous lovers, she'd been the one to decide when it was over. They'd treated her well or poorly, and she'd stuck with the relationships until she could be bothered to deal with the logistics of breaking them off. She had been diverted by them, but she hadn't needed them for her happiness. When she thought about Mace leaving, it was as though a void opened up at her feet.

So she was back to her debate—tell him and risk finding that they couldn't come to terms or live with the hollowness? Put that way, it wasn't really much of a decision. The worst that could happen was what was going to happen anyway, and she'd never been one to shrink from unpleasant tasks. If they both wanted a future, they could find a way. If Mace didn't...

If Mace didn't, he was already lost to her.

She'd just go in there and join him and have the conversation. Resolved, she got up to take a step—

And nerves assaulted her, dampening her palms and sending adrenaline surging through her veins. She sat back down on the bed. Probably best to wait a minute or two while she figured out what to say, maybe even wait for him to get out of the shower. When the timing was right, she'd start that discussion. Just put herself out there, let him know what she felt and see what happened. She'd do it, too, Becka thought. Really. Just as soon as she checked the weather.

She fiddled with the remote, flipping through channels, noticing none of them. Then suddenly she stopped dead. On the screen was an image of a heartbreakingly beautiful actress, one who'd been a big star just a couple of years before.

And standing with his arm around her, was Mace.

MACE STOOD under the hot water, letting it beat onto his shoulders. In a matter of days, his time with the Lowell Weavers would be over. A couple of weeks with the southern teams and the season would be complete. But he wouldn't be, not without Becka.

In the time since he'd left Florida, he'd found new meaning to his life, an energy, a reason. Part of that was the teaching, he had to hand it to Stan. Part of it, though, was a certain cat-eyed redhead who prowled through his days and filled his dreams. But how did he even know what he felt? Certainly in the past when he'd thought he'd found the one, he'd been sadly mistaken. Why did he think now was any different?

Because it was, and deep down, he knew it. If he left Lowell without talking with Becka about where they went next, he knew he would regret it. He didn't need the Trenton job, he could keep doing what he was doing. They'd find a way to make it work.

Because deep down, he knew he loved her. And it was time to tell her that.

BECKA STARED at the television as the image changed. It was a shot of Mace from years before, his hair cropped short as it had been in his playing days. The blond, waifish woman on his arm whispered in his ear.

Even though Becka knew that she was looking at photos taken years before, jealousy pricked at her. The shot faded to a live television studio, and the same woman cozily ensconced on a couch with the talk show host. She knew the face, Becka thought. An actress, and what was her name? Carolyn…Catherine…Ca… She notched the sound up, fascinated. "I'm Jessamine Maffrey. We're here with Calista Stockton to talk about her newly released tell-all book *Calista Confidential.* Thanks for being here with us."

Calista smiled and fluffed her hair.

Jessamine leaned in. "I have to tell you, all the Hollywood dish aside, the thing I found most fascinating about your book was the story of your relationship with Mace Duvall. I was absolutely riveted." The screen behind them changed to a shot of Mace in his baseball uniform, with that focused look Becka knew he wore when he was at the plate. In the current context, though, it just made him look hard and cold. "The pregnancy and miscarriage right when your relationship ended…" Behind her glasses, the host's eyes were bright with malice. "He was the father of the child, right? Your book doesn't really ever say how it actually happened."

The hairs on the back of Becka's neck began to prick up one by one.

Calista's face wore an expression of lingering pain. "Well, Jessamine, it's just time to get past it. I'm streamlining my life, and ending the secrecy is part of that."

"Oh, but your book is just as tantalizing for what it doesn't tell as what it does. Mace Duvall was the father of the child you lost, wasn't he? You're among friends who care for you. Won't you tell us what happened?"

"That's why I put out the book, so I couldn't run away anymore." Calista gave a laugh that rang just a little hollow.

"It doesn't sound like you were the one who ran away at all," the host said flatly. "Now you were involved with Mace Duvall for six months, is that right? Were you living together?"

"He moved into my house in L.A. He hadn't bought a place yet. I thought we were building a life together. I thought—" She broke off, misting over daintily. Jessamine handed her a box of tissues.

Becka watched, transfixed.

"You thought that he was serious. According to your book, you'd talked about marriage."

Calista nodded. "I thought he wanted the same things that I did. A family. A home." Her voice faltered.

"When did you find out you were pregnant?"

She stared down at her hands. "In February. Mace was upset because it meant I'd deliver in October, and he was hoping his team would make the World Series."

Jessamine gave her one of her patented empathetic stares. "You must have been really hurt by that."

Calista raised her head bravely. "I knew he'd love the baby when it came, and if he couldn't be there for the birth, well, I figured it was just part of being a player's wife."

"But he didn't ask you to marry him right away when you told him."

Becka's hands curled into fists, the nails cutting into her palms, unnoticed.

"Well, no, he didn't. He'd been working out a lot, spending late nights at the gym getting ready for spring training. I just put it down to preoccupation. I knew he loved me, you see." Her chin wobbled. "Or I thought I did."

Jessamine lowered her voice, touching Calista's shoulder gently. "Tell us about the night of the charity auction. According to your book, that was the night you miscarried, but you don't say exactly what happened."

Calista looked down at her lap, silky blond hair falling to screen her face. The seconds ticked by while she gathered her strength. While Becka tried to absorb what she was hearing.

"Calista?" The host said gently. "Are you sure you want to do this?"

Calista looked up, blinking away tears. "Oh yes." She dashed them away and took a deep breath, visibly composing herself. "I'd been at an industry function. It was scheduled to run quite late, but I'd begun feeling ill, so I came home in the early evening. I walked in…" her voice cracked.

"Take your time," Jessamine said gently.

Calista pushed her shoulders back with determination. "Imagine being pregnant and sick, coming to your home, looking for comfort. Imagine instead finding the father of your child in bed with another woman, having him tell you that he doesn't want the child, that you're trapping him and interfering with his career. Imagine having him tell you that he doesn't love you anymore." She reached out for Jessamine's supporting hand. On the screen behind her, a montage of shots appeared, Mace with actresses, models, pop stars, seemingly every famous woman in the world on his arm. "That night…I lost the baby." Her face crumbled and sobs choked her voice as she fell into Jessamine's comforting arms.

Becka stared at the screen numbly.

Behind her, the bathroom door opened and Mace walked out, naked, toweling his hair. "Hey, I thought you were going to take a shower with me."

Becka sat absolutely still. Something must have shown in the lines of her body because he stepped forward.

"What's wrong?" he asked in concern.

She couldn't speak, just gestured at the screen as she tried to reconcile the face she loved with the odious tale she'd just heard.

On the screen, the two women broke apart, Calista wiping at her eyes.

"What a devastating experience," Jessamine said softly.

Mace snorted. "Ah, darling Calista," he said sardonically. "Well if it's her life and she's telling it, I'm sure it was devastating. So what's the story this time?" He combed his wet hair back with his fingers.

Becka turned slowly to look at him. "You."

On screen, Calista blinked eyes still damp with tears. "I'll never forget that night as long as I live. What a beautiful baby we might have had." The montage switched from shots of Mace on the town, back to his merciless look, then the show broke for commercial.

"What the hell is this about?" Mace asked slowly, his eyes narrowing. "What night?"

"The night you broke things off with her. Don't tell me it's slipped your mind, you were there," Becka said astringently.

"What is she saying?" he demanded.

"That when she was pregnant with your child, she came home to find you in bed with another woman." She needed to move, Becka realized, and badly. Pacing wasn't nearly enough. She needed to be running, running somewhere miles and miles away from there. "She miscarried that night, after you told her you were done with her."

"*What?*"

"Guess babies didn't fit in with your career. At least that's what she says," Becka managed, unable to make herself look at him. She wanted him to tell her it was lies, that it wasn't true, but the awful choking horror clenched around her heart made her very afraid it was.

"My God." The words exploded out of him. She did look then, to see his face bone white. It told her all she needed to know.

"Oh yes," Becka said miserably. "It's all in her new book, available at bookstores everywhere." Inside her, a thousand voices were screaming that this could not be, it could simply not be. When she looked at him, he was Mace, the man she loved. Could that be an illusion? Could he really be the kind of monster who would have done something like that?

"Jesus," he said softly and sat down slowly on the bed. Becka stared at him, torn between wanting to offer comfort and wanting to be anywhere but there. Mace looked up. "The media is going to have a field day with this. I've got to call my family and warn them," he said with sudden urgency, snatching his cell phone off the dresser and punching keys as he walked into the other room to pull on a pair of jeans.

"So were you ever going to tell me what happened with her?" Becka asked bleakly. "'Nothing much,' you said. 'Just one of those relationship things.'"

Mace looked at her blankly and put the phone down. "What?" he asked in a barely audible voice.

"Were you even going to tell me about Calista? Didn't you think it was going to come out some day?"

He shook his head. "You don't honestly buy that story."

Becka gave a short laugh. "Mace, the woman just told the whole country on national television. She wrote it in her memoirs. And you're not telling me anything. What do you expect me to believe?"

He looked at her oddly, then stood up. "I guess I expect you to believe in me. But then that's been our problem all along, hasn't it? What I say has never held as much weight with you as the dirt and the sleaze."

"Then tell me what really happened." She despised herself for pleading, for, after everything, holding out the faint hope that there was an explanation.

Mace leaned against the connecting door and looked at her. "Why should I bother? It sounds like Calista's already taken care of that. You've got your mind made up." He turned into his room. "You'll excuse me. I've got some calls to make. I'll see you tomorr—"

The phone jangled for attention until Becka picked it up. "Hello? Yes, this is Becka. What? Oh my God, where?" Her voice sharpened with concern. "Yes. I'll be there as soon as I can." She hung up the phone and looked at Mace. "That was Sammy," she said bleakly. "Morelli's in the hospital. He got cut in a bar fight. I've got to go." She shucked her wet clothes swiftly and pulled on dry ones.

Mace walked into his room and came back wearing a shirt. "I'm coming with you," he said, tucking it in.

"Don't be ridiculous," Becka snapped. "There's no reason for you to come, and anyway, how would we explain it? I woke you up in the middle of the night? Stay here, Mace, I don't need you." Somewhere deep inside, a part of her was shrieking and wailing, but she couldn't afford the luxury of indulging it. Sometime soon, she'd be alone and then she could deal with it. In the meantime, maybe if she told herself often enough that she didn't need him, in time she'd get used to saying it. And maybe, in time, she might even come to believe it.

"Whether you want me there or not, I'm coming," Mace said flatly. "The kid is hurt, and maybe if I'd done my job and talked to him weeks ago he wouldn't be in the shape he's in."

"Mace, he's been headed this way all summer. I doubt there was much any of us could have done. You tried." Then they were out in the hall, and the question of whether he was coming with her was moot.

THE BATTLE-SCARRED HOSPITAL was crowded with late-night emergency cases. A harried-looking intern checked their identification. "He's cut, but it's not life-threatening," she said briefly. "The knife bounced off a rib. He'll be stiff for a couple of weeks and he'll have an interesting scar, but that's about it."

"Where is he?"

"Back in bay three. We haven't given him any pain-killers because his blood alcohol level was too high, so he'll probably be glad of the distraction."

Becka and Mace walked past several patients until they spotted Morelli, looking pale and wan. He mustered up a smile when he saw them. "Hey."

"Hey yourself," Becka said.

"How you feeling, champ?" Mace asked.

"Like I got kicked by a horse," Morelli said. "Just don't make me laugh, okay? Even breathing hurts right now."

"What's under here?" Mace pointed toward a pad taped to Morelli's jaw.

"Guy did a warm-up on my face before he tried to fillet me."

"Yeah, well, you go looking for trouble, you're likely to find it."

"Tell me something I don't already know," Morelli said and gave a weak cough. He winced. "Oh man, that hurts."

"Where's Sammy?" Becka asked.

"He went out to make some phone calls."

"I should go find him. Okay if I leave you guys?"

Mace nodded. "We'll be fine." Not exactly true, he thought as he watched her walk away. Morelli's cuts would heal eventually, but he wasn't sure if the Becka-shaped hole in his gut would ever fill in.

He pulled the drape around the bay for privacy and turned back to Morelli. "So what happened?"

"Guy went off on me."

"Morelli, for once, cut the crap, okay?" Macc's voice was hard, without a trace of sympathy. "You've been looking for trouble all summer and you finally found it. Now what happened?''

Morelli blinked. "I was out having a couple of drinks after the game. I saw this woman over at the jukebox. Real looker. You know the type, wearing something little and tight. So I figure, hey, I'll go over and be sociable. She sort of plays it cool, but she's still giving me the look and kind of turning that body toward me." He craned his neck to look at Mace. "Hey, I'm a smart guy, I can read a woman's body language and know when she's coming on to me, but at the same time she's acting like she's not interested. So I say fine and go back to my drink. I figure it's her problem."

"First smart thing I've heard you say." Mace pulled a chair over and straddled it, resting his arms on the back.

"Well, then I look over a little while later and she's standing by the pool table watching this lump of meat play. And he's ignoring her, except every so often he'll come over and give her a squeeze, feel her up. So I see what's going on. She wants me, but this dumbass boyfriend of hers is here, so she's having to play it cool."

"And you decided not to."

"I walked over and said to her, hey, how tight are you with this guy? Asked her if she wanted to go somewhere else."

Mace snorted. "Smooth move, Morelli."

"Hey, she was turning that little body my way, but then she looks over at the meat and says, 'No, I'm here with someone.' I tell her that doesn't matter, she can still go with me."

"Maybe she didn't want to."

He shook his head. "Not a chance. She wanted me, she was just afraid of the meat."

"Maybe you should have been."

The sarcasm went over Morelli's head. "So the meat asks her is there a problem, and she says yeah, this guy won't leave me alone. Next thing I know, he's got a blade out and he's trying to carve me up." Morelli grimaced. "What is it with this place? When are they going to give me something for the pain?"

"You've got too much alcohol in you. They don't want to risk it."

"I'll risk it for them."

"Morelli." Something steely in Mace's tone finally penetrated through the haze of alcohol and pugnacity in Morelli's brain. "This is a wake-up call, and if you've got a brain in your head, you'll listen to it. You've had a lot of talent handed to you on a platter, but you've been doing nothing with it and the organization knows it. Now you've gotten yourself injured so that you can't play, which is going to directly impact the team's performance, and if you don't think that management is going to come after you about this, then you don't know much about how baseball really works."

"But..." Morelli opened his mouth, but Mace cut him off.

"You're done with talking for now. You talked tonight in that bar and see where that got you? This sport is littered with players who had tons of skill but zero control. Teams won't touch 'em because they know they're problems. You're not good enough for a team to stick its neck out for. Yeah, maybe if you were in the majors and had had a couple of all-star years they'd take a risk on you, but if you keep screwing up at this level, buddy, they'll just let you rot, because there are way too many guys standing in line behind you."

"But you did the partying and they kept you on."

"That was hype, not reality, and management knew the

difference. I made a few mistakes when I was starting out, but I was lucky.'' Was he really, Mace wondered. Was he really if something he'd done a decade before had torn away the one person he wanted most in his life?

BECKA WALKED back to Morelli's bedside. The drape was pulled around the bed, lending the illusion of privacy, but she could hear the two men talking through the barrier.

"So it worked out for you, then," Morelli said.

"I said one or two mistakes. I didn't go around picking bar fights."

"No, you just picked up babes."

Frustration shaded Mace's voice. "Morelli, stop being impressed. What I did didn't mean anything at all. It was for show, and it turned me into a collector's item. That was it."

"Oh come on, Duvall. You had some of the most beautiful women in the world on your arm. Don't act one way and then come around lecturing me."

"I'm trying to tell you that I screwed up," Mace said angrily. "I'm trying to get you to stop and look at yourself so that you don't throw away your career. Little stuff, stuff you think is over and done with can dog you. Your past is always there, you know? I fight against mine all the time. Tonight, I had something that happened ten years ago bite me, and I may have lost someone who's really important to me."

Hope and despair filled Becka at his words.

"You mean Florence, right?" Morelli's voice came through the barrier. "Don't give me that look, I'm not blind, you know. I see the way you guys are together. It looks pretty hot."

"And now it's pretty well not. She won't get over my past, and maybe I shouldn't be trying to. Trust me, you don't want to be the guy with rep. You're whoever they say you are, and you can never get away from it. But we're not talking about me.''

''Sure sounds to me like we are.''

Mace sighed. ''Morelli, something stupid that I did ten years ago has just blown apart my future, something nobody would have even known or cared about if I hadn't had the profile I do.''

How could he throw it off like some small dating snafu? Becka pressed her palms to her temples, willing the pain to stop. How could he talk so seriously about caring for her and yet be so callous about his past?

''Morelli, are you even getting this at all? You're at a crossroads right now. You can get your act together and maybe wind up in the Hall of Fame someday or you can wind up drinking yourself blind in a sports bar somewhere, talking about the career you almost had. You decide.''

A doctor brushed past Becka and walked into the bay. ''Okay, let's get you stitched up.''

Becka followed him in, not looking at Mace, fighting to remain expressionless. The doctor would put in some sutures and give the usual tetanus injection. Morelli would heal. Maybe he'd even get straightened out and have a successful career.

Now if they just had some sutures for the heart.

19
_____

BECKA SAT in the training room at her desk, turning a white envelope over in her hands. She should be happy, she knew, she should be thrilled. The envelope contained the passport to her future. Inside was a contract with the Lowell Weavers for the following season. It was everything she'd hoped for.

It meant nothing to her at all.

How to make things matter at a time when it felt as if nothing did, this was the riddle she struggled with every day. Another time, she might have cried on Ryan's shoulder, but Ryan was on a beach somewhere in the Greek isles. Ryan, the romantic, would search for hope in what had happened, she'd search for love.

She wouldn't understand that just then Becka's life held neither. In the three days that they'd been back from the New York road trip, she and Mace had barely spoken. It seemed there was nothing to say.

The Weavers were one win from clinching their league title. Morelli had bounced back surprisingly well from his ordeal, chastened and subdued, but healing rapidly. Even Mace was on his way out, slated to leave the next day. His work—even where she was concerned—was done.

MACE WALKED into the diner, looking around for Stan.

"Yo, Duvall, over here," Stan called from where he sat in a booth along the wall, a cup of coffee in front of him.

Mace eased himself down on the dark blue vinyl seat and waved to the waitress. "Bernice, coffee please?"

She gave him a hard look. "When I get time."

He sighed, knowing from experience that fallout from Calista's little stunt was just going to keep hitting him unexpectedly.

"What's going on, buddy? You don't look so good, if you don't mind me saying so."

Mace gave a humorless grin. "I take it you haven't been looking at the entertainment news lately."

Stan shook his head. "No. What's up?"

"Calista Stockton released her memoirs a couple of days ago, and yours truly figured into it pretty heavily," Mace said grimly.

"How's she playing it?"

"According to her, she wanted home and baby and I was the louse who got her pregnant, cheated on her, booted her out of my life, and indirectly made her have a miscarriage."

Stan blanched. "But it's a pack of lies!" he burst out.

"You know that and I know that, but she's hitting the talk show circuit and I'm a washed up has-been. Who do you think people are going to believe?"

Stan looked out the window for a moment. "Well, I can see why she's doing it," he said thoughtfully. "Her career's been in a slide for years. So she decides to write a book, and what better way to rack up sales and get free press than to attach a nice, juicy scandal? What I don't get is why you? Why not some big Hollywood name?"

"That's easy," Mace said, wondering if he'd ever get his coffee. "I'm a safe target. People still recognize the name and face. No career means no money, and no money means no threat of a lawsuit."

Stan shook his head, bewildered. "Yeah, but you've got plenty of money."

"She doesn't know that. Trust me, Stan, I know the way her mind works."

"Well, you can sue her over what she's saying, get her for slander or libel or whatever it is."

"She's too clever for that. According to Wally, she never came out and said the words, just implied it. And even if she had, first I'd have to prove slander, and that gets into some pretty ugly territory."

Bernice came up with her order pad. "What'll it be, hon?" she asked Stan.

"Uh, short stack and ham."

"We got blueberry pancakes on special this morning," she said, pencil poised over her pad.

"Sign me up."

"Good move," she approved, then flicked an unfriendly glance at Mace. "You?" she asked simply.

"Farmer's breakfast, scrambled, and coffee," Mace ordered. "Oh, and I'd like some water, too, when you get a chance."

"You'll get it when I'm ready," she said rudely and walked off.

"What's up with her?" Stan asked as she walked away. "That ain't the way to get repeat customers."

"I've been getting a lot of that the last couple of days." He stared moodily into space.

"How's Becka taking it?"

Mace winced. As usual, Stan had unerringly hit upon what was bothering him. "Becka's out the door. She saw Calista in an interview and that told her everything she thought she needed to know."

"Did you tell her it wasn't true?"

Mace turned his palms up in a gesture of futility. "What's the point? Ever since we met she's been convinced that I'm some worthless creep. I finally get her to trust that I'm not and then she hears this story."

"But you didn't tell her your side of what happened?"

"Why bother?" Mace shrugged. "It wouldn't have done any good. You saw how Bernice was just now. It doesn't take much to destroy your credibility."

"Yeah, well, Bernice ain't sleeping with you." Stan gave her a squint. "At least I hope she's not."

"Funny."

"Becka cares about you, Mace, she knows you. She's going to want to know the real story."

"Not anymore. She's done with me. And I'm done with her," he said, with a finality he didn't feel. "I don't want to keep fighting to get her to believe in me. There comes a point where you have to trust."

Stan gave him a level stare. "She matters to you."

"Yeah? So?" Mace looked up as Bernice thumped down a coffee cup in front of him and poured steaming brew into it. She ignored his thank-you and walked away.

"Duvall, I can count the number of women you've been with since Calista on one hand, and you never brought any of them along to meet your friends."

Mace shrugged. "I didn't feel like it, or it wasn't convenient. Look, why are you harping on this?"

"Because you can't see the difference in you. When I stopped by your house in Florida, you were like some kind of hermit, hiding away, doing your hobbies, trying to pretend it was okay. I know you weren't happy that I pushed you out of your little cave, but you're alive again. And Becka's part of that. It wasn't just finding the right job, Duvall, it was finding the right woman."

"Maybe. Or maybe I'm just falling on her as a way to escape," he countered in frustration. "I can't even figure out if I can trust my own feelings, and she can't figure out if she can trust me. It's not a real promising basis for a future, Stan. And let's not even get into the question of what would happen if we did decide to try—we live in different states, we work all over the place. You can't have a relationship if you're never together.''

"Oh, cry me a river, Duvall." Stan's voice rose. "You really learned to feel sorry for yourself when you were in the hospital, didn't you?"

"Spare me the pop psychology," Mace snarled.

"Then spare me the self-pity," Stan threw back at him. "You know, I remember times playing with you when we'd be behind in the bottom of the ninth, maybe one or two outs, and you'd still go up to the plate convinced you were gonna make us win."

"This isn't baseball, Stan."

"Bullshit." Stan slapped the table. "Baseball isn't about baseball, it's about what's inside you, what you bring to the game. Same thing with life. Don't tell me you don't know how you feel about this woman, you know. And if you want her, then fight for her. Convince her. As far as futures, hell, you've got enough dough you can spend the off-season anywhere you want. During the season, you're set if you want it—they want you as batting coach in Pawtucket."

"Pawtucket?" Mace's head snapped up. "The triple A club?"

Stan grinned. "Yep. It's yours if you want it."

"Hell yes!"

"Am I talking with the guy who told me he didn't want anything to do with teaching?"

"You're just dying to say I told you so, aren't you?"

"I don't want to waste it when I know you're going to have a few more coming to you. Get the rest of your life straightened out. Then I can give you a blanket version."

"You never let up."

"Not when it's for a good cause. You know," Stan said casually, "Pawtucket, Rhode Island, is only about an hour from Lowell."

"First place," Stats whooped after the game that night. "We got to go out and celebrate, guys. Wings and beer. Morelli, you're in. Who else?"

Morelli shook his head. "I'll leave the hard living up to you guys for a while."

Stats stared. "Seriously?"

"Seriously." He yawned. "I'm going to head back to the dorms for some sleep."

"But you were part of the team all season, you gotta go," Stats protested. "You're part of the reason we're here."

Across the room, Chico nodded in agreement. "Stats is right. Come out with us."

Morelli's face brightened. "Thanks for asking, guys. I'm going to pass, but I appreciate the invitation."

"Ah, you turning into a wuss in your old age, Morelli?" Chico razzed him.

"No," he said soberly. "I'm turning smart."

Becka slid onto a bar stool at Double Play. This early in the week, the bar was quiet. A pair of guys sat at a table watching ESPN. At the end of the bar, a lone drinker hunched over a beer.

Mallory wiped the surface of the bar. She tossed a bar mat down in front of Becka. "What'll it be?"

"A shot of Dewar's."

"Whoa." Mallory stepped back. "Okay, what's going on? It wouldn't possibly have anything to do with a man, would it?"

Becka raised dark smudged eyes to her. "It's not a joke anymore, Mallory."

Mallory studied her. "I can see that. I'm sorry, hon," she said gently. "Let me get you your drink."

Becka held up the glass of whiskey, studying the warm, golden liquid. The color of Mace's eyes, she thought, and the emotion swamped her again. "So what do you do when every blessed thing in your gut tells you that a guy is on the level, but people on the outside say he's scum?"

Mallory blinked and set down her bar towel. "Well, they are pretty serious charges. What does Mace say?"

Becka looked at the ceiling as though the answer hovered there. "He won't say anything, keeps telling me that I won't believe him anyway. I mean, if he would at least talk with me, maybe I'd understand." She took a deep drink of the whiskey and felt the liquid flame through her veins. It didn't warm her heart, though. That remained chilled. "Maybe there's something to explain it. I know he's not who the papers make him out to be. Maybe there's something about this whole mess, too, but he won't say anything."

"Have you tried asking him?"

"I asked him the night I found out about it, but he said I'd already made up my mind."

"Had you?"

Becka hesitated. "I don't know. Maybe, at first. I mean, I'd been sitting there thinking how impossible it all was, but I'd finally convinced myself to tell him how I felt about him. And then she came on the television." Becka looked directly at Mallory. "I was just so horrified, you know? And she was breaking down in the interview. It was awful, and I kept thinking he had done that to her, but it doesn't fit with the guy I know. If you'd asked me a week ago, I'd have told you Mace would never have intentionally hurt anyone ever, but here she is crying her eyes out on national television, twelve years later.''

Mallory crossed her arms and raised an eyebrow. ''Twelve years later, huh?''

Becka glanced at her over the rim of her glass. ''Yeah, why?''

''Well, she is an actress.''

''Meaning?''

''Meaning if she hasn't gotten to the point that she can talk about this without crying twelve years later, she should ask her therapist for a refund.''

''Okay, you might have a point there.''

Mallory shrugged. ''People always want to believe the worst of anyone, and once a rumor's out there, it's hard to quash. The whole time I was growing up, all my aunt ever told me was that I was no good. I got to where I wouldn't even fight it if some outrageous rumor came out about me. I just figured there wasn't any point.''

Mallory broke away to attend to another customer. Becka studied her glass. Anguish on demand was Calista's stock in trade. Could she be playing up the whole incident for publicity? The truth, Becka thought impatiently, she needed the truth.

''Becka?'' a voice behind her asked. She turned to see Stan Angelo at her elbow.

It was all she needed, one more reminder of Mace. One more reminder of the good times. ''Hi, Stan. How are you?'' she said briefly. ''I saw you at the game but...'' she flapped her hand vaguely and didn't finish the sentence, hoping he'd leave so she could talk with Mallory.

Meanwhile, Mallory returned, nodding her head at Stan with a questioning look. Becka sighed. ''Mallory Carson, this is Stan Angelo. Stan used to play baseball with Mace.''

Mallory cocked her head and looked at him, and a broad

smile bloomed on her face. "Pleased to meet you, Stan. I'm Becka's neighbor. Why don't you take a seat and I'll get you something to drink?" She placed a bar mat in front of him, ignoring Becka's pop-eyed look. Stan sat and ordered a beer, staring moodily at Becka.

"That stuff…that trash Calista's spouting about Mace? It's all a load of hogwash. But you probably already know that." He hoisted the beer that Mallory brought him, taking a deep drink before putting it down. "So the team's in first place, now, huh? You must be happy about that. I think that's the best that—"

"Go back a minute," Becka said. "What do you mean, it's hogwash? What's hogwash? What really happened?"

"Not my place to say. I'm sure Mace told you."

"No," Becka said. "I don't know about what happened with Mace and Calista, at least not his side."

Stan blinked at her. "Really? I'd figure that's the first thing you'd ask."

"I did, but he wouldn't tell me."

"Did you ask because you wanted to hear his side or did you just want to see him try to talk his way out of it?"

"I didn't…I just thought…" her words trailed off.

"You just thought because it fit all the rest of the hype it was the truth?" he asked gently.

Becka looked down at what was left of her drink as though the answer would appear.

"You've been involved with him for weeks, Becka," Stan said softly. "Haven't you figured out yet that there's not a dishonorable bone in his body? If I were you and I cared about the guy, I'd at least want to go see what he had to say about it." He cut her off before she could speak. "And if he didn't want to tell me, I'd make him."

Mallory looked at her. "You know you need to."

Becka's gaze flicked between the two of them. She nodded, slowly at first, then faster. "You're right. You guys are right." She was on her feet the next moment. "Thanks."

"Where are you going?" Mallory called.

"Gotta find Loverboy," Becka returned as she walked out the door.

She missed the wink that passed between Mallory and Stan.

BECKA KNOCKED on Mace's door, but there was no answer. She knocked again. Silence.

Defeated, she took the elevator down to the lobby and turned to leave. Then she heard the clack of pool balls. She walked toward the sound, rounding the corner to a small, shadowed rec room. A pair of video games flashed light and color. A Ping-Pong table sat silent. And Mace Duvall played pool, alone.

"Mind if I join you?"

He was leaning over the table to get a shot. Only his eyes moved when she spoke. The cue stick shot forward, balls clicked, and the two ball went into the pocket.

He straightened up. "Becka."

She walked across the room to him, feeling as though she was moving through mud, fighting to keep herself moving. "I need you to talk to me," she said, her voice shaking a bit. "I need to know what really happened with you and Calista."

"It's ancient history." He turned back to the table and lined up another shot. The balls clacked.

"Not any more it isn't. It's part of the present, and the only way to put it to rest is to deal with it."

He straightened up and looked at her, expressionless. Becka reached out to touch his cheek with her fingertips. "Talk to me," she said softly. "I'll listen this time."

Mace started to line up another shot, focusing on the table.

"Please," she blurted. "I need to know."

He looked at her, his eyes shadowed, then nodded slowly. "Seems like I'm always telling you stories these days."

Becka swallowed. Now was the time to take a risk. "That's what you do when you're in love with someone. You share your lives."

He sucked in a breath. "In lo—"

"Talk to me."

Mace let the breath out slowly. "All right. Get a cue and we'll play while I'm telling you." He grabbed the triangle from where it hung on the light fixture hanging over the table and began setting up the balls as if glad of something to do. "I told you how I got into the business of escorting women to events," he said, arranging the balls and pulling off the rack. "For a couple of weeks, it went fine. I'd show up at these things, I'd meet a few more people, the press would take their pictures, and the whole thing just sort of snowballed."

He gestured to Becka to break. Stepping forward, she stroked the cue a few times and slammed the balls all over the table. "Keep going," she prompted.

Mace aimed a shot that went wide. "It was a whole new world for me."

"I can imagine." Becka set up a shot and put one in, grateful to have something to keep her hands busy. She missed the next one.

Mace moved from where he'd been standing, staring at her. "I dated one or two of them, nothing serious, and then I met Calista at a gallery opening." He stepped in to take a shot. "I'd gone my whole life without falling in love and boom, I went like a ton of bricks. Her first movie came out a couple months later, and suddenly she was famous, I mean really famous.'' He shook his head as he circled the table. ''I think about it now, and it was probably mostly infatuation, because we never had much to talk about, but it felt real, you know?''

Becka nodded.

''Anyway, one morning I came in to find her getting sick, and when I asked her about it, she told me she was pregnant.'' He lined up a shot, then glanced up at Becka. ''I'd always figured I'd have kids some day, so it was fine. I thought we'd get married. Where I come from, that's what you do. Calista had different ideas, I found out later.'' He stood up, the pool game forgotten. ''I was hosting a fundraiser one night. Calista was supposed to go, but she'd said she didn't feel well, so I ducked out early to check on her. I walked in to find her in bed with some one-hit-wonder actor. We fought and she told me...'' He stopped for a moment. ''She told me that she'd aborted our child. And that I was trying to smother her and destroy her career by wanting to marry her. When I got angry, she told me she wasn't even sure it had been my child, that she'd been sleeping with other men the whole time.''

Becka looked at him in horror. ''She said it was you who'd done all that,'' she breathed.

''No,'' he corrected, ''she implied it and let everyone else fill in the blanks.''

''I'm so sorry,'' Becka whispered.

Mace shrugged. ''It pretty much flattened me back then. I used to dream about the kid.'' He raked his hair out of his eyes. ''It also taught me a lot about people, about the important things. After that, I just did the appearances, none of the dating. No involvement.''

She searched for the right words, knowing there really weren't any. ''It must have been brutal for you.''

"What was brutal was knowing you believed it," he said quietly.

"But I didn't, not really," Becka protested. "I wanted you to tell me your side because I didn't want to think that you'd have done something like that."

"I figured there was no point. You should have seen your face. I mean, it was chalk white, with these huge eyes. You'd always believed all the newspaper stuff. I just assumed you'd believed this, too." He took a slow step toward her, then another. "I'd been in the shower trying to figure out a way to talk to you about what came next. To tell you I loved you."

Becka caught her breath as she watched him move. "I was working up my nerve to do the same thing."

They stared at each other.

"And what are you thinking now?" Mace asked softly.

"That I do love you. What are you thinking?"

"That I love you."

Becka raised her head toward his, thinking he was going to kiss her, but he didn't. "Love isn't enough, Becka. There's got to be trust there, too."

She nodded, understanding. "I went to Mallory's bar after the game. Stan was there. He seemed surprised that you and I hadn't talked about what happened. He told me that I should have trusted you enough to ask for your side of the story."

"That operator." One corner of Mace's mouth tugged up into a grin of reluctant admiration. "I had breakfast with Stan this morning. He told me I should have trusted you to believe me instead of just assuming you wouldn't."

They looked at each other and laughed.

Mace shook his head. "Stan missed his calling. He should have been a couples' counselor. He told me something else, by the way. I'm going to be batting coach at the

Pawtucket Red Sox next year.'' He reached out to brush his knuckles across her cheek. ''It's only an hour away from Lowell. I'll go on the road with the team, but no more than you will. In the off-season, we can do whatever you want.'' He took her hands in his. ''I want a future with you, Becka.''

''I want that, too,'' she whispered.

They kissed, a slow, gentle touch of mouth to mouth that was more heart to heart. Then Mace backed away.

''Okay, one more game,'' he said briskly, pulling balls from the pockets and tossing them in the triangle. ''Nine ball. Why don't we add a little bet, just to make it interesting?''

''What do you have in mind?'' she asked, chalking her cue.

''I win, you marry me.''

Her mouth curved. ''What happens if I win?''

He held up the two ball. ''You win, I marry you.''

Becka gave him a grin full of sunlight and threw her arms around his neck. ''Now that's what I'd call scoring.''

1

SHAY BLINKED. She was his pleasure, if he was honest, though he had a pretty good idea that she wouldn't be all that impressed with that response. He'd watched her progress across the room in a lithe, flowing walk that managed to be far more provocative than any hipsway might be. Why she'd decided to come his way, he wasn't sure, but he was certainly interested in finding out. Up close, she was everything the glance from afar had promised and more. In another century, she would have had men dueling over that aristocratic beauty, vying to tease a smile from that wide, mobile mouth.

One slim brow arched as she looked down at him. "I get the impression from the way you were looking that we're not doing a very good job entertaining you."

Shay smiled. "Quite the contrary. I'm very entertained right now. And I'll take a beer when you get a chance. You have Guinness?"

"No Guinness, at least not yet. We've got Bud, Bud Light, Miller and Heineken."

"Heineken, then," Shay said. She was in a whole different class from the rest of the bartenders in the place. Whoever had hired her had known what they were doing.

She leaned over to collect bottles from the shelf behind him, setting them on the tray. "Is this your first time at Bad Reputation?"

Shay nodded, watching her. She had the kind of face that

sucked a man in, that made it impossible to look away, because the minute you did, you started wondering if anyone could really be that beautiful. "Just stopped by to see if what I've heard was true." Not just beauty, he thought. Sex. Something in the curve of her lips and the tilt of those dark eyes suggested abandonment, disregard for rules. Come with me, they said, and I'll show you things you've never even thought of.

"And what have you heard?" The brunette propped her tray on the shelf and looked at him under her lashes.

His mouth curved. "Something about half-naked women dancing on the bar."

"Well, you've got to admit, they're on the bar and they're dancing." She glanced over her shoulder to where the blonde was whipping her hair to the music.

"Like college girls having a wild night."

"You're calling us girls?" She smiled, but her eyes narrowed a trifle in warning.

"Not you, darlin'." He ran his gaze from her long, smooth legs to the sleek curve of hip and waist, to the dark hair tumbling down her back, and up to that fabulous face. "You're a whole different breed from girls."

A little buzz went through Mallory at his look, and she gave herself a mental shake. She might be giving the appearance of flirting, but she was supposed to be working a customer. It definitely didn't do to get caught up in it. "And here I thought I'd heard about every line out there."

"I didn't intend it as a line." His teeth gleamed, and something of the pirate came out in him then. "Did you want it to be?"

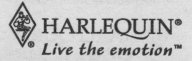

A "Mother of the Year" contest brings
overwhelming response as thousands of women
vie for the luxurious grand prize....

Kate Hoffmann

Jacqueline Diamond

Jill Shalvis

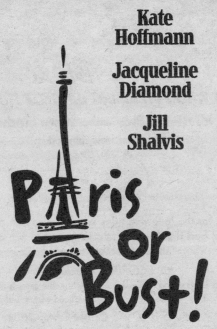

Paris or Bust!

A hilarious and romantic trio of new stories!

With a trip to Paris at stake, these women are
determined to win! But the laughs are many as three of
them discover that being finalists isn't the most
excitement they'll ever have.... Falling in love is!

Available in April 2003.

If you enjoyed what you just read,
then we've got an offer you can't resist!

Take 2 bestselling
love stories FREE!
Plus get a FREE surprise gift!

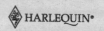

COOPER'S CORNER

Welcome to Cooper's Corner...
a small town with very big surprises!

Coming in April 2003...
JUST ONE LOOK
by Joanna Wayne

Check-in: After a lifetime of teasing, Cooper's Corner postmistress Alison Fairchild finally had the cutest nose ever—thanks to recent plastic surgery! At her friend's wedding, all eyes were on her, except those of the gorgeous stranger in the dark glasses—then she realized he was blind.

Checkout: Ethan Granger wasn't the sightless teacher everyone thought, but an undercover FBI agent. When he met Alison, he was thankful for those dark glasses. If she could see into his eyes, she'd know he was in love....

HARLEQUIN®
Makes any time special ®

CC-CNM9